Hagar's Daughter

Hagar's Daughter

A Story of Southern Caste Prejudice

Pauline E. Hopkins

MINT EDITIONS

Hagar's Daughter: A Story of Southern Caste Prejudice was first published in 1902.

This edition published by Mint Editions 2021.

ISBN 9781513280134 | E-ISBN 9781513285153

Published by Mint Editions®

 MINT
EDITIONS

minteditionsbooks.com

Publishing Director: Jennifer Newens
Design & Production: Rachel Lopez Metzger
Project Manager: Micaela Clark
Typesetting: Westchester Publishing Services

Contents

I

In the fall of 1860 a stranger visiting the United States would have thought that nothing short of a miracle could preserve the union of states so proudly proclaimed by the signers of the Declaration of Independence, and so gloriously maintained by the gallant Washington.

The nomination of Abraham Lincoln for the presidency by the Republican party was inevitable. The pro-slavery Democracy was drunk with rage at the prospect of losing control of the situation, which, up to that time, had needed scarcely an effort to bind in riveted chains impenetrable alike to the power of man or the frowns of the Godhead; they had inaugurated a system of mob-law and terrorism against all sympathizers with the despised party. The columns of partisan newspapers teemed each day in the year with descriptions of disgraceful scenes enacted North and South by pro-slavery men, due more to the long-accustomed subserviency of Northern people to the slaveholders than to a real, personal hatred of the Negro.

The free negroes North and South, and those slaves with the hearts of freemen who had boldly taken the liberty denied by man, felt the general spirit of unrest and uncertainty which was spreading over the country to such an alarming extent. The subdued tone of the liberal portion of the press, the humiliating offers of compromise from Northern political leaders, and the numerous cases of surrendering fugitive slaves to their former masters, sent a thrill of mortal fear into the very heart of many a household where peace and comfort had reigned for many years. The fugitive slave had perhaps won the heart of some Northern free woman; they had married, prospered, and were happy. Now came the haunting dread of a stealthy tread, an ominous knock, a muffled cry at midnight, and the sunlight of the new day would smile upon a broken-hearted woman with baby hands clinging to her skirts, and children's voices asking in vain for their father lost to them forever. The Negro felt that there was no safety for him beneath the Stars and Stripes, and, so feeling, sacrificed his home and personal effects and fled to Canada.

The Southerners were in earnest, and would listen to no proposals in favor of their continuance in the Union under existing conditions; namely, Lincoln and the Republican party. The vast wealth of the South made them feel that they were independent of the world. Cotton was not merely king; it was God. Moral considerations were nothing.

Drunk with power and dazzled with prosperity, monopolizing cotton and raising it to the influence of a veritable fetich, the authors of the Rebellion did not admit a doubt of the success of their attack on the Federal government. They dreamed of perpetuating slavery, though all history shows the decline of the system as industry, commerce, and knowledge advance. The slaveholders proposed nothing less than to reverse the currents of humanity, and to make barbarism flourish in the bosom of civilization.

The South argued that the principle of right would have no influence over starving operatives; and England and France, as well as the Eastern States of the Union, would stand aghast, and yield to the master stroke which should deprive them of the material of their labor. Millions of the laboring class were dependent upon it in all the great centers of civilization; it was only necessary to wave this sceptre over the nations and all of them would acknowledge the power which wielded it. But, alas! the supreme error of this anticipation was in omitting from the calculation the power of principle. Right still had authority in the councils of nations. Factories might be closed, men and woman out of employment, but truth and justice still commanded respect among men. The pro-slavery men in the North encouraged the rebels before the breaking out of the war. They promised the South that civil war should reign in every free state in case of an uprising of the Southern oligarchy, and that men should not be permitted to go South to put down their brothers in rebellion.

Weak as were the Southern people in point of numbers and political power, compared with those of the North, yet they easily persuaded themselves that they could successfully cope in arms with a Northern foe, whom they affected to despise for his cowardly and mercenary disposition. They indulged the belief, in proud confidence, that their great political prestige would continue to serve them among party associates at the North, and that the counsels of the adversary would be distracted and his power weakened by the effects of dissension.

When the Republican banner bearing the names of Abraham Lincoln for President and Hannibal Hamlin for Vice-President flung its folds to the breeze in 1860, there was a panic of apprehension at such bold manoeuvering; mob-law reigned in Boston, Utica and New York City, which witnessed the greatest destruction of property in the endeavor to put down the growing public desire to abolish slavery. Elijah Lovejoy's innocent blood spoke in trumpet tones to the reformer from his quiet grave by the rolling river. William Lloyd Garrison's outraged manhood brought the blush of shame to the cheek of the honest American who loved his country's honor better than any individual institution. The memory of Charles Sumner's brutal beating by Preston Brooks stamped the mad passions of the hour indelibly upon history's page. Debate in the Senate became fiery and dangerous as the crisis approached in the absorbing question of the perpetuation of slavery.

At the South laws were enacted abridging the freedom of speech and press; it was difficult for Northerners to travel in slave states. Rev. Charles T. Torrey was sentenced to the Maryland penitentiary for aiding slaves to escape; Jonathan Walker had been branded with a red-hot iron for the same offense. In the midst of the tumult came the "Dred Scott Decision," and the smouldering fire broke forth with renewed vigor. Each side waited impatiently for the result of the balloting.

In November the Rubicon was passed, and Abraham Lincoln was duly elected President contrary to the wishes and in defiance of the will of the haughty South. There was much talk of a conspiracy to prevent by fraud or violence a declaration of the result of the election by the Vice-President before the two Houses, as provided by law. As the eventful day drew near patriotic hearts were sick with fear or filled with forebodings. Would the certificates fail to appear; would they be wrested by violence from the hands ordered to bear them across the rotunda from the Senate Chamber to the hall of the House, or would they be suppressed by the only official who could open them, John C. Breckenridge of Kentucky, himself a candidate and in full sympathy with the rebellion.

A breathless silence, painfully intense, reigned in the crowded chamber as the Vice-President arose to declare the result of the election. Six feet in height, lofty in carriage, youthful, dashing, he stood before them pale and nervous. The galleries were packed with hostile conspirators. It was the supreme moment in the life of the Republic. With unfaltering utterance his voice broke the oppressive stillness:

"I therefore declare Abraham Lincoln duly elected President of the United States for the term of four years from the fourth of March next."

It was the signal for secession, and the South let loose the dogs of war.

II

During the week preceding the memorable 20th of December, 1860, the streets of Charleston, S.C., were filled with excited citizens who had come from all parts of the South to participate in the preparations for seceding from the Union. The hotels were full; every available space was occupied in the homes of private citizens. Bands paraded the streets heading processions of excited politicians who came as delegates from every section south of Mason and Dixon's line; there was shouting and singing by the populace, liberally mingled with barrelhead orations from excited orators with more zeal than worth; there were cheers for the South and oaths for the government at Washington.

Scattered through the crowd traders could be seen journeying to the far South with gangs of slaves chained together like helpless animals destined for the slaughter-house. These slaves were hurriedly sent off by their master in obedience to orders from headquarters, which called for the removal of all human property from the immediate scene of the invasion so soon to come. The traders paused in their hurried journey to participate in the festivities which ushered in the birth of the glorious Confederate States of America. Words cannot describe the scene.

> "The wingèd heralds by command
> Of sovereign power, with awful ceremony
> And trumpet sound, proclaimed
> A solemn council forthwith to be held
> At Pandæmonium, the high capital
> Of Satan and his peers."

Among the traders the most conspicuous was a noted man from St. Louis, by the name of Walker. He was the terror of the whole Southwest among the Negro population, bond and free; for it often happened that free persons were kidnapped and sold to the far South. Uncouth, ill-bred, hardhearted, illiterate, Walker had started in St. Louis as a dray-driver, and now found himself a rich man. He was a repulsive-looking person, tall, lean and lank, with high cheekbones and face pitted with the small-pox, gray eyes, with red eyebrows and sandy whiskers.

Walker, upon his arrival in Charleston, took up his quarters with his gang of human cattle in a two-story flat building, surrounded by a stone wall some twelve feet high, the top of which was covered with bits of glass, so that there could be no passage over it without great personal injury. The rooms in this building resembled prison cells, and in the office were to be seen iron collars, hobbles, handcuffs, thumbscrews, cowhides, chains, gags and yokes.

Walker's servant Pompey had charge of fitting the stock for the market-place. Pompey had been so long under the instructions of the heartless speculator that he appeared perfectly indifferent to the heart-rending scenes which daily confronted him.

On this particular morning, Walker brought in a number of customers to view his stock; among them a noted divine, who was considered deeply religious. The slaves were congregated in a back yard enclosed by the high wall before referred to. There were swings and benches, which made the place very much like a New England schoolyard.

Among themselves the Negroes talked. There was one woman who had been separated from her husband, and another woman whose looks expressed the anguish of her heart. There was old "Uncle Jeems," with his whiskers off, his face clean shaven, and all his gray hairs plucked out, ready to be sold for ten years younger than he was. There was Tobias, a gentleman's body servant educated at Paris, in medicine, along with his late master, sold to the speculator because of his intelligence and the temptation which the confusion of the times offered for him to attempt an escape from bondage.

"O, my God!" cried one woman, "send dy angel down once mo' ter tell me dat you's gwine ter keep yer word, Massa Lord."

"O Lord, we's been a-watchin' an' a-prayin', but de 'liverer done fergit us!" cried another, as she rocked her body violently back and forth.

It was now ten o' clock, and the daily examination of the stock began with the entrance of Walker and several customers.

"What are you wiping your eyes for?" inquired a fat, red-faced man, with a white hat set on one side of his head and a cigar in his mouth, of the woman seated on a bench.

"'Cause I left my mon behin'."

"Oh, if I buy you, I'll furnish you with a better man than you left. I've got lots of young bucks on my farm," replied the man.

"I don't want anudder mon, an' I tell you, massa, I nebber will hab anudder mon."

"What's your name?" asked a man in a straw hat, of a Negro standing with arms folded across his breast and leaning against the wall.

"Aaron, sar."

"How old are you?"

"Twenty-five."

"Where were you raised?"

"In Virginny, sar."

"How many men have owned you?"

"Fo."

"Do you enjoy good health?"

"Yas, sar."

"Whipped much?"

"No, sar. I s'pose I didn't desarve it, sar."

"I must see your back, so as to know how much you've been whipped, before I conclude a bargain."

"Cum, unharness yoseff, ole boy. Don't you hear the gemman say he wants to zammin yer?" said Pompey.

The speculator, meanwhile, was showing particular attention to the most noted and influential physician of Charleston. The doctor picked out a man and a woman as articles that he desired for his plantation, and Walker proceeded to examine them.

"Well, my boy, speak up and tell the doctor what's your name."

"Sam, sar, is my name."

"How old are you?"

"Ef I live ter see next corn plantin' I'll be twenty-seven, or thirty, or thirty-five, I dunno which."

"Ha, ha ha! Well, doctor, this is a green boy. Are you sound?"

"Yas, sar; I spec' I is."

"Open your mouth, and let me see your teeth. I allers judge a nigger's age by his teeth, same as I do a hoss. Good appetite?"

"Yas, sar."

"Get out on that plank and dance. I want to see how supple you are."

"I don't like to dance, massa; I'se got religion."

"Got religion, have you? So much the better. I like to deal in the gospel, doctor. He'll suit you. Now, my gal, what's your name?"

"I is Big Jane, sar."

"How old are you?"

"Don' know, sar; but I was born at sweet pertater time."

"Well, do you know who made you?"

PAULINE E. HOPKINS

"I hev heard who it was in de Bible, but I done fergit de gemman's name."

"Well, doctor, this is the greenest lot of niggers I've had for some time, but you may have Sam for a thousand dollars and Jane for nine hundred. They are worth all I ask for them."

"Well, Walter, I reckon I'll take them," replied the doctor.

"I'll put the handcuffs on 'em, and then you can pay me."

"Why," remarked the doctor, "there comes Reverend Pinchen."

"It is Mr. Pinchen as I live; jest the very man I want to see." As the reverend gentleman entered the enclosure, the trader grasped his hand, saying: "Why, how do you do, Mr. Pinchen? Come down to Charleston to the Convention, I s'pose? Glorious time, sir, glorious; but it will be gloriouser when the new government has spread our institootions all over the conquered North. Gloriouser and gloriouser. Any camp-meetin's, revivals, death-bed scenes, or other things in your line going on down here? How's religion prospering now, Mr. Pinchen? I always like to hear about religion."

"Well, Mr. Walker, the Lord's work is in good condition everywhere now. Mr. Walker, I've been in the gospel ministry these thirteen years, and I know that the heart of man is full of sin and desperately wicked. Religion is a good thing to live by, and we'll want it when we die. And a man in your business of buying and selling slaves needs religion more than anybody else, for it makes you treat your people well. Now there's Mr. Haskins—he's a slave-trader like yourself. Well, I converted him. Before he got religion he was one of the worst men to his niggers I ever saw; his heart was as hard as a stone. But religion has made his heart as soft as a piece of cotton. Before I converted him he would sell husbands from their wives and delight in doing it; but now he won't sell a man from his wife if he can get anyone to buy them together. I tell you, sir, religion has done a wonderful work for him."

"I know, Mr. Pinchen, that I ought to have religion, and that I am a great sinner; and whenever I get with good, pious people, like you and the doctor, I feel desperate wicked. I know that I would be happier with religion, and the first spare time I have I'm going to get it. I'll go to a protracted meeting, and won't stop till I get religion."

Walker then invited the gentlemen to his office, and Pompey was dispatched to purchase wine and other refreshments for the guests.

Within the magnificent hall of the St. Charles Hotel a far different scene was enacted in the afternoon. The leading Southern politicians were gathered there to discuss the election of Lincoln, the "sectional" candidate, and to give due weight and emphasis to the future acts of the new government. There was exaltation in every movement of the delegates, and they were surrounded by the glitter of a rich and powerful assemblage in a high state of suppressed excitement, albeit this meeting was but preliminary to the decisive acts of the following week.

The vast hall, always used for dancing, was filled with tables which spread their snow-white wings to receive the glittering mass of glass, plate and flowers. The spacious galleries were crowded to suffocation by beautiful Southern belles in festive attire. Palms and fragrant shrubs were everywhere; garlands of flowers decorated the walls and fell, mingled with the new flag—the stars and bars—gracefully above the seat of the chairman.In the gallery opposite the speaker's desk a band was stationed; Negro servants in liveries of white linen hurried noiselessly to and fro. The delegates filed in to their places at table to the crashing strains of "Dixie"; someone raised the new flag aloft and waved it furiously; the whole assembly rose *en masse* and cheered vociferously, and the ladies waved their handkerchiefs. Mirth and hilarity reigned. The first attention of the diners was given to the good things before them. After cigars were served the music stopped, and the business of the day began in earnest.

There was the chairman, Hon. Robert Toombs of Georgia; there was John C. Breckenridge of Kentucky, Stephen A. Douglas, Alexander H. Stevens, and Jefferson Davis.

"Silence!" was the cry, as Hon. Robert Toombs, the chairman, arose.

"*Fellow Delegates and Fellow Citizens:*I find myself in a most remarkable situation, and I feel that every Southern gentleman sympathizes with me. Here am I, chairman of a meeting of the most loyal, high-spirited and patriotic body of men and their guests and friends, that ever assembled to discuss the rights of humanity and Christian progress, and yet unable to propose a single toast with which we have been wont to sanction such a meeting as this. With grief that consumes my soul, I am compelled to bury in the silence of mortification, contempt and detestation the name of the government at Washington.

"I can only counsel you, friends, to listen to no vain babbling, to no treacherous jargon about overt acts; they have already been committed. Defend yourselves; the enemy is at your door; wait not to meet him at the hearthstone,—meet him at the door-sill, and rive him from the temple of liberty, or pull down its pillars and involve him in a common ruin. Never permit this federal government to pass into the traitorous hands of the black Republican party.

"My language may appear strong; but it is mild when we consider the attempt being made to wrest from us the exclusive power of making laws for our own community. The repose of our homes, the honor of our color, and the prosperity of the South demand that we resist innovation.

"I rejoice to see around me fellow-laborers worthy to lead in the glorious cause of resisting oppression, and defending our ancient privileges which have been set by an Almighty hand. We denounce once and for all the practices proposed by crazy enthusiasts, seconded by designing knaves, and destined to be executed by demons in human form. We shall conquer in this pending struggle; we will subdue the North, and call the roll of our slaves beneath the very shadow of Bunker Hill. 'It is a consummation devoutly to be wished.'

"And now, I call upon all true patriots in token of their faith, to drink deep of one deserving their fealty,—the guardian and savior of the South, Jefferson Davis."

Vociferous cheers broke forth and shook the building. The crowd surrounding the hotel took it up, and the name "Davis!" "Davis!" was repeated again and again. He arose in his seat and bowed profoundly; the band played "See the Conquering Hero Comes"; a lady in the gallery back of him skilfully dropped a crown of laurel upon his head. The crowd went mad; they tore the decorations from the walls and pelted their laurel-crowned hero until he would gladly have had them cease; but such is fame. When the cheers had somewhat subsided, Mr. Davis said:

"I must acknowledge, my fellow-citizens, the truth of the remarks just made by our illustrious friend, Senator Toombs. I was never more satisfied with regard to the future history of our country than I am at present. I believe in state rights, slavery, and the Confederacy that we are about to inaugurate.

"The principle of slavery is in itself right, and does not depend upon difference of complexion. Make the laboring man the slave of *one* man, instead of the slave of society, and he would be far better off. Slavery, black or white, is necessary. Nature has made the weak in mind or body for slaves.

"In five days your delegates from all the loyal Southern States will meet here in convention. I feel the necessity that every eye be fixed upon the course which will be adopted by this assembly of patriots. You know our plans. South Carolina will lead the march of the gallant band who will give us the liberty we crave. We are all united in will and views, and therefore powerful. I see before me in my colleagues men to whom the tranquility of our government may be safely confided—men devoted and zealous in their interest—senators and representatives who have managed everything for our aid and comfort. Few of the vessels of the navy are available at home; the army is scattered on the Western frontier, while all the trained officers of the army are with us. Within our limits we have control of the entire government property—mints, custom-houses, post-offices, dock-yards, revenue-cutters, arsenals and forts. The national finances have been levied upon to fill our treasury by our faithful Southern members of the late cabinet. Yes, friends, all is ready; every preparation is made for a brief and successful fight for that supremacy in the government of this nation which is our birthright. (Tremendous applause.)

"By the election just thrust upon us by the Republican party the Constitution is violated; and were we not strong to sustain our rights, we should soon find ourselves driven to prison at the point of the bayonet (cries of 'Never, never!'), ousted from the council of state, oblivion everywhere, and nothing remaining but ourselves to represent Truth and Justice. We believe that our ideas are the desires of the majority of the people, and the people represent the supreme and sovereign power of Right! (Hear! hear! cheers.) For Abraham Lincoln (hisses) nothing is inviolate, nothing sacred; he menaces, in his election, our ancient ideas and privileges. The danger grows greater. Let us arise in our strength and meet it more than half way. Are you ready, men?"

"We are ready!" came in a roar like unto the waters of the mighty Niagara. "What shall we do?"

"No half measures; let it be a deed of grandeur!"

"It shall be done!" came in another mighty chorus.

"In such a crisis there must be no vacuum. There must be a well-established government before the people. You, citizens, shall take up arms; we will solicit foreign re-enforcements; we will rise up before this rail-splitting ignoramus a terrible power; we will overwhelm this miserable apology for a gentleman and a statesman as a terrible revolutionary power. Do you accept my proposition?"

"Yes, yes!" came as a unanimous shout from the soul of the vast assembly.

PAULINE E. HOPKINS

"Our Northern friends make a great talk about free society. We sicken of the name. What is it but a conglomeration of greasy mechanics, filthy operatives, small-fisted farmers, and moonstruck Abolitionists? All the Northern States, and particularly the New England States, are devoid of society fitted for well-bred gentlemen. The prevailing class one meets with is that of mechanics struggling to be genteel, and farmers who do their own drudgery, and yet who are hardly fit for association with a gentleman's slave.

We have settled this matter in the minds of the people of the South by long years of practice and observation; and I believe that when our principles shall have been triumphantly established over the entire country—North, South, West—a long age of peace and prosperity will ensue for the entire country. Under our jurisdiction wise laws shall be passed for the benefit of the supreme and subordinate interests of our communities. And when we have settled all these vexed questions I see a season of calm and fruitful prosperity, in which our children's children may enjoy their lives without a thought of fear or apprehension of change."

Then the band played; there was more cheering and waving of handkerchiefs, in the midst of which John C. Breckenridge arose and gracefully proposed the health of the first President of the Confederate States of America. It was drunk by every man, standing. Other speakers followed, and the most intemperate sentiments were voiced by the zealots in the great cause. The vast crowd went wild with enthusiasm.

St. Clair Enson, one of the most trusted delegates, and the slave-trader Walker sat side by side at the table, and in the excitement of the moment all the prejudices of the Maryland aristocrat toward the vile dealer in human flesh were forgotten.

The convention had now passed the bounds of all calmness. Many of the men stood on chairs, gesticulating wildly, each trying to be heard above his neighbor. In vain the Chair rapped for order. Pandemonium reigned. At one end of the long table two men were locked in deadly embrace, each struggling to enforce his views upon the other by brute strength.

One man had swept the dishes aside, and was standing upon the table, demanding clamorously to be heard, and above all the band still crashed its brazen notes of triumph in the familiar strains of "Dixie."

A Negro boy handed a letter to Mr. Enson. He turned it over in his hand, curiously examining the postmark.

"When did this come, Cato?"

"More'n a munf, massa," was the reply.

Mr. Enson tore open the envelope and glanced over its contents with a frowning face.

"Bad news?" ventured Walker, with unusual familiarity.

"The worst possible for me. My brother is married, and announces the birth of a daughter."

"Well, daughters are born every day. I don't see how that can hurt you."

"It happens in this case, however, that this particular daughter will inherit the Enson fortune," returned Enson with a short laugh.

Walker gave a long, low whistle. "Who was your brother's wife? Any money?"

"Clark Sargeant's daughter. Money enough on both sides; but the trouble is, it will never be mine." Another sharp, bitter laugh.

"Sargeant, Sargeant," said Walker, musingly. "'Pears to me I've had business with a gentleman of the same name years ago, in St. Louis. However, it can't be the same one, 'cause this man hadn't any children. Leastways, I never heard on eny."

"Perhaps it is the same man. Clark Sargeant was from St. Louis; moved to Baltimore when the little girl was five years old. Mr. and Mrs. Sargeant are dead."

"Same man, same man. Um, um," saidWalker, scratching the flesh beneath his sandy whiskers meditatively, as he gazed at the ceiling. "Both dead, eh? Come to think of it, I moight be mistaken about the little gal. Has she got black hair and eyes and a cream-colored skin, and has she growed up to be a all-fired pesky fine woman?"

"Can't say," replied Enson, with a yawn as he rose to his feet. "I've never had the pleasure of meeting my sister-in-law."

"When you going up to Baltimore?" asked Walker.

"Next week, on 'The Planter.'"

"Think I'll take a trip up with you. You don't mind my calling with you on your brother's family, do you, Mr. Enson? I would admire to introduce myself to Clark Sargeant's little gal. She moight not remember me at first, but I reckon I could bring back recollections of me to her mind, ef it's jes' the same to you, Mr. Enson."

"O, be hanged to you. Go where you please. Go to the devil," replied Enson, as he swung down the hall and elbowed his way out.

"No need of goin' to the devil when he's right side of you, Mr. Enson," muttered Walker, as he watched the young man out of sight. "You d—d aristocrats carry things with a high hand; I'll be glad to take a reef in your sails, and I'll do it, too, or my name's not Walker."

III

S t. Clair Enson was the second son of an aristocratic Maryland family. He had a fiery temper that knew no bounds when once aroused. Motherless from infancy, and born at a period in the life of his parents when no more children were expected, he grew up wild and self-willed. As his character developed it became evident that an unsavory future was before him. There was no malicious mischief in which he was not found, and older heads predicted that he would end on the gallows. Sensual, cruel to ferocity, he was a terror to the God-fearing community where he lived. With women he was successful from earliest youth, being possessed of the diabolical beauty of Satan himself. There was great rejoicing in the quiet village near which Enson Hall was situated when it was known that the young scapegrace had gone to college.

The atmosphere of college life suited him well, and he was soon the leader of the fastest set there. He was the instigator of innumerable broils, insulted his teachers, and finally fought a duel, killing his man instantly. According to the code of honor of the time, this was not murder; but expulsion from the halls of learning followed for St. Clair, and much to his surprise and chagrin, his father, who had always indulged and excused his acts as the thoughtlessness of youth's high spirits, was thoroughly enraged.

There was a curious scene between them, and no one ever knew just what passed, but it was ended by his father's saying:

"You have disgraced the name of Enson, and now you dare make a joke to me of your wickedness. Let me not see your face in this house again. Henceforth, until you have redeemed yourself by an honest man's career, I have but one son, your brother Ellis."

"As you please, sir," replied St. Clair nonchalantly, as he placed the check his father handed him in his pocket, bowed, and passed from the room.

That was the last heard of him for five years, when at his father's death he went home to attend the funeral.

By the terms of the will St. Clair received a small annuity, to be enlarged at the discretion of his brother, and in event of the latter's death without issue, the estate was to revert to St. Clair's heirs "if any there be who are an honor to the name of Enson," was the wording of the will. In the event of St. Clair's continuing in disgrace and "having no honorable and lawful issue," the property was to revert to a distant branch of cousins, "for I have no mind that debauchery and crime shall find a home at Enson Hall."

After this St. Clair seemingly dropped his wildest habits, but was still noted on all the river routes of the South as a reckless and daring gambler.

His man Isaac was as much of a character as himself, and many a game they worked together on the inexperienced, and many a time but for Isaac, St. Clair would have fared ill at the hands of his victims. Isaac was given to his young master at the age of ten years. The only saving grace about the scion of aristocracy appeared in his treatment of Isaac. Master and slave were devoted to each other.

As a last resource young Enson had gone in for politics, and the luck that had recently deserted him at cards and dice, favored him here. The unsettled state of the country and the threatening war-clouds were a boon to the tired child of chance, which he hailed as harbingers of better times for recreant Southern sons. He would gain fame and fortune in the service of the new government.

All through the dramatic action of the next week when history made so fast in the United States, when the South Carolina convention declared that "the union then subsisting between herself and other states of America, was dissolved" and her example followed by Mississippi, Florida, Alabama, Georgia, Louisiana, Texas, Virginia, Arkansas, North Carolina and Tennessee, all through that time when politics reached the boiling point, St. Clair, although in the thickest of the controversy, busy making himself indispensable to the officials of the new government, was thinking of the heiress of Enson Hall. He was bitter over his loss, and ready to blame anyone but himself.

In his opinion, Ellis was humdrum; he was mild and peaceful in his disposition, because his blood was too sluggish and his natural characteristics too womanish for the life of a gentleman. Then, too, Ellis, was old, fifteen years his senior, and he was twenty-five.

St. Clair shared the universal opinion of his world (and to him the world did not exist north of Mason and Dixon's line), that a reckless career of gambling, wine and women was the only true course of development for a typical Southern gentleman. As he thought of the infant heiress his face grew black with a frown of rage that for the time completely spoiled the beauty women raved over. His man Isaac, furtively watching him from the corner of his eye, said to himself:

"I know dat dar's gwine to be a rippit; Marse St. Clair never look dat a way widout de debbil himself am broked loose." In which view of the case Isaac was about right.

St. Clair made up his mind to go home and see this fair woman who had come to blast his hopes and steal his patrimony for her children. Perhaps as she was young, and presumably susceptible, something might be done. He was handsome—Ah, well! and he laughed a wicked laugh at his reflection in the mirror; he would trust to luck to help him out. He ordered Isaac to pack up.

"Good Lawd, Marse St. Clair! I thought you'd done settled here fer good. How comes we go right off?"

"We're going home, Isaac, to see the new mistress Enson and my niece. Haven't I told you that your master, Ellis was married, and had a daughter?"

"Bress my soul! no sar!" replied Isaac, dropping the clothes he held upon the floor. His master left the room.

"Now de Lawd help de mistress an' de little baby. I love my master, but he's a borned debbil. He's jes' gwine home to tare up brass, dat's de whole collusion ob de mystery."

St. Clair Enson took passage on board "The Planter," which was ready to start upon its last trip up Chesapeake Bay before going into the service of the Confederate government. At that time this historic vessel was a side-wheel steamer storing about fourteen hundred bales of cotton as freight, but having accommodations for a moderate number of passengers. No one of the proud supporters of the new government dreamed of her ultimate fate. The position of the South was defined, and given to the world with a loud flourish of trumpets. By their reasoning, a few short months would make them masters of the entire country. Wedded to their idols, they knew not the force of the "dire arms" which Omnipotence would wield upon the side of Right. One of the most daring and heroic adventures of the Civil War was successfully accomplished by a party of Negroes, Robert Small commanding, when the rebel gunboat "The Planter" ran by the forts and batteries of Charleston Harbor, and reaching the flagship "Wabash" was duly received into the service of the United States government.

St. Clair Enson went on board the steamer with mixed feelings of triumph and chagrin—triumph because of the place he had made for himself in the councils of the new government and the adulation meted out to him by the public; chagrin because of his brother's new family ties and his own consequent poverty.

For a while he wandered aimlessly about, resisting all the tempting invitations extended by his numerous admirers in the sporting and political world to "have something" at the glittering bar. But his pockets were empty—they always were—and he finally allowed himself to be cajolled to join in a quiet game in the hope of replenishing his purse, where he saw the chances were all in his favor.

The saloon was alight with music and gaiety; the jolly company of travelers and the gaudy furniture were reflected many times over in the gilded mirrors that caught the rays of a large chandelier depending from the center of the ceiling. To the eye and ear merriment held high carnival; some strolled about, many sought the refreshment bar, but a greater number—men and even women—took part in the play or bet lightly on the players, sotto voce, for pastime. The clink and gleam of gold was there as it passed from hand to hand. Six men at a table played baccarat; farther on, a party of very young people—both sexes—played loo for small stakes. There were quartets of whist players, too; but the most popular game was poker, for high stakes made by reckless and inveterate gamblers.

St. Clair and his party found an empty table, and Isaac, obedient to a sign from his master, brought him the box containing implements for a game of poker. All the men were inveterate gamblers, but Enson was an expert. Gradually the on-lookers gathered about that one particular table. Not a word was said; the men gripped their cards and held their breaths, with now and then an oath to punctuate a loss more severe than usual.

The slaver-trader Walker sauntered up to the place where St. Clair sat, and stood behind him.

"What's the stakes?" he asked of his next neighbor. The man addressed smiled significantly: "Not a bagatelle to begin with; they've raised them three times."

"Whew!" with a whistle. "And who is winning?"

"Oh, Enson, of course."

"Why 'of course?'" asked Walker with a wicked smile on his ugly face.

"He always wins."

"I reckon not now," returned Walker, as he pointed to the play just made.

PAULINE E. HOPKINS

"He's dealing above board and square, and luck's agin him."

It was true. From this time on Enson played again and again, and lost. The other players left their seats and stood near watching the famous gambler make his play. Finally, with a muttered curse, he staggered up from his chair and started to leave the table with desperate eyes and reeling gate. But he stopped as if struck by a sudden inspiration, and resumed his seat.

"What will he do now?" was the unspoken thought of the crowd.

"Isaac, come here," called out Enson. "I will see you and five hundred better," he continued, addressing his opponent, as the boy approached, and at a signal from him climbed upon the table. The crowd watched the strange scene in breathless silence.

"What price do you set on the boy?" asked the winner, whose name was Johnson, taking a large roll of bills from his pocket.

"He will bring eighteen hundred dollars any day in the New Orleans market."

"I reckon he ain't noways vicious?" asked Johnson, looking in the Negro's smiling face.

"I've never seen him angry."

"I'll give you fifteen hundred for him."

"Eighteen," returned Enson, with an ominous tightening about the mouth.

"Well, I'll tell you what I'll do, the very best; I'll make it sixteen hundred, no more, no less. That's fair. Is it a bargain?"

Enson nodded assent. The crowd heaved a sigh of relief.

"Then you bet the whole of this boy, do you?" continued Johnson.

"Yes."

"I call you, then," said Johnson.

"I've got three queens," replied Enson.

"Not enough," said the other.

"Then if you beat three queens, you beat me."

"I have four jacks, and the boy is mine." The crowd heaved another sigh as one man.

"Hold on! Not so fast!" shouted Enson. "You don't take him till you *show* me that you beat three queens." Johnson threw his five cards upon the table, and four of them were jacks! "Sure," said Johnson, as he looked at Enson and then at the crowd.

"Sure!" came in a hoarse murmur from many throats. For a moment all things whirled and danced before Enson's eyes as he realized what he had lost. The lights from the chandelier shot out sparkles from piles of golden coin, the table heaved, faces were indistinct. He seemed to hear his father's voice again in stern condemnation, as he had heard it for the last time on earth. His face was white and set. He was a man ready for desperate needs. It seemed an hour to him, that short second. Then he turned to the winner:

"Mr. Johnson, I quit you."

Isaac was standing upon the table with the money at his feet. As he stepped down, Johnson said:

"You will not forget that you belong to me."

"No, sir."

"Be up in time to brush my clothes and clean my boots; do you hear?"

"Yas, sir," responded Isaac, with a good-natured smile and a long side-glance at Enson, in which one might have seen the lurking deviltry of a spirit kindred to his master's. Enson turned to leave the saloon, saying:

"I claim the right of redeeming that boy, Mr. Johnson. My father gave him to me when I was a lad. I promised never to part with him."

"Most certainly, sir; the boy shall be yours whenever you hand me over a cool sixteen hundred," returned Johnson. As Enson moved away, chewing the bitter curd of disappointment, Walker strolled up to him.

"That's a bad bargain Johnson's got in your man, Mr. Enson."

"How? Explain yourself."

"If he finds him after tomorrow morning, it's my belief it won't be the fault of Isaac's legs."

"Do you mean to say, sir, that I would connive at robbing a gentleman in fair play?"

"Oh, no; it won't be your fault," replied Walker with a familiar slap on Enson's back, that made the latter wince; "but he's a cute darkey that you can sell in good faith to a man, but he won't stay with him. Bet you the nigger'll be in Baltimore time you are."

"I'll take you. Make your bet."

Walker shook his head. "No, don't you do it. Luck's agin you, an' I won't rob you. That nigger'll lose you, sure."

Enson made no reply, but stood gazing moodily out upon the dark waters of the Atlantic, through which the steamer swiftly ploughed her way. Finally Walker continued:

"Why don't you try another game? Keep it up; luck may change. I'll lend you."

PAULINE E. HOPKINS

Enson waved his hand impatiently and said: "No; no more tonight. I have not a cent in the world until I eat humble pie and beg money from my brother."

"Tough!"

"Thank you. I do not want your sympathy."

"My help, then. Perhaps I can help you. Enson smiled derisively at the endless black waves and the moonless sky.

"No man can do that. I have made my bed hard and must abide the issue."

"Oh, rot! Be a man, and keep on fighting 'em. You'll be all right presently. Never say die."

"Perhaps you have a plan to compass the impossible," returned Enson with a sneer.

"I should say so. I've been thinking a good deal about your brother's marriage, and my old friends, the Sargeants. What would it be worth to you now to find a way to break off this marriage?"

"Break it off! Why man, that can't be done. What are you driving at?"

"Easy there, now. I said 'break if off,' and I meant 'break it off.' They used to tell me when I was a boy that two heads was better'n one ef one was a sheep's head. Same case here. Job's worth ten thou. I can see three thou right in sight, that would make your bill about seven thou." Walker settled his hat at the back of his head, thrust his hands deep in his hip pockets, and gazed out over the dark waters with a glance from his ferret-like gray eyes that seemed to pierce the blackness.

"I don't understand you, Walker; explain yourself."

"I understand myself, and that's enough. All you've got to do is to put your I O U to a paper calling for seven thousand dollars conditional on my rendering you valuable service in a financial matter. Savey?"

"I'd do anything that would break this cursed luck I'm having. Can you do anything? What do you mean, anyhow, Walker?"

"Never mind what I mean. You meet me at Enson Hall. Wait for me if you get there first. Be ready to sign the paper, and I'll show you as neat a job as was ever put up by any man on earth. That's all." Walker turned as he finished speaking and walked away. St. Clair looked after him, uncertain what to think of his strange words and actions.

IV

The morning sun poured its golden light upon the picturesque old house standing in its own grounds in one of the suburban towns adjacent to Baltimore—the Baltimore of 1858 or 1860.

The old house seemed to command one to render homage to its beauty and stateliness. It was a sturdy brick building flanked with offices and having outbuildings touching the very edge of the deep, mysterious woods where the trees waved their beckoning arms in every soft breeze that came to revel in their rich foliage. This was Enson Hall. The Hall was reached through a long dim stretch of these woods—locusts and beeches—from ten to twelve acres in extent; its mellow, red-brick walls framed by a background of beechtrees reminded one of English residences with their immense extent of private grounds. In the rear of the mansion was the garden, with its huge conservatories gay with shrubs and flowers. Piazzas and porticoes promised delightful retreats for sultry weather. The interior of the house was in the style that came in after the Revolution. An immense hall with outer door standing invitingly open gave greeting to the guest. The stairs wound from the lower floor to the rooms above. The grand stairway was richly embellished with carving, and overhead a graceful arch added much to the impressive beauty which met the stranger's first view. The rooms, spacious and designed for entertaining largely, had panelled wainscotting and carved chimney-pieces.

Ellis Enson, the master of the Hall, was a well-made man, verging on forty. "Born with a silver spoon in his mouth," for the vast estate and all invested money was absolutely at his disposal, he was the envy of the men of his class and the despair of the ladies. He was extremely good-looking, slight, elegant, with wavy dark hair, and an air of distinction. Since his father's death he had lived at the Hall, surrounded by his slaves in lonely meditation, fancy free. This handsome recluse had earned the reputation of being morose, so little had he mixed with society, so cold had been his politeness to the fair sex. His farms, his lonely rides, his favorite books, had sufficed for him. He was a good manager, and what was more wonderful, considering his Southern temperament, a thorough man of business. His crops, his poultry, his dairy products, were of the very first quality. Sure it was that his plantation was a paying investment. Meanwhile the great house, with all its beautiful rooms and fine furniture, remained closed to the public, and was the despair of managing mammas with many daughters to provide with eligible husbands. Enson was second to none as a "catch," but he was utterly indifferent to women.

Just about this time when to quarry the master of Enson Hall seemed a hopeless task, Hagar Sargeant came home from a four years' sojourn at the North in a young ladies' seminary.

The Sargeant estate was the one next adjoining Enson Hall; not so large and imposing, but a valuable patrimony that had descended in a long line of Sargeants and was well preserved. For many years before Hagar's birth the estate had been rented because of financial misfortunes, and they had lived in St. Louis, where Mr. Sargeant had engaged in trade so successfully that when Hagar was six years old they were enabled to return to their ancestral home and resume a life of luxurious leisure. Since that time Mr. Sargeant had died. On a trip to St. Louis, where he had gone to settle his business affairs, he contracted cholera, then ravaging many large cities of the Southwest, and had finally succumbed to the scourge. Hagar, their only child, then became her mother's sole joy and inspiration. Determined to cultivate her daughter's rare intellectual gifts, she had sent her North to school when every throb of her heart demanded her presence at home. She had developed into a beautiful girl, the admiration and delight of the neighborhood to which she returned, almost a stranger after her long absence.

A golden May morning poured its light through the open window of the Sargeant breakfast-room. A pleasanter room could scarcely be found, though the furniture was not of latest fashion, and the carpet slightly faded. There was a bay window that opened on the terrace, below which was a garden; there was a table in the recess spread with dainty china and silver, and the remains of breakfast; honeysuckles played hide-and-seek at the open window. Aunt Henny, a coal-black Negress of kindly face, brought in the little brass-bound oaken tub filled with hot water and soap, and the linen towels. Hagar stood at the window contemplating the scene before her. It was her duty to wash the heirlooms of colonial china and silver. From their bath they were dried only by her dainty fingers, and carefully replaced in the corner cupboard. Not for the world would she have dropped one of these treasures. Her care for them, and the placing of every one in its proper niche, was wonderful to behold. Not the royal jewels of Victoria were ever more carefully guarded than these family heirlooms.

This morning Hagar was filled with a delicious excitement, caused by she knew not what. The china and silver were an anxiety unusual to her. She felt a physical exhilaration, inspired, no doubt, by the delicious weather. She always lamented at this season of the year the lost privileges of the house of Sargeant, when their right of way led directly from the house to the shining waters of the bay. There was a path that led to the water still, but it was across the land of their neighbor Enson. Sometimes Hagar would trespass; would cross the parklike stretch of pasture, bordered by the woodland through which it ran, and sit on the edge of the remnant of a wharf, by which ran a small, rapid river, an arm of Chesapeake Bay, chafing among wet stones and leaping gaily over rocky barriers. There she would dream of life before the Revolution, and in these dreams participate in the joys of the colonial dames. She longed to mix and mingle with the gay world; she had a feeling that her own talents, if developed, would end in something far different from the calm routine, the housekeeping and churchgoing which stretched before her. Sometimes softer thoughts possessed her, and she speculated about love and lovers. This peaceful life was too tranquil and uneventful. Oh, for a break in the humdrum recurral of the same events day after day.

She had never met Ellis Enson. He was away a great part of the time before she left home for school, and since she had returned. If she remembered him at all, it was with the thought of a girl just past her eighteenth birthday for a man forty.

This morning Hagar washed the silver with the sleeves of her morning robe turned up to the shoulder, giving a view of rosy, dimpled. arms. "A fairer vision was never seen," thought the man who paused a moment at the open window to gaze again upon the pretty, homelike scene. As Hagar turned from replacing the last of the china, she was startled out of her usual gay indifference at the sight of a handsome pair of dark eyes regarding her intently from the open window. A quick wonder flashed in the eyes that met hers; the color deepened in his face as he saw he was observed. The girl's beauty startled him so, that for a moment he lost the self-control that convention dictates. Then he bared his head in courteous acknowledgement of youth and beauty, with an apology for his seeming intrusion.

"I beg pardon," Enson said in his soft, musical tones; "is Mrs. Sargeant at home? I did not know she had company."

"I am not company; I am Hagar. Yes, mamma is at home; if you will come in, I will take you to her."

He turned and entered the hall door and followed her through the dark, cool hall to the small morning-room, where Mrs. Sargeant spent her mornings in semi-invalid fashion. Then a proper introduction followed, and Ellis Enson and Hagar Sargeant were duly acquainted.

At forty Enson still retained his faith in womanhood, although he had been so persistently pursued by all the women of the vicinity. He believed there were women in the world capable of loving a man for himself alone without a thought of worldly advantage, only he had not been fortunate enough to meet them.

He had a very poor opinion of himself. Adulation had not made him vain. His face indicated strong passions and much pride; but it was pride of caste, not self. There was great tenderness of the eye and lip, and signs of a sensitive nature that could not bear disgrace or downfall that might touch his ancient name. After he left the Sargeant home Hagar's face haunted him; the pure creamy skin, the curved crimson lips ready to smile,—lips sweet and firm,—the broad, low brow, and great, lustrous, long-lashed eyes of brilliant black—soft as velvet, and full of light with the earnest, cloudless gaze of childhood; and there was heart and soul and mind in this countenance of a mere girl. Such beauty as this was a perpetual delight to feast the eyes and charm the senses—aye, to witch a man's heart from him; for here there was not only the glory of form and tints, but more besides,—heart that could throb, soul that could aspire, mind that could think. She was not shy and self-conscious as young girls so often are; she seemed quite at her ease, as one who has no thought of self. He was conscious of his own enthralment. He knew that he had set his feet in the perilous path of love at a late day, but knowing this, he none the less went forward to his fate.

After that the young girl and the man met frequently. She did not realize when the time came that she had grown to look for his coming. There were walks and drives and accidental meetings in the woods. The sun was brighter and the songs of the birds sweeter that summer than ever before.

Ellis fell to day-dreaming, and the dreams were tinged with gold, bringing a flush to his face and a thrill to his heart. Still he would have denied, if accused, that this was love at first sight—bah! That was a well-exploded theory. And yet if it was not love that had suddenly come into his being for this slender, dark-eyed girl, what was it? A change had come into Ellis Enson's life. The greatest changes, too, are always unexpected.

It was a sultry day; there was absolutely no chance to catch a refreshing breeze within four walls. It was one of the rare occasions when Mrs. Sargeant felt obliged to make a business call alone. From the fields came the sound of voices singing: the voices of slaves. Aunt Henny's good-natured laugh occasionally broke the stillness.

"Now I shall have a nice quiet afternoon," thought Hagar, as she left the house for the shadow of the trees. Under the strong, straight branches of a beech she tied three old shawls, hammock-like, one under another, for strength and safety. It was not very far from the ground. If it should come down, she might be bruised slightly, but not killed. She crawled cautiously into her nest; she had let down the long braids of her hair, and as she lolled back in her retreat, they fell over the sides of the hammock and swept the top of the long, soft grass. Lying there, with nothing in sight but the leafy branches of the trees high above her head, through which gleams of the deep blue sky came softly, she felt as if she had left the world, and was floating, Ariel-like, in midair.

After an hour of tranquility, footsteps were audible on the soft grass. There was a momentary pause, then someone came to a standstill beside her fairy couch.

"Back so soon, mamma? I wish you could come up here with me; it is just heavenly."

"Then I suppose you must be one of the heavenly inhabitants, an angel, but I never can pay compliments as I ought," said a voice.

"Mr. Enson!" Hagar was conscious of a distinct quickening of heart-action and a rush of crimson to her cheeks; with a pretty, hurried movement she rose to a sitting position in her hammock; "I really am ashamed of myself. I thought you were mamma."

"Yes," he answered, smiling at her dainty confusion.

"Mr. Enson," she said again, this time gravely, "politeness demands that I receive you properly, but decency forbids I should do it unless you will kindly turn your back to me while I step to earth once more."

The man was inwardly shaking with laughter at the grave importance with which she viewed the business in hand, but not for worlds would he have had her conscious of his mirth.

"I can help you out all right," he said.

PAULINE E. HOPKINS

"No, I am too heavy. I think I will stay here until you go."

"Oh—but—say now, Miss Hagar, that is hard to drive me away when I have just come; and such an afternoon, too, hot enough to kill a darkey. Do let me help you down."

"No; I can get out myself if I must. Please turn your back."

Thus entreated, he turned his back and commenced an exhaustive study of the landscape. Hagar arose; the hammock turned up, and Ellis was just in time to receive her in his arms as she fell.

"Hagar—my darling—you are not hurt?" he asks anxiously, still holding her in a close embrace.

"No; of course not. It is so good of you to be by to care for me so nicely," she said in some confusion.

"Hagar—my darling," he said again, with a desperate resolve to let her know the state of his feelings, "will you marry me?" She trembled as his lips pressed passionate kisses on hers. The veil was drawn away. She understood—this was the realization of the dreams that had come to her dimly all the tender springtime. Never in all her young life had she felt so happy, so strangely happy. A soft flush mounted to cheek and brow under his caresses.

"I don't understand," murmured the girl, trembling with excitement.

"My darling, I think I have said it more plainly that most men do. Hagar, I think you must know it; I have made no secret of my love for you. Have you not understood me all the days of the spring and summer?"

"Are you quite sure that you love me? You are so old and wise, and I so ignorant to be the wife of so grand a man as you."

She glanced up fleetingly, and flushed more deeply under the look she met. He folded her closer still in his arms. His next words were whispered:

"My love! lift your eyes to mine, and say you love me."

Hagar had not dreamed that such passion as this existed in the world. It seemed to take the breath of her inner life and leave her powerless, with no separate existence, no distinct mental utterance.

Gently Ellis drew back the bright head against him, and bent over the sweet lips that half sought his kiss; and so for one long moment he knew a lifetime of happiness. Then he released her.

"Heaven helping me, you shall be so loved and shielded that sorrow shall never touch you. You shall never repent trusting your young life to me. May I speak to your mother tonight?"

"Yes," she whispered.

And so they were betrothed. Ellis felt and meant all that he said under the stress of the emotion of the moment; but who calculates the effect of time and cruel circumstance? Mrs. Sargeant was more than pleased at the turn of events. Soon Ellis was taking the bulk of the business of managing her estates upon his own strong shoulders. These two seemed favored children of the gods all that long, happy summer. She was his, and he was hers.

The days glided by like a dream, and soon brought the early fall which was fixed for the wedding festivities. All was sunshine. The wedding day was set for October. On the morning of the day before, Hagar entered her mother's room as was her usual custom, to give her a loving morning greeting, and found nothing but the cold, unresponsive body, from which the spirit had fled. Then followed days that were a nightmare to Hagar, but under Ellis' protecting care the storm of grief spent itself and settled into quiet sadness. There was no one at the Sargeant home but the bereaved girl and her servants. At the end of a month Ellis put the case plainly before her, and she yielded to his persuasions to have the marriage solemnized at once, so that he might assume his place as her rightful protector. A month later than the time originally set there was a quiet wedding, very different from the gay celebration originally planned by a loving mother, and the young mistress took her place in the stately rooms of Enson Hall. When a twelve-month had passed there was a little queen born—the heiress of the hall. Ellis' happiness was complete.

V

It was past the breakfast hour in the Hall kitchen, but Marthy still lingered. It was cold outside; snow had fallen the night before; the clouds were dull and threatening. The raw northern blasts cut like bits of ice; the change was very sudden from the pleasant coolness of autumn. The kitchen was an inviting place; the blaze shot up gleefully from between the logs, played hide-and-seek in dark corners and sported merrily across the faces of the pickaninnies sprawling on the floor and constantly under Aunt Henny's feet.

Aunt Henny now reigned supreme in the culinary department of the Hall. Her head was held a little higher, if possible, in honor of the new dignity that had come to the family from the union of the houses of Enson and Sargeant.

"'Twarn't my 'sires fer a weddin' so close to a fun'ral, but Lor', chile, dars a diffurunce in doin' things, an' it 'pears dis weddin's comin' out all right. Dem two is a sight fer sore eyes, an' as fer de baby"—Aunt Henny rolled up her eyes in silent ecstasy.

"Look hyar, mammy," said Marthy, Mrs. Enson's maid and Aunt Henny's daughter, "why don' you see Unc' Demus? He'd guv you a charm fer Miss Hagar to wear; she needn't know nuthin' 'bout it."

"Sho, honey, wha' you take me fo'? I done went down to Demus soon as dat weddin' wus brung up."

"Wha' he say, mammy?"

"Let me 'lone now tell I tells you." Aunt Henny was singeing pin-feathers from a pile of birds on the floor in front of the fire. She dropped her task to give emphasis to her words. "I carried him Miss Hagar's pocket-hankercher and he guv me a bag made outen de skin ob a rattlesnake, an' he put in it a rabbit's foot an' er sarpint's toof, an' er squorerpin's tail wid a leetle dust outen de graveyard an' he sewed up de bag. Den he tied all dat up in de hankercher an' tell me solemn: 'Long as yer mistis keep dis 'bout her, trouble'll neber stay so long dat joy won't conquer him in de end.' So, honey, I done put dat charm in Missee Hagar draw 'long wid her tickler fixins an' I wants yer, Marthy, to take keer ob it," she concluded, with a grave shake of her turbanned head. Marthy was duly impressed, and stood looking at her mother with awe in every feature of her little brown face.

"'Deed an' I will, mammy."

"My young Miss will be all right ef dat St. Clair Enson keeps 'way from hyar," continued the woman reflectively.

"Who's St. Clar Enson?" asked Marthy.

"Nemmin' 'bout him. Sometime I'll tell you when you gits older. All you got ter do now is ter take mighty good keer o' your mistis and de baby," replied her mother, with a knowing wag of her head. "Fling anudder chunk on dat fire!" she called to one of the boys playing on the floor. "Gittin' mighty cole fer dis time ob year, de a'r small pow'rful lack mo' snow."

A shadow fell across the doorsill shutting out the light for a moment, that came through the half-open doorway. Marthy gave a shriek that ended in a giggle as a young Negro, tall, black, smiling, sauntered into the kitchen; it was Isaac. Aunt Henny threw her arms high above her head in unbounded astonishment.

"En de name ob de Lawd! Isaac! What's gwine ter happen ter dis fambly now, Ike, dat you's come sneakin' home?"

Isaac grinned. "Isn't you pow'rful glad ter see me, Aunt Henny? I is ter see you an' Marthy. Marfy's a mighty likely lookin' gal, I 'low." He gave a sly roll of his eye in the direction where the girl stood regarding the athletic young Negro with undisguised admiration.

"Non o' dat," sputtered Aunt Henny. "Don' you go tryin' ter fool wid dat gal, you lim' ob de debbil. Take yo'sef right off! What yer doin' hyar, enyhow? Dis ain't no place for you."

"My marse tell'd me ter come," replied Isaac, not at all ruffled by his reception. "I ain't gwine ter go right off; ain't tell'd none o' de folks howdy yit."

"*Your marse tell'd you ter come!* What fer he tell'd yer to come?" stormed Aunt Henny, with a derisive snort. "Dat's what I want ter know. *My* marse'll have somethin' ter say I reckon, ef *yer* marse *did* tell'd yer ter come. An' I b'lieve you's a liar, 'deed I do. I don' b'lieve yer marser knows whar you is at, dis blessid minnit."

Isaac chuckled. "I'se come home ter see de new mistis an' de leetle baby; I cert'n'y hope dey is well. Marse St. Clar'll be hyar hisself bimeby."

Aunt Henny stood a moment silently regarding the boy. Fear, amazement and curiosity were blended in her honest face. Plainly, she was puzzled. "De debbil turn' sain'," she muttered to herself, with a long look at the unconscious Isaac, who sat toasting his cold bare toes before the roaring fire. "Dis house got mo' peace in it, an' Marse Ellis happier den he been since his mar, ol' Missee Enson, died; but," and she shook her turbanned head ominously, "'tain't fer long. I ain't fergit nuffin'; I isn't lived nex' dis Enson Hall so many years fer nuffin."

"I'se walk'd a long way slippin' officers"—began Isaac.

"Um!" grunted Aunt Henny, with the look of alarm still in her eyes, "officers! dat's what's de matter."

"Dey'll hab ter see Marse St. Clar, tain't me. He sol' me. I runned 'way. I come home, dat's all. Kain't I hab suthin' to eat?"

"Ef 'tain't one it's t'odder. Befo' God, I 'lieve you an' yo' marse bof onhuman. Been sol'! runned 'way! hump!" again grunted Aunt Henny.

Meanwhile Marthy had made coffee and baked a corncake in the hot ashes. Isaac sniffed the aroma of the fragrant coffee hungrily. There was chicken and rice, too, he noticed as she placed food on the end of a table and motioned him to help himself. Isaac needed no pressing, and in a moment was eating ravenously.

"Tell you de troof, Aunt Henny," he said at last, as he waited for a fourth help, "Marse St. Clar git hard up de oder night in a little play comin' up de bay, an' he sell me to a gempleman fer sixteen hundred dollars. But, Lor', dat don' hol' Isaac, chile, while he's got legs."

"Dat's jes' what I thought. No use yer lyin' ter me, Isaac, yer Aunt Henny *was born wif a veil.* I knows a heap o' things by seein' 'em fo' dey happens. I don' tell all I sees, but I keeps up a steddyin' 'bout it."

"Dar's no mon can keep me, I don't keer how much Marse St. Clar sells me; he's my onlies' marser," continued Isaac, as he kept on devouring food a little more slowly than at first.

"Lawd sakes, honey; you's de mos' pow'rfulles' eater I'se seed fer many a day. Don' reckon you's had a good meal sence yer was home five years ago. Dog my cats ef I don' hope Marse Ellis will jes' make yer trot."

"He kin sen' me back, but I isn't gwine stay wid 'em," replied Isaac, with his mouth full of food.

"You cain't he'p yo'se'f."

"I kin walk," persisted Isaac doggedly.

"Put you in de caboose an' give yer hundred lashes," Aunt Henny called back, as she waddled out of the kitchen to find her master.

"Don' keer fer dat, nudder."

Isaac improved the time between the going and coming of Aunt Henny by making fierce love to Marthy, who was willing to meet him more than half way.

The breakfast-room was redolent with the scent of flowers, freshly cut from the greenhouses; the waxed floor gleamed like polished glass beneath the fur rugs scattered over it, and the table, with its service for two, was drawn in front of the cheerful fire that crackled and sparkled in the open fireplace. All the luxuries that wealth could give were gathered about the young matron. It was a happy household; the hurry and rush of warlike preparations had not reached its members, and the sting of slavery, with its demoralizing brutality, was unknown on these plantations so recently joined. Happiness was everywhere, from the master in his carriage to the slave singing in the fields at his humble task. Breakfast was over, and as Ellis glanced over the top of his morning paper at his wife and baby, he felt a thrill of intense pride and love.

As compared with her girlhood, Hagar's married life had been one round of excitement. Washington and many other large cities had been visited on their brief honeymoon. They were royally entertained by all the friends and relatives of both families, and the beautiful bride had been the belle of every assembly. Ellis was wrapped up in her; intimate acquaintance but deepened his love. Her nature was pure, spiritual, and open as the day. Gowned in spotless white, her slender form lost in a large armchair, she sat opposite him, dandling the baby in her arms. She looked across at him and smiled.

"Well, pet," he smiled back at her, "going to ride?"

She shook her head and set every little curl in motion.

"I won't go out today, it is so cold; we are so comfortable here before the fire, baby and I."

"What a lazy little woman it is," he laughed, rising from his seat and going over to stand behind her chair, stroke the bright hair, and clasp mother and child in his arms. Hagar rested her head against him, and held the infant at arm's length for his admiration.

"Isn't she a darling? See, Ellis, she knows you," as the child cooed and laughed and gurgled at them both, in a vain effort to clinch something in her little red fists.

"This little beggar has spoiled our honeymoon with a vengeance," he replied with a laugh. "I cannot realize that it is indeed over, and we have settled down to the humdrum life of old married folk."

"Can anything ever spoil that and its memories?" she asked, with a sweet upward look into his face. "Indeed, I often wonder if I am too happy; is it right for any human being to be so favored in life as I have been."

"Gather your roses while you may, there will be dark clouds enough in life, heaven knows. No gloomy thoughts, Mignon; let us be happy in the present." He kissed the lips raised so temptingly for his caress, and then one for the child. He thought humbly of his own career beside the spotless creature he had won for life. While not given to excesses, yet there were things in the past that he regretted. Since the birth of their child, the days had been full of emotion for these two people, who were, perhaps, endowed with over-sensitive natures given to making too much of the commonplace happenings of life. Now, as he watched the head of the child resting against the mother's breast, he ran the gamut of human feelings in his sensations. Love and thanksgiving for these unspeakable gifts of God—his wife and child—swept the inmost recesses of his heart.

"Please, Marse Ellis!" cried Aunt Henny's voice from the doorway, "please, sah, Marse St. Clar's Isaac done jes' dis minnit come home. What's I gwine ter do wid him?"

"What, Henny!" Ellis cried in astonishment; "St. Clair's Isaac? Where's his master?"

"Dunno Marse Ellis, but dar's allers truble, sho, when dat lim' o' Satan turns up; 'deed dar is."

Ellis left the room hurriedly, followed by Aunt Henny. Hagar sat there, fondling the child, a perfect picture of sweet womanhood. She had matured wonderfully in the few months of married life; her girlish manner had dropped from her like a garment. Eve's perfect daughter, she accomplished her destiny in sweet content. Presently the door opened, and her husband stood beside her chair again; his face wore a troubled look.

"What is it?" she asked, with a sweeping upward glance that noted every change of his countenance.

"St. Clair's Isaac."

"Well, and is he so serious a matter that you must look so grave?"

"My dear, the slaves all look upon him as a bird of evil omen; for myself, I look upon it as mere ignorant superstition, but still I have a feeling of uneasiness. They have neither of them been at the Hall for five years. Isaac says his master is coming—that he expected to find him here. What brings them is the puzzler."

"News of your marriage, Ellis; a natural desire to see his new relative. I see nothing strange in that, dear."

"He can't feel very happy about it, according to the terms of the will; probably he has been counting on my not marrying, and now, being disappointed, comes for me to pay his debts, or perform some impossible favor."

"Why impossible?"

"St. Clair is an unsavory fellow, and his desires are not likely to appeal to a man of honor," replied Ellis, with a short, bitter laugh.

"So bad as that?" said his wife regretfully; it was the first shadow since the beginning of their honeymoon. She continued: "Promise me, Ellis, to bear with him kindly and grant him anything in reason, in memory of our happiness."

In the kitchen Aunt Henny, with little braids of hair sticking out from under turban, talked to Marthy.

"Ef Marse Ellis listen to me, he gwine ter make dat Isaac quit dese diggin's."

"Law, mammy," laughed Marthy, showing her tiny white teeth and tossing her head, "you don' want ter drive de po' boy 'way from whar he was born, does yer?" Marthy was a born coquette, and Isaac was very gallant to her.

"Dat all I gwine ter say. Nobody knows dat Marse St. Clar an' his Isaac better'n I does. I done part raise 'em bof. I reckon my ha'r'd all turn plum' white ef dem two hadn't don lef' dese parts."

"How you come to raise 'em, mammy, an' what made 'em try ter turn yo' ha'r plum' white?"

"Dev'ment, honey, pur' dev'ment! It 'pears lack 'twas only yisterday dat I was a gal wurkin' right yere in dis same ol' kitchen. Marse Sargeant he lose heap money, an' all ob dem move ter St. Louis ter 'trench an' git rich ergin; Marse Enson he want me fer ol' Miss, an' so Marse Sargeant done leave me hyar at Enson Hall. While I was hyar bof ob dem imps was born, but Marse St. Clar he good bit older dan Isaac. Many's de time he run me all ober dis plantation when he no bigger'n dat Thomus Jefferson, 'cause I wouldn't give dat Isaac fus' help from de chickuns jes' roasted fer dinner befo' de fambly done seed nary leg ob 'em. Chase me, chile, wid a pissle pinted plum' at me."

"Lordy! wha' you reckon he do ef he come back hyar now?"

"I don' reckon on nuffin but dev'ment, jes' same as he done time an' time agin when he were a boy—jes' dev'ment."

"Mammy, you say oder day when Missee Hagar git married to Marse Ellis: 'Now dat St. Clar'll stan' no chance ob gittin' de property'; what you mean by dat?"

"Didn't mean nuffin," snapped her mother, with a suspicious look at her. "G' 'long 'bout yo' bisness; you's gittin' mighty pert since you git to be Miss Hagar's maid; you's axin' too many questions."

In a day or so the family settled down to Isaac's presence as a matter of course. Aunt Henny's predictions about the weather were verified, and the week was unpleasant. The wind blew the bare branches of the trees against the veranda posts and roared down the wide fireplaces; snowflakes were in the air. Hagar and Ellis had just come in from a canter over the country roads; she went immediately to her room to dress for dinner, but Ellis tarried a moment in the inviting room which seemed to command his admiration. The luxuries addressed themselves to his physical sense, and he was conscious of complete satisfaction in the knowledge that his wealth could procure a fitting setting for the gem he had won. Other thoughts, too, crept in, aroused by the talk of a friend where they had called on the way home. He had not thought of war, and was not interested in politics; still, if it were true that complications were arising that demanded a settlement by a trial of arms, he was ready. "Perhaps we are too happy for it to last," he muttered; "but, come what will, I have been blessed." His gaze followed Marthy's movements mechanically, as she lighted the wax candles and let fall the heavy curtains, shutting the gloom outside in the gathering darkness. He was aroused from the deep revery into which he had fallen by the sound of wheels on the carriage drive. In a moment, before he could cross the room, the door opened and St. Clair Enson entered, followed by the slave-trader, Walker.

"St. Clair! Is it possible!" he cried, striding forward to grasp his brother's hand. "Is it really you? Welcome home!" They shook hands warmly, and then Ellis threw his arm about St. Clair's shoulders, and for a moment the two men gazed in the depths of each other's eyes with emotion too deep for words. The younger man *did* feel for an instant a wave of fraternal love for this elder brother against whom he meditated (an evil) deed.

"Why, Ellis, I do believe you're glad to see me. You're ready to kill the fatted calf to feast the prodigal," St. Clair said, as they fell apart. "My friend, Mr. Walker—Walker, my brother."

"Glad to see you and welcome you to Enson Hall," said Ellis in cordial greeting, his hospitable nature overcoming his repugnance for this man of unsavory reputation.

"Thanky, thanky," said Walker, as he awkwardly accepted the armchair Ellis offered him, and drew near the blazing fire.

"Just in time for dinner; you will dine with us, Mr. Walker." Walker nodded assent.

"Well, Ellis, how's the world using you? You're married, lucky dog. Got your letter while I was at the nominating convention; it must have followed me about for more than a month. Thought I'd come up and make the acquaintance of my new sister and niece," remarked St. Clair, with careless ease.

"Yes," replied Ellis. Somehow his brother's nonchalant air and careless words jarred upon his ear. "You are always welcome to come when you like and stay as long as you please. This is your home."

"Home with a difference," replied St. Clair, as an evil smile for an instant marred his perfect features.

"He won't stand much show of gittin' eny of this prop'ty now you's got a missus, Mr. Enson," ventured Walker, with a grin. "He's been mighty anxious to meet your missus. Most fellers isn't so oneasy about a sister-in-law, but I reckon this one is different, being report says she's a high-stepper," said Walker, as he grinned at Ellis and cleared his mouth by spitting foul tobacco juice on the polished hearth. Ellis bowed coldly in acknowledgment of his words.

"Mrs. Enson will be down presently. This certainly is a joyful surprise," he said, turning to St. Clair. "Why didn't you send word, and the carriage would have met you at the station?"

"Oh, we came out all right in Walker's trap."

"I'll have it put up." Ellis rose as he spoke.

"No, no; my man will drive me back to the city shortly," Walker broke in.

"I hope you are doing well, St. Clair; where are you from now?"

"Just from Charleston, where I have made a place for myself at last. Politics," he added significantly.

"Ah!"

"Great doin's down in Charleston; great doin's," Walker broke in again.

"No doubt of it; how do you think this matter will end?"

"It's goin' to be the greatest time the world ever saw, Mr. Enson. When we git a-goin' thar'll be no holdin' us. The whole South, sah, is full of sodjers, er-gittin' ready to whup the Yanks t'uther side of nex' week. That's how it's goin' to end."

"Then it will really be war?"

"The greatest one the worl' ever seen, sah, unless the Yanks git on their knees and asks our pardon, and gives up this govinment to their natral rulers. Why, man, ain't yer heard? You's a patriot, ain't you? Yer a son of the sunny South, ain't yer?"

Ellis smiled at this enthusiasm, although filled with disgust for the man.

"When one has his family to think of, there are times when he forgets the world and thinks of nothing but his home. Be that as it may, I am no recreant son of the South. I stand by her with all I possess. I can imagine nothing that would turn me a traitor to my section."

"Spoken like a man. That's the talk, eh, Enson?" he said, appealing to St. Clair, who nodded in approval.

"Do all you can, I say, for the Confederate States of America, from givin' 'em yer money down to helpin' 'em cuss."

"When the time comes I shall not be found wanting. By the way, St. Clair, your boy Isaac is here. Came on us suddenly the other day."

"Ha, ha, ha! the little black rascal. Didn't I tell you he'd do Johnson out of that money? He's the very devil, that boy."

"Like master, like man," replied St. Clair, with a shrug of his handsome shoulders.

"What is it?" asked Ellis sternly; "no cheating or swindling, is there?"

"He's a runaway. I sold him to a gentleman about a week ago," was St. Clair's careless answer.

"What is the man's name, and where is he to be found? he must be reimbursed or Isaac returned to him," said Ellis, looking sternly at his brother. "Enson Hall is no party to fraudulent dealings."

"I'm glad to hear you say that, Mr. Enson; I'm up here lookin' for a piece of property belonging to me, and said to be stopping on this very plantation."

"Impossible, sir; all our slaves have been here from childhood, or have grown old with us. You have been misinformed."

"I reckon not. As I was tellin' your brother here, it's a mighty onpleasant job I've got before me, but I must do my dooty." Walker put on a sardonic smile, and continued:

"I see, sah, that you don' understan' me. Let me explain further: Fourteen years ago I bought a slave child from a man in St. Louis, and not being able to find a ready sale for her on account of her white complexion, I lent her to a Mr. Sargeant. I understand that you have her in your employ. I've come to get her." Here the slave-trader took out his large sheepskin pocketbook, and took from it a paper which he handed to Ellis.

Ellis gazed at Walker in bewilderment; he took the paper in his hand and mechanically glanced at it. "Still your meaning is not clear to me,

Mr. Walker. I tell you we have no slave of yours on this plantation," but his face had grown white, and large drops of perspiration stood on his forehead.

"Well, sah, I'll explain a leetle more. Mr. and Mrs. Sargeant lived a number of years in St. Louis; they took a female child from me to bring up—*a nigger*—and they passed her off on the commoonity here as their own, and you have *married* her. Is my meaning clear now, sah?"

"Good God!" exclaimed Ellis, as he fell back against the wainscotting, "then this paper, if it means anything, must mean my wife."

"I can't help who it means or what it means," replied Walker, "this yer's the bill of sale, an' there's an officer outside there in the cart to git me my nigger."

"This paper proves nothing. You'll take no property from this house without proper authority," replied Ellis with ominous calm. Walker lost his temper, apparently.

"I hold you in my hand, sah!" he stormed; "you are a brave man to try to face me down with stolen property."

Ellis rose slowly to his fee. Pale, teeth set, lips half parted, eyes flashing lightning—furious, terrible, superb in his wrath. His eyes were fixed on Walker, who, frightened at his desperate look, rose to his feet also, with his hand on his pistol. "You would murder me," he gasped.

Ellis laughed a strange, discordant laugh.

"There is, there must be some mistake here. My wife was the daughter of Mr. Sargeant. There is not a drop of Negro blood in her veins; I doubt, sir, if you have ever seen her. And, Mr. Walker, if you do not prove the charges you have this day insulted me by making, your life shall pay the penalty."

"Well, sah, fetch her in the room here; I reckon she'll know me. She warn't so leetle as to fergit me altogether."

Just at this moment Hagar opened the door, pausing on the threshold, a fair vision in purest white; seeing her husband's visitors, she hesitated. Ellis stepped quickly to her side and took her hand.

"My dear, are you acquainted with this gentleman? Do you remember ever seeing him before?"

She looked a moment, hesitated, and then said: "I think not."

Walker stepped to the mantel where the wax-light would fall full upon his face, and said:

"Why, Hagar, have you forgotten me? It's only about fourteen years ago that I bought you, a leetle shaver, from Rose Valley, and lent you to Mrs. Sargeant, ha, ha, ha!"

Hagar put her hand to her head in a dazed way as she heard the coarse laugh of the rough, brutal slave-trader. She looked at Ellis, put out her hand to him in a blind way, and with a heartrending shriek fell fainting to the floor.

VI

"I thought she'd remember," exclaimed Walker.

Ellis raised his wife in his arms and placed her upon a sofa. St. Clair stood watching the scene with a countenance in which curiosity and satisfaction struggled for the mastery.

"Throw a leetle water in her face, and that'll bring her to. I've seen 'em faint befo', but they allers come to."

Ellis was deathly white; he turned his flaming eyes upon the trader:

"The less you say, the better. By God! I have a mind to put a ball in you now, you infernal hound!"

"Yes, but she's mine; I want to see that she's all right," and Walker shrank away from the infuriated man.

Ellis took his wife in his arms and bore her from the room. Shortly, Aunt Henny brought them word to dine without him, their rooms were ready, and he would see Mr. Walker in the morning after he had communicated with his lawyer. The officer was dismissed, and drove back to the town. As they sat at the table enjoying the sumptuous fare and perfect appointments, St. Clair said to Walker.

"Is this thing true?"

"True as gospel. The only man who could prove the girl's birth is the one I took her from, and he's dead."

"Well, you've done me a mighty good turn, blame me if you have'nt. I shan't forget it. Here's to our future prosperity," and he touched his wineglass to his friend's.

"I don't mean you shall forget," was Walker's reply as he sat his glass down empty. "Now, siree, you hang about here for a spell and watch the movements. He'll pay me all right, but you mustn't let him snake her off or anything. Ef things look queer, jes' touch the wires and I'll be with you instanter."

On the following morning Ellis Enson's lawyer, one of the ablest men of the Maryland Bar, pronounced the bill of sale genuine, for it had been drawn up by a justice, and witnessed by men who sent their affadavits under oath.

"There is but one thing to be done, Mr. Walker," Ellis said, after listening to his lawyer's words. "What do you want? How much money will it take to satisfy you to say no more about the matter?"

"I don't bear you any malice for nothing you've said ter me; perhaps

PAULINE E. HOPKINS

I'd do about the same as you have ef it was my case. Five thou, cash, will git her, though ef I toted her to New Orleans market, a handsome polished wench like her would bring me any gentleman's seven or eight thou, without a remark. As for the pickaninny—"

"What!" thundered Ellis, "the child, too?"

"In course," replied Walker, drawing his finger in and out his scraggy whiskers, "the child follows the condition of the mother, so I scoop the pile."

Ellis groaned aloud.

"As I was sayin'," continued Walker, "the pickaninny will cost you another thou, and cheap at that."

"I would willingly give the money twice over, even my whole fortune, if it did not prove my wife to be of Negro blood," replied Ellis, with such despair in his tones that even these men, inured to such scenes from infancy, were touched with awe.

The money was paid, and within the hour the house had resumed its wonted quiet and all was apparently as before; but the happiness of Enson Hall had fled forever.

VII

Marthy was horrified to see how her mistress arose from the couch where her husband placed her, fall on her knees beside it, and burst into wild tempestuous sobbing.

"Lor', Missee Hagar! Lor', honey! Don' cry so, don', honey!"

Hagar suddenly arose, caught her by the shoulders and turned her toward the light, minutely examining the black skin, crinkled hair, flat nose and protruding lips. So might her grandmother have looked.

"Fo' mercy sake, is you sick, Miss Hagar?" cried the girl, frightened at the strange glare in the large dark eyes. But Hagar turned away without replying. Marthy hurried down stairs.

"My soul, Mammy," she cried as she burst into the kitchen, "Miss Hagar done gone clean destructed."

Once more Hagar crouched upon the floor. She felt like writhing and screaming, only her tongue seemed paralyzed. She thought and thought with agonizing intensity. Vaguely, as in a dream, she recalled her stay in Rose Valley and the terror of her childish heart caused by the rough slave-trader. Could it be true, or was it but a hideous nightmare from which she would soon awake? Her mother a slave! She wondered that the very thought did not strike her dead. With shrinking horror she contemplated the black abyss into which the day's events had hurled her, leaving her there to grovel and suffer the tortures of the damned. Her name gone, her pride of birth shattered at one blow! Was she, indeed, a descendant of naked black savages of the horrible African jungles? Could it be that the blood of generations of these unfortunate ones flowed through her veins? Her education, beauty, refinement, what did they profit her now if—horrible thought—Ellis, her husband, repudiated her? Her heart almost ceased beating with the thought, and she crouched still lower in the dust of utter humiliation.

Then she rose and walked about the room; it was crowded with her wedding finery. She touched an article here and there with the solemnity that we give to the dead—they were relics of a time that would never return to her. She examined her features in the mirror, but even to her prejudiced eyes there was not a trace of the despised chattel. One blow with her open hand shattered its shining surface and the pieces flew about in a thousand tiny particles; she did not notice in her frenzy that the hand was torn and bleeding. Then she laughed a dreadful laugh:

first, silently; then in a whisper; then a peal that clashed through the quiet house and reached the sorrow-stricken man in the silent library. He shuddered, but did not move; he could not face her yet. Aunt Henny and Marthy stood outside the locked door and whispered to each other: "Missee Hagar done gone mad!"

She paused an instant, in her ceaseless promenade about the room, beside the dressing table where her husband's picture reposed in its nest of silk and lace; she paled and shuddered. Could she expect him to forget all his prejudices, which were also her own? Slavery—its degradation, the pining and fretting of the Negro race in bondage—had always seemed right to her. Although innocent of cruelty to them, yet their wrongs were coming home to her in a two-fold harvest. Yes, Ellis would give her up; he must; it was his duty. Only this morning she was his wife, the honored mistress of his home; tonight what? His slave, his concubine! Horrible fatality that had named her Hagar. Somewhere she had read lines that came back to her vividly now:

> "Farewell! I go, but Egypt's mighty gods
> Will go with me, and my avengers be,
> And in whatever distant land your god,
> Your cruel god of Israel, is known,
> There, too, the wrongs that you have done this day
> To Hagar and your first-born,
> Shall waken and uncoil themselves, and hiss
> Like adders at the name of Abraham."

Then she gazed once more upon the pictured face with the strained look we place upon the face of the dead before they are hidden from us forever. They brought the child to the door and begged her to open to it. She heeded it not. Let it die; it, too, was now a slave.

The night passed; it was dawn again. There were sounds of life from the house below. Some one came slowly up the stairs and paused at her door. Then Ellis's voice, sounding harsh and discordant, said:

"It is I, Hagar."

She opened the door. She nerved herself to hear what he might say. The sense of her bitter shame overpowered her, and she shrank before him, cowering as he closed the door, and stood within the room.

Twice he essayed to speak, and twice a groan issued from his white lips. How could he bear it! She stood before him with clasped hands and hanging head as became a slave before her master. How changed, too, he thought, a blight had even fallen upon her glorious beauty. He who had always upheld the institution as a God-given principle of humanity and Christianity, suddenly beheld his idol, stripped of its gilded trappings, in all its filthiness. Then in his heart he cursed slavery.

"Hagar, I have bought you of that man—Walker—he will not annoy you again."

She did not speak or raise her eyes. Ellis bit his lips until the blood ran in the effort to restrain himself for her sake.

"I have thought the matter over and much as I wish it might be otherwise, much as I would sacrifice for you, I feel it my duty as a Southern gentleman, the representative of a proud old family, to think of others beside myself and not allow my own inclinations to darken the escutcheon of a good old name. I cannot, I dare not, and the law forbids me to acknowledge as my wife a woman in whose veins courses a drop of the accursed blood of the Negro slave."

Still she stood there motionless.

Ellis was in torture. Why did she stand there like a forlorn outcast, in stony despair?

"Speak!" he cried at last, "for God sake say something or I shall die!"

Then she raised her eyes to his for one fleeting moment.

"I do not blame you. You can do nothing else."

He moved a step toward her with a smothered groan, "Dearest, dearest," he whispered, and the tone of his voice carried in it his unshaken love.

"Do not,—do not,—" broke from her white lips and with a smothered cry of agony her reserve broke down and she flung herself upon the couch face down.

Ellis went to her and knelt beside her with his arms about her. Five minutes must have passed while they communed in spirit. There was no sound but the girl's hysterical sobbing.

"I am going away," he said at length: "I cannot stay here and live. I may never return, but I shall leave you amply provided for." Then he rose to his feet and rushed from the room. She heard his footsteps echoing down the empty corridor and pause before the door of the nursery.

Ellis loved his wife devotedly, but the shame of public ostracism and condemnation seemed too much for inherited principles. An hour passed. Once more Ellis resumed his measured pacing in the library.

The clock ticked slowly on the mantel, but the beating of his heart outstripped it. He could not follow the plans he had laid out as the path of duty. His visit to the nursery had upset them; parental love, love for his innocent wife, was too strong to be easily cast aside. The ticking of the clock maddened him. It seemed the voice of doom pursuing him—condemning him as a coward—coward—coward. He could stand it no longer. Once more he mounted the stairs to his wife's room.

"Hagar, I cannot do it. We cannot alter the fact that we are bound by all the laws of God and man for better or worse. I have thought it all out, and I have planned a way."

"It is impossible," she said in quiet despair. "You cannot overcome this fearful thing that has fallen upon us. I myself think and feel as you do. It is enough; I accept my fate."

"Oh, no, no; do not say that!"

"Yes, Ellis," she repeated, her face like snow in its pallor.

"Hagar, you do not know what you are saying. You love me, and I love you as my very soul. How were we to know? How could we tell? Therefore, having committed a sin in innocence—if sin it be, and I do not so believe it, for things appear in a different light to me now—we will together live it down. Surely heaven cannot fix the seal of this crime on us forever." The supplication of his voice, his speaking eyes, shook Hagar's heart, so tired and worn with emotion. Her eyes were full of compassion as they rested on him, her lips firm and cold. "I love you, Ellis; you know that, and by that love, although I am your slave and chattel, I know that your love demands naught for your wife but honor. The force of circumstances cannot degrade you—cannot change your chivalrous nature."

"Great heavens! You misunderstand me. I have no hope, no life, apart from you, and I hold you as I cling to salvation, my love, my soul! Listen, Hagar, I have a plan." Bending over her he rapidly outlined a plan of life abroad. They would be remarried, and sail from a Northern port for Europe; there, where the shadow of this crime could not come, they would begin life anew. He had mapped it all out carefully and as she listened she was convinced—it was feasible; it could be done.

Neither of them noticed that the door was ajar; neither did they hear the light footfall that paused beside it. It was St. Clair.

"Walker was right. We must stop that game," he muttered to himself.

VIII

Two weeks had passed since Ellis left his home on the pretext of urgent business, but in reality to make necessary arrangements for an indefinite stay abroad. Ill news travels fast and it was well known all over the plantations and in the neighborhood that the terrible discovery of Hagar's origin had broken up the home life at Enson Hall. Save for St. Clair's presence, the Hall had settled back into its old bachelor state with one difference—in the mistress's suite a beautiful despairing woman sat day after day, with her infant across her knees, eating her heart out in an agony of hope and fear waiting the reprieve from a living death that Ellis's return would bring her.

Here was a woman raised as one of a superior race, refined, cultured, possessed of all the Christian virtues, who would have remained in this social sphere all her life, beloved and respected by her descendants, her blood mingling with the best blood of the country if untoward circumstances had not exposed her ancestry. But the one drop of black blood neutralized all her virtues, and she became, from the moment of exposure, an unclean thing. Can anything more unjust be imagined in a republican form of government whose excuse for existence is the upbuilding of mankind!

These were sorrowful days for the Negroes who could not bring themselves to look upon their beloved mistress as one of their race, a share in their sad destiny.

Aunt Henny spent most of her spare time praying and coaxing Hagar out of the apathy into which she had fallen.

"Bless de Lawd! I know'd dev'ment was on han' when Marse St. Cla'r done comed home," she said one morning to Marthy. "Las' time he was here ol' Marse he bus' a blud vessel in his head an' never know'd a blessed thing fer a munf, den he die. 'Fore dat he shoot a mon to de college an' beat de prefesser 'mos' to def. Dais a cuss on dat boy, sho."

"How you tink it come so, Mammy?"

"I hern tell from Aunt Di, who nussed Missee Enson. See hyar, chile, I don' no 'bout tellin' a disrespons'ble gal like you fambly secrets,—an' ef you goes to 'peatin' my words all 'roun' de plantation, I hope Marse Ellis whop yer back." Marthy rolled her eyes in terror and promised to keep her mammy's revelations as sacred as Scripture.

PAULINE E. HOPKINS

"You know's dat no one neber goes nigh de old summer house down dar close to de wharf at de foot ob de garden, don' you?"

Marthy nodded, and her eyes grew larger as she listened with bated breath for the ghostly story she was sure would follow.

"Jes' 'fore Marse St. Cla'r was born, ole Missee Enson was settin' in there an' a turrible thunder storm came up an' jes' raised Jeemes Henry with houses an' trees, an' tored up eberythin'. Ol' Miss so dar 'feared to move even one teeny bit her li'l' finger. While she sot dar all white an' trimbly de debbil jes' showed he face to her an' grinned."

"Sure nuff debbil, mammy?" whispered Marthy in awed accents. Her mammy nodded solemnly in reply.

"Ol' Miss jes' went onto conwulshuns an' when dey fin' her she in dead faint. Dat night Marse St. Clair was born, an' ef de debbil ain't de daddy den dat ol' rapscalion neber had a borned servant in dis sinful wurl'."

"Mammy what you tink de reason de debbil show hisse'f to old Missee Enson?"

"De trubble wid you is, Marthy, dat you is de mos' 'quis'tive gal on dis plantation; you want to know too much, but de ol' fo'ks been hyar long time say dat ol' Marse git mad one day wid Unc' Ned, and' tell oberseer 'whop him.' Unc' Ned conjure man; neber been whopped in all he life. He jes' rub hisse'f all ober wid goopher, put a snake skin 'roun' he neck, a frog in one pocket an' a dry lizard in de oder, an' den he pray to de debbil: 'Dear debbil, I ax you to stan' by me in dis' my trial hour, an' I'll neber 'sert you as long as I live. I's had de power, continer de power; make me strong in your cause, make me faithful to you, an' help me to conquer my enemies, an' I will try to deserve a seat at your right han'!'"

As Marthy listened an ashy hue overspread her face and she asked breathlessly:

"Did dey whop him?"

"Bless yer soul, gal, dat was de afternoon 'fore dey was 'gwine ter whop him in de mornin', an' dat bery night de debbil 'pear to ole Miss, an' Unc' Ned neber was whopped tell de day he died, neber."

"He must a been a power, mammy, he cert'nly must."

"But de strangest part was dis: At de bery time ole Miss seen de debbil in de summer house, de oberseer was in de barn an' he 'clar' dat ober in de east corner he saw de lightnin' play, an' while he looked he see hell wid all its torments an' de debbil dar, too, wid his cloven foot, an' a struttin' 'bout like he know'd he was boss; de oberseer was so skeered dat he run, an he run, an' he run an' he neber stop runnin' tell he git plum inter Baltymo'."

"'Spec' he know'd he 'long'd to be debbil."

"Course! An' den he sen' ol' Marse word to sen' him his clo's: 'neber lib on dat plantation agin fer twice yer money; money no 'ducemen'."

"Mammy, mammy," this in a whisper, "do you b'lieve Miss Hagar got nigger blud in her?"

"Course not, honey. Somebody roun' hyar done conjured her. Dat debbil, St. Cla'r, I spec. Now, Marthy, take dat big silver tray of things up dar to dat po' li'le chile, an' you keep a poundin' 'tell she ope de do,' po' li'le chile."

Marthy obediently disappeared to execute orders and Aunt Henny with a dubious shake of her head lifted up her voice in song:

> *I'm a gwine to keep a climbin' high,*
> *See de hebbenly lan';*
> *Till I meet dem er angels in a de sky,*
> *See de hebbenly lan'.*
> *Dem pooty angels I shall see,*
> *See de hebbenly lan';*
> *Why don' de debbil let-a-me be,*
> *See de hebbenly lan'.*

DAY SUCCEEDED DAY. THERE WAS little communication between the town and Enson Hall. Inclement weather prevailed for it was now the latter part of January. The fire of curiosity still burned fiercely among the rich planters over the "Enson horror," as it was called, but up at the Hall all seemed quiet. One bitter morning St. Clair sat at breakfast the picture of luxurious ease. He felt himself master of the situation already, and had assumed all the airs of ownership. Aunt Henny felt drawn, sometimes, to "shy a plate at him," as she expressed it to herself.

The odor of roses and lilies mingled pleasantly with that of muffins and chocolate. A man came striding up the avenue. It was Dr. Gaines, the family physician, who owned a neighboring plantation.

"Where is Mr. Enson?" he asked of Isaac, who answered his clamorous call on the resounding brass knocker.

"At breakfas', massa."

"I must see him at once. I have news for him."

PAULINE E. HOPKINS

As the doctor entered the room, St. Clair Enson was leaning back in his chair snapping his fingers at a hound stretched on a rug at his side. The doctor was unceremonious:—

"I regret to say, that I come as the bearer of evil tidings."

"Shall I bid Isaac set another plate, doctor? No? You have taken breakfast? At this hour? You are a primitive people in this rural district, truly. You should mingle with the world as I have and become capable of enjoying the delights and privileges of civilized life. May I ask the nature of the news you bring?" The doctor was a kind old man though somewhat brusque. He averted his eyes, and answered in a low voice.

"It relates to your brother. Mr. Enson, when did Ellis leave home, and when was he expected back?"

"My brother Ellis? He left home about two weeks ago, for what reason he did not state. I do not know when to look for his return; he may drop in, unexpectedly, at any moment."

The doctor was preternaturally grave.

"And you have heard nothing from him since?"

"No, I have not."

The doctor grew graver yet.

"My dear sir, early this morning my boy Sam had occasion to cross the foot of your land, where the remains of the old wharf enter the stream, and there he stumbled upon a frightful thing—the dead body of a man!"

"Not a pleasant sight," said St. Clair as he helped himself to another hot cake.

"Evidently, the body has been there two or three days. There is an ugly wound in the head that completely disfigures the face, and an empty pistol by the side of the body tells its own pitiful tale. St. Clair Enson that dead man was—"

St. Clair shifted uneasily in his chair as he looked the speaker in the eye, then started to his feet.

"My brother?"

"Your brother!"

To Dr. Gaines's eyes the cold, pale face into which he gazed did not change, only the gaze sought the floor.

"That is strange. Was he robbed also?"

"No. A large sum of money is on the body; papers and his watch. Sam ran home to me, and I summoned help, and was among the first to reach the spot."

The hound leaped suddenly to his feet and began to howl.

"Was it murder or suicide?" asked St. Clair in a calm voice.

"That cannot be decided yet. Finding his valuables untouched, and his hand frozen to his pistol, seems to point to suicide; that will be determined at the inquest." Dr. Gaines turned from the window by which he was standing, and said: "The remains of your brother are being brought home."

A little procession of Negroes, with heads uncovered, advanced up the avenue, slowly, between the grand old beeches, their tread-echoing in a solemn thud upon the frozen ground. A cloth was spread decently over the mangled face. In the silence and majesty of death the master returned to his home. His unlucky life had come to a sudden close. In midnight solitude and shadowed by mystery the curtain fell on the tragedy.

St. Clair advanced with a firm step to meet the bearers; there was no sign of grief in his face. The servants crowded the hall, standing in terrified silence broken only by Aunt Henny's sobs and lamentations. St. Clair lifted the cloth that covered the dead face with a hand that did not tremble, under the curious gaze of Dr. Gaines.

"Mr. Enson," said the doctor at length, "your brother had a wife or one whom we believed his wife," he corrected at St. Clair's negative gesture. "Will you not notify her of his death? She must be suffering anxiety concerning him."

"True; I had forgotten her," muttered St. Clair with a shrug of his handsome shoulders. "Yes, doctor, you break the news to her." The doctor left the room. Presently there was a scream in a woman's voice as of one in mortal agony, an opening and closing of doors and a hurrying of feet; then silence broken only by the pitiful wail of a young child.

There was an inquest at which Walker, the speculator, corroborated the evidence of St. Clair Enson—that the deceased was laboring under great depression at the time of his leaving home, and of his avowed purpose to shoot himself as the shortest way out of his family difficulties. This testimony so clearly given produced a profound impression upon the listeners. It was hoped by many that Hagar would testify, but they were doomed to disappointment. The pistol was well-known to many friends as well as to his servants, as the one Ellis Enson always carried. The watch was the old-fashioned timepiece that his father had carried before him. The papers were legal documents made by the family lawyer and having no bearing on the case.

PAULINE E. HOPKINS

The jury rendered a verdict of suicide. Plainly, Ellis Enson had died by his own hand.

There was a stately funeral: St. Clair Enson buried his brother with every outward mark of wealth and pomp. The servants moved about the house with red eyes and stealthy steps while from the quarters the wind bore the sound of mournful wailing.

It was a bleak night. The new master of the Hall and the slave-trader, now his inseparable companion, sat before the fire consulting about the disposal of the slaves.

"I'm going to let them all go, Walker, and only keep a small working gang to till the ground and look after the Hall."

"Jes' so," replied Walker, as he folded a fat bundle of bills into his pocket-book and carefully replaced the same in his hip pocket.

"That's a sensible thing to do. It won't be six months from now before we'll all be fighting Yankees like mad, and then where'd your niggers be so nigh as this plantation is to Washington. Best be on the safe side is my idee. And there's the missis—" At this moment the door opened unceremoniously and Hagar came straight up to the two men, seated before the blazing fire. Her dark eyes shone like stars, her face was white as the snow that covered the fields outside, her long hair hung in a straggling mass, rough and unkept, about her shoulders and over her sombre dress. A more startled apparition could not well be imagined. An exclamation broke from the lips of both men.

"I have come without your bidding, sir, for I have something to say to you," she said, addressing St. Clair without bestowing a glance on the man Walker. She cast a wild look around the sumptuous room.

"So you take your ease while he sleeps in his coffin. You need not frown. I do not fear you. Life has no terrors to offer me now." She towered above him as he sat crouched in his chair, and she looked down upon him with a wicked glare in her eyes.

"The question I came to ask is this—St. Clair Enson, do you believe that your brother died by his own hand?"

"Most certainly," Enson constrained his white lips to answer.

"Ellis was killed, murdered—shot down like a dog! What did the pistol prove? Nothing. His pockets had not been rifled. That proves nothing. Neither his great trouble brought to him by his marriage with me—a Negro—would have driven him to self-destruction. He was murdered!"

A chill crept over her listeners. No one had ever seen the gentle Hagar Sargeant in her present character.

"Murdered?" gasped St. Clair.

"Yes," she shouted. "You are his murderer!"

He recoiled as if she had struck him a blow.

"Mad woman! You are mad I say, trouble has turned your brain!"

"It was you who drove him forth from a happy home. You who found your twin demon and brought home the story that broke his heart, ruined his life and gained for you the wealth you have always coveted. I repeat, you are his murderer!"

St. Clair cringed; then he sprang to his feet and seized her by the arm.

"This is too much for any man to stand from a nigger wench. You have sealed your own fate. Off you go, my fine madam, to the Washington market in short meter. I would have kept you near me, and made your life as easy as it has been in the past, but this settles it. Walker," he said as he turned to the speculator, "you have my permission to take this nigger and her brat whenever it pleases you." Then he released her.

Hagar eyed the man critically from head to foot.

"Selfish, devilish, cruel," she said slowly; "think not that your taunts or cruelties can harm me; I care not for them. No heart in your bosom; no blood in your veins! You are his slayer, and his blood is crying from the ground against you this very hour."

It was more than he could bear. Again he sprang from his seat and seized her arm. Walker took her by the other one and between them they dragged her toward the entrance.

"Easy, easy!" exclaimed Walker in a warning voice to St. Clair. "Don't injure the sale of your property, Enson." St. Clair dropped his hold and again returned to his seat by the fire.

"There, there, my dear, you're a leetle bit excited an' no wonder. Go to your room and rest yourself, my dear, I recommend gin. Gin with a leetle hot water, sugar and spice is very nice, very nice for hysterics, and soothing, very soothing to a gal's nerves." Walker punctuated his remarks with many a little thump and pat in her back.

With a defiant smile, Hagar paused on the threshold and said:

"It's the truth! you're his murderer, and in spite of the wealth and position you have played for and won, you have seen the last on this earth of peace or happiness." Then striking her breast, she added:

"As I have parted with the same friends! Pleasant dreams to you, St. Clair Enson, master of Enson Hall!"

IX

It will be remembered that on February 4, 1861, a provisional government was formed for the "Confederate States of America." This provisional government was soon superseded by a "permanent" one, under whose constitution Jefferson Davis, Alexander H. Stevens and other officials were to serve six years, from February 22, 1862. A Peace Congress composed of delegates from twenty states, held a session for three weeks at Washington, in February, 1862. In March, same year, a Commission also went to the Capital City to negotiate for a settlement of difficulties; but all these overtures failed. Being called to Washington as a leading delegate, with power to help settle all these great questions that were then agitating the country, St. Clair Enson and Walker decided that it would be best to close the Hall, leaving Isaac, Aunt Henny and Marthy in charge of the house, and take the rest of the hands to Washington, where so many rich and influential men would congregate from the most southern parts of the country, that they would be assured of quick sales and large profits.

On the morning of departure, the small colony of black men and women sat and stood about the familiar grounds stunned and hopeless. Here most of them were born, and here they had hoped to die and be buried. The unknown future was a gulf of despair. Ellis was a good master, kind and considerate; their sincere mourning for him was mingled with grief at their own fate.

In the midst of a motley group Hagar stood with her child clasped in her arms,—hopeless, despairing. She had felt her degradation before, but not until now had she drained the bitter cup of misery.

Ellis Enson's lawyer had questioned her about her husband's business.

"Did he give you free papers?" with a pitying glance at the fair, crushed woman.

"When he returned, he intended to take me and the child abroad after making ample settlements."

The legal gentleman sighed.

"It was a great oversight—a great mistake."

So no papers, bearing upon the case, being found, all the Sargeant fortune reverted by law to the master. Nothing could be done.

Then began the humiliating journey to Washington, herding with slaves, confined in pens like cattle, the delicately nurtured lady tasted of the torments of those accursed. Her brain grew wild; she folded her infant closer to her breast—sang, whispered, laughed and wept.

Upon reaching the private slave-pen, a number of which then disgraced the national capital, she fell into a state of melancholy from which nothing aroused her but the needs of the child.

A purchaser was soon found for the handsome slave, in a New Orleans merchant who agreed to take the child, too, for the sake of getting the mother out of the city without trouble.

At the dusk of the evening, previous to the day she was to be sent off, as the prison was being closed for the night, Hagar, with her child closely clasped in her arms, darted past the keeper and ran for her life. It was not far from the prison to the long bridge which passes from the lower part of the city, across the Potomac, to the forests of Arlington Heights. Thither the fugitive directed her flight. The keeper by this time had recovered from the confusion incident to such a daring and unexpected attempt, he rallied his assistants and started in pursuit. On and on she flew, seeming tireless in her desperate resolve. It was an hour when horses could not be easily obtained; no bloodhounds were at hand to run her down. It was a trial of speed and endurance.

The pursuers raised the hue-and-cry as they followed, gaining steadily upon the fugitive. Astonished citizens poured forth from their dwellings to learn the cause of the alarm, and learning the nature of the case fell in with the motley throng in pursuit. With the speed of a bird, having passed the avenue, she began to gain, and presently she was upon the Long Bridge. Panting, gasping, she hushed her babe, appealed to God in broken sentences, and gathered all her courage to dash across the bridge and lose herself in the friendly shelter of the woods. Oh, will she,—can she, make it! Already her heart began to beat high with hope. Courage! She had only to pass three-quarters of a mile more and all would be well, the woods would shelter her, night would cover her and save her.

Just as the pursuers passed the draw they beheld three men slowly approaching from the Virginia shore. They called to them to help arrest the runaway slave. As she drew near they formed a line across the bridge to intercept her. Now the panting woman, hard-pressed on every side, suddenly stopped.

She looked wildly and anxiously around to see if all hope were indeed gone; far below the ridge rolled the dark waters, sullen, angry, threatening. Before and behind were the voices of the profane, inhuman monsters into whose hands she must inevitably fall. Her resolution was taken. She kissed her babe, clasped it convulsively in her arms, saying:

"Alas, poor innocent, there is one gift for thee yet left for your unfortunate mother to bestow,—It is death. Better so than the fate reserved for us both."

Then she raised her tearful, imploring eyes to heaven as if seeking for mercy and compassion, and with one bound sprang over the railing of the bridge, and sank beneath the waters of the Potomac river.

X

Twenty Years Later

It was a fine afternoon in early winter in the year 1882, in the city of Washington, the beautiful capital of our great Republic. Pennsylvania Avenue was literally crammed with foot-passengers and many merry sleighing parties, intent on getting as much enjoyment as possible out of the day.

Freezing weather had been followed by a generous fall of frozen, down-like flakes. Quick to take advantage of a short-lived pleasure, vehicles of every description were flying along the avenue filled with the elite of the gay city. The stream of well-dressed pedestrians moved swiftly over the snowy pavements, for the air was too cold for prolonged lingering, watching with interest, in which envy mingled to some extent, the occupants of the handsome carriages gliding along so rapidly on polished runners. Every notable of the capital was there from the President in his double-runner to the humble clerk in a single-seated modest rig.

A sumptuous Russian sleigh drawn by two splendid black horses, with a statuesque driver in ebony handling the ribbons, attracted the attention of the crowd as it dashed down the avenue and paused near the capitol steps. Two ladies were its occupants. The elder was handsome enough to demand more than a passing glance from the most indifferent, but her young companion was a picture as she nestled in luxurious ease among the costly robes, wrapped in rich furs, from which her delicate face shone out like a star upon the curious throng. That she was a stranger to the crowd could be easily told from the questioning glances which followed the turnout.

As they passed the Treasury Department two men, both past their first youth, though one was at least twenty years older than the other, came down the steps, and paused a moment, to follow with their eyes the Russian sleigh with the beautiful girl, before mingling with the living stream that flowed from between the great stone columns and spread itself through the magnificent streets of the national capital.

"Really, Benson," remarked the elder man as they resumed their walk, "the most beautiful girl I have seen for many a day. You know everyone worth knowing; who is she?"

At this moment an elderly man of dark complexion, in stylish street costume, but with a decidedly Western air, came down the capitol steps followed by a young man. Both were warmly greeted by the occupants of the sleigh. The dark man spoke a few words to the driver, then both men entered the carriage and it dashed off rapidly.

"That is Senator Bowen, his wife and daughter. He is the new millionaire senator from California. I am not acquainted with the ladies, but after their ball I intend to become assiduous in my attentions."

"Oh! then they are the Bowens! How I wish I knew them. I predict a sensation over the young beauty. Who's the young man?"

"Cuthbert Sumner, my private secretary. Deuced fine fellow, too."

The conversation drifted away from the Bowens, and they were apparently forgotten.

"How was it at the Clarks' last night, Benson, as bad as you expected?"

"Worse if possible. It was dev'lish slow! Nothing stronger than bouillon, not a chance to buck the tiger even for one moment, not a decent looking woman in the rooms. All the women fit for pleasant company give that woman's house a wide berth. Dashed if I blame 'em. The only thing that gives the Clarks a standing is his position. I can't see how he puts up with her. If I had a sanctimonious woman like her for a wife I'd cut and run for it, dashed I wouldn't."

His companion laughed long and loud.

"No fun for you there, eh, Benson? My boy, you'll never fit into the dignified position of a father of this country, I fear. Oh, well; it's hard to teach an old dog new tricks." "Yes, but think of not being able to give your friends a decent time, because your wife has a fad on temperance and thinks it a sin to smell a claret cup or a brandy-and-soda. A man with a wife of that sort ought to leave her at home, where she could rule the roost to her heart's content. The seat of government is no place for a missionary." "Well, there's always a way to remedy such things when you know your hostess."

"Of course, of course," General Benson hastened to reply. "Our bouillon was washed down with Russian tea a la Russe. We doctored it in the coatroom."

The two men indulged in a hearty laugh.

"Well, Benson, you'll do," remarked the elder when their mirth had somewhat subsided. "For a dignified chief of a division you're a rare bird."

After a moment's silence, General Benson asked:

"Is Amelia come?"

"Yes, got here last night?"

"Good. It's a relief to be with a woman who can join a man in a social glass, have a cigar with him, or hold her own in winning or losing a game with no Sunday-school nonsense about her. It's hard work keeping up to it, Major; one needs a friend to help one out."

"When's the session end?"

"Next week, thank heaven."

"Sick of politics, too, old man?"

"No; but it's been nothing but wind. Words—words—words—"

"And mutual abuse," broke in the Major, laughing. "Exactly; with nothing accomplished. Can't seem to throw much dust in the eyes of these old fossils."

"The truth is, Benson, the South has a hard, rough road before her to even things up with the North; we've got to go slow until some of the old fire-eaters die out and a new generation comes in."

"It'll be slow enough, never you fear. At present we are in a Slough of Despond; heaven knows when we'll get out of it. My position in the Treasury brings the secret workings under my eye. I know."

"Slough!" retorted the Major; "call it a bog at once. And to think of the money we have lost for the Cause."

"And my exile abroad that my mix-up in the Lincoln assassination caused me. Do you know, Major, if it were known that I am my father's son, they'd hang me even now with little ceremony."

"Thank God they don't know it, my boy, and take courage."

"I'll get mine out of it by hook or by crook," replied Benson with a savage look. "The country owes me a fortune, and I'm bound to have it."

The two had reached the corner made historical by the time-honored political headquarters, Willard's Hotel. They paused before separating.

"By the by, Major, I'll get you cards for the Bowens' ball if you like. It would be a great chance for Amelia."

"If I like! Why, man, I'll be your everlasting debtor."

"Very well; consider it done."

"A thousand thanks." The friends parted.

General Benson entered the hotel, where he had apartments, and the Major wended his way to his home, a handsome house in a quiet side street.

PAULINE E. HOPKINS

XI

The Family of a Millionaire

Senator Zenas Bowen, newly elected senator from California, and many times a millionaire, occupied a mansion on 16th Street, N. W., in close proximity to the homes of many politicians who have made the city of Washington famous at home and abroad.

There were three persons in the Bowen family—the Honorable Zenas Bowen, his wife Estelle and his daughter Jewel. This was his second season in Washington. The first year he was in the House and his work there was so satisfactory to his constituents that the next season he was elected with a great flourish of trumpets to fill the seat in the Senate, made vacant by a retiring senator.

The Honorable Zenas was an example of the possibilities of individual expansion under the rule of popular government. Every characteristic of his was of the self-made pattern. In familiar conversation with intimate friends, it was his habit to fall into the use of ungrammatical phrases, and, in this, one might easily trace the rugged windings of a life of hardship among the great unwashed before success had crowned his labors and steered his bark into its present smooth harbor. He possessed a rare nature: one of those genial men whom the West is constantly sending out to enrich society. He had begun life as a mate on a Mississippi steamboat. When the Civil War broke out, he joined the Federal forces and at its close was mustered out as "Major Bowen." His wife dying about this time, he took his child, Jewel, and journeyed to California, invested his small savings in mining property in the Black Hills. His profits were fabulous; he counted his pile way up in the millions.

His appearance was peculiar. Middle height, lank and graceless. He had the hair and skin of an Indian, but his eyes were a shrewd and steely gray, wherein one saw the spirit of the man of the world, experienced in business and having that courage, when aroused, which is common to genial men of deadly disposition. Firm lips that suggested sternness gave greater character to his face, but his temper was known to be most mild. He dressed with scrupulous neatness, generally in black broadcloth. There was no denying his awkwardness; no amount of polish could make him otherwise. His relation to his family was most tender, his wife and daughter literally worshipping the noble soul that dwelt within its ungainly casket.

After Fortune had smiled on him, one day while stopping at the Bohemian, a favorite resort in 'Frisco, he was waited on by a young woman of great beauty. The Senator fell in love with her immediately and at the end of a week proposed marriage. Fortunate it was for him that Estelle Marks, as she was called, was an honorable woman who would not betray his confidence. She accepted his offer, vowing he should never have cause to regret his act. One might have thought from her eager acceptance that in it she found escape, liberty, hope.

"Yes," she said, "I will marry you."

He was dazed. He could not speak for one moment so choked was he with ecstasy at his own good fortune. He covered his eyes with his hand, and then he said in a hoarse voice: "I swear to make you happy. My own happiness seems more than I can believe."

Then she stooped suddenly and kissed his hand. He asked her where she would like to live.

"Anywhere you think best," was her reply.

He assured her that the North Pole, Egypt, Africa—all were one to him, with her and his little daughter. And so they were married.

He had never regretted the step. Estelle was a mother to the motherless child, and being a well-educated woman, versed in the usages of polite society, despite her recent position as a waitress in a hotel, soon had Jewel at a first-class school, where she could be fitted for the position that her father's wealth would give her. Nor did Estelle's good work end there. She recognized her husband's sterling worth in business and morals, and insisted upon his entering the arena of politics. Thanks to her cleverness, he made no mistakes and many hits which no one thought of tracing to his wife's rare talents. Not that Bowen was a fool; far from it. Mrs. Bowen simply fulfilled woman's mission in making her husband's career successful by the exercise of her own intuitive powers. His public speeches were marked by rugged good sense. His advice was sagacious. He soon had enthusiastic partisans and became at last a powerful leader in the politics of the Pacific Slope. All in all, Mrs. Bowen was a grand woman and Senator Bowen took great delight in trying to further her plans for a high social position for himself and the child.

Jewel Bowen's beauty was of the Saxon type, dazzling fair, with creamy roseate skin. Her hair was fair, with streaks of copper in it; her eyes, gray with thick short lashes, at times iridescent. Her nose superbly Grecian. Her lips beautifully firm, but rather serious than smiling.

Jewell was not unconscious of her attractions. She had been loved, flattered, worshipped for twenty years. She was proud with the pride of conscious worth that demanded homage as a tribute to her beauty—to herself.

Her tastes were luxuriously simple; she reveled in the dainty accessories of the toilet. To the outside world her dress was severely plain, but her dressmaker's bill attested to the cost of her elegant simplicity.

It was but a short time since Jewel had been transported from her quiet Canadian convent into the whirl of Washington life, a splendid house, more pretty dresses than she could number, a beautiful mother, albeit a step-mother, more indulgent than most mothers, fairly adoring the sweet and graceful girl so full of youth's alluring charm, and a father who was the noblest, tenderest and wisest of men. But she was a happy-hearted girl, full of the joy of youth and perfect health. She presented a bright image to the eye all through the fall, as she galloped over the surrounding country on her thoroughbred mare, followed by her groom and two or three dogs yapping at her heels.

There was perfect accord between her and her step-mother. Mrs. Bowen shared the Senator's worship of Jewel. From the moment the two had met and the child had held her little arms toward her, blinking her great gray eyes in the light that had awakened her from her slumbers, and had nestled her downy head in the new mother's neck with a sigh of content, almost instantly falling asleep again, with the words: "Oh, pitty, pitty lady!"

Estelle Bowen had kissed her passionately again and again, and from that time Jewel had been like her very own. The young step-mother trained the child carefully for five years, then very reluctantly sent her to the convent of the Sacred Heart at Montreal, where she had remained until she was eighteen. Then followed a year abroad, and her meeting with Cuthbert Sumner.

About this time events crowded upon each other in her young life. Her father's rise was rapid in the money world and, together with his political record, gave his family access to the wealthiest and most influential society of the country.

Cuthbert Sumner, her acknowledged lover, was an only child of New England ancestry favored by fortune like herself. His father, a wealthy manufacturer, was the owner of a business that had been in the Sumner family for many generations. His mother had died while he was yet a lad. It was a dull home. The son just leaving Harvard, had been expected to assume the responsibilities of his father's establishment, but having no taste for a commercial life, and being fitted by nature as well as education for a career in politics, his father reluctantly gave his consent that Cuthbert should have his wish after a few years spent in travel had acquainted him with the great world.

Mr. Sumner, senior, finding his son's desires still unchanged upon his return from abroad, used his influence and obtained for him a position in the Treasury as private secretary in General Benson's department. So young Sumner was duly launched upon the sea of politics. The world of fashion surged about him and he soon found himself a welcome guest in certain homes. He had little leisure for society, but sought it more after he attended Jewel Bowen's "coming-out" reception, a year previous to this chronicle. There he had seen a maiden in white, her arms laden with fragrant flowers, with beautiful fearless eyes which looked directly into the secret depths of his heart.

Sumner was twenty-six and this was not his first experience with women. He had been in love with the sex, more or less, since the day he left off knee-breeches. As he looked into Jewel's eyes he remembered some of his experiences with a pang of regret. He was no better, no worse than most young fellows. He had played some, flirted some, had even been gloriously hilarious once, for all of which his conscience nowwhipped him soundly. Jewel looked upon him with mingled feelings, in which curiosity was uppermost. In her world money was the potent factor; but in this man she saw the result of generations of culture and wealth combined.

One afternoon when they were calling, about the time of her "coming-out" party, a friend of Mrs. Bowen had mentioned him: "Such a fascinating man! and so handsome! Will you let me bring him? He's a man you must know, of course, and the sooner the better."

"We shall be very pleased," Mrs. Bowen replied; "any friend of yours is welcome."

"Thanks. That's settled then."

"He looks very different from the most of the men one meets in Washington," remarked Jewel, who was examining the pictured face that smiled at her from its ornate frame on the mantel.

"How?"

"Oh, I don't know. More manly, I suppose would explain it."

"Wait till you know him," returned the matron with a meaning smile.

"Cuthbert Sumner," Jewel repeated to herself. "Yes, they talk so much of him, all the women seem to have lost their hearts to him. I wonder if he will, after all, be worth the knowing."

That was the beginning. The end was in sight from the time they first met. It was a desperate case on both sides. None was surprised at the announcement of the engagement the previous winter. It was understood that the wedding would take place at Easter.

"THE BOWENS ARE IN TOWN." That meant a vast deal to the important section of Washington's world which constitutes "society," for the splendid mansion, closed since the daughter's brief introduction to society, it was rumored, would be added to the list of places where one could dance, dine and flirt. Festivities were to open with a ball—a marvel of splendor, for which five hundred invitations had been issued.

Senator Bowen was walking down the avenue the next afternoon, on his way home, when he was joined by General Benson, who had developed lately a passion for his society. The two men frequented the same clubs and transacted much official business together, but there had been nothing approaching intimacy between them. If the shrewd Westerner had given expression to his secret thoughts they would have run somewhat in the following vein:

"Got a hang-dog look about that off eye which tells me he's a tarnation mean cuss on occasion. He's all good looks and soft sawder. However, that don't worry me any; it's none o' my funeral."

After the two men had exchanged the usual civilities, the latest political question looming up on the horizon was discussed; finally, the conversation turned upon the coming ball.

"By the by, Senator, I wish I dared ask for cards for a friend of mine and his daughter. They have just arrived in town for the season, and know no one. He, the father, is the newly-appointed president of the Arrow-Head mines; the daughter is lovely; a fine foil for Miss Jewel. Unexceptional people, and all that."

"Certainly, General," the Senator hastened to reply, "What address?"

With profuse thanks, General Benson handed him a card, on which appeared the name:

"I will speak to Mrs. Bowen right away."

Mrs. Bowen and Jewel were enjoying a leisure hour before dinner, in lounging chairs before the blazing grate-fire in the former's sitting-room. There was a little purr of gratification from both women as they heard a well-known step in the hall.

"Well, here you both are," was Senator Bowen's greeting as he kissed his wife and daughter and flung himself wearily into a chair.

"Tired?" asked his wife.

"Yes, some of these dumb-headed aristocrats are worse to steer into a good paying bit of business for the benefit of the government treasury, than a bucking bronco."

"How late you are, papa," here broke in Jewel from her perch on her father's knee, where she was diligently searching his pockets. It had been her custom from babyhood, and never yet had her search been unrewarded.

"I'd have been here earlier only I met General Benson and he always has so many questions to ask, especially about my little lass, that he kept me no end of time."

"Don't be wicked, papa," smiled Jewel, "because you spoil me; you think everyone must see with your eyes."

"Ah! pet; it's just wonderful how well all the old and young single fellows know me since you have grown up. But we won't listen to 'em just yet, Blossom; not even Sumner shall part us for a good bit; your pa just can't lose you for a good spell, I reckon."

"No man shall part us, dad; if he takes me, he must take the whole family," replied Jewel with a loving pat on the sallow cheek.

"We'll see, we'll see. There's another bid for an invite to your shindig," he continued, with a laugh, as he tossed the card given him by General Benson into his wife's lap. "It's mighty pleasant to be made much of; it's worth while getting rich just to see how money can change the complexion of things, and how cordial the whole world can be to one man if he's got the spondulix."

"My dear Zenas," said Mrs. Bowen, with a shake of her head and a comical smile on her face, "don't talk the vernacular of the gold mines here in Washington. You'll be eternally disgraced."

"Well, Mrs. Senator, I've fit the enemy, tackled grizzlies, starved, been locked up in the pens of Libby Prison, and I've come out first best every time, but this thing you call society beats me. The women make me dizzy, the men make me sick, and a mighty little of it makes me ready to quit, fairly squashed. Them's my sentiments."

A cry of delight broke from Jewel,—"O dad!" as she brought to view a package in a white paper. Mrs. Bowen left her seat to join in the frolic that ensued to gain possession of it. At last the mysterious bundle was unwrapped, the box opened and a pearl necklace brought to view of wonderful beauty and value. The senator's eyes were full of the glint and glister of love and pride as he watched the faces of his wife and daughter. After a moment he brought out another package, which he gave to his wife.

"There, Mrs. Senator, there's your diamond star you've been pining after for a month. I ordered them quite a while ago; happened to be passing Smith's and stopped in, found 'em ready and here they be. What women see in such gewgaws is a puzzler to me. I can tolerate such hankering in a young 'un, but being you're not a chicken, Mrs. Senator, and not in the market, and still good looking enough to make any man restless with no ornaments but a clean calico frock, your fancies are a conundrum to yours truly. But these women folks must be humored, I suppose."

With this the Senator plunged into his dressing-room, which adjoined his wife's sitting-room, and began the work of dressing for dinner and the theatre.

"Cuthbert coming?" he called to his daughter, who still lingered.

"Yes, papa."

"Jewel, dear, have Venus be particular with your toilet tonight; I will overlook you when she has finished."

"That the name of your new maid, Blossom?" the Senator's voice demanded. There were many grunts, groans and growls issuing from the privacy where his evening toilet was progressing because of refractory collar buttons and other unruly accessories.

"Yes, papa."

"Hump! Name enough to hang her: Venus, the goddess of love and beauty! Can she earn her salt?"

He appeared at the door now struggling into an evening vest. He employed no man, declaring that no valley de chamber should boss him around. He'd always been free and didn't propose to end his days in slavery to any slick-pated fashion-plate who didn't know the color of gold from the inside of a brass kettle.

"I don't know what I would do without her. I have been intending to speak to you for some time concerning her brother. He is a genius, and Venus has given up her hopes of becoming a school teacher among her people to earn money to help develop his talents. Can't we do something for them, papa? I have said nothing to her yet."

"Hump! You're always picking up lame animals, Blossom; from a little shaver it's been the same. If you keep it up in Washington, you'll have all the black beggars in the city ringing the area bell. However, I'll look the matter up. If the girl ain't too proud to go out as a servant to help herself along, there may be something in her."

XII

Who is She?

At eight that evening—Theatre was filled to overflowing, for Modjeska was to interpret the heart-breaking story of "Camille." Senator Bowen and his handsome wife; Jewel and Cuthbert Sumner occupied a box, and were watching intently the mimic portrayal of life. Jewel was listening earnestly to Modjeska's words; the grand rendering of the life story of a passionate, loving, erring, noble woman's heart touched her deeply. The high-bred grace, the dainty foreign accent, the naturalness of the actress, held her in thrall and she did not take her eyes from the stage. As the curtain went down on the second act she lifted her glass and slowly scanned the house. Suddenly she paused with a heart that throbbed strangely. Directly across from her sat a woman—young in years, but with a mature air of a woman of the world. "Surely," thought Jewel, "I know that face." The girl had a woman's voluptuous beauty with great dusky eyes and wonderful red-gold hair. Her dress of moss-green satin and gold fell away from snowy neck and arms on which diamonds gleamed. Just then Sumner uttered an exclamation of surprise. He had turned, almost at the same moment with Jewel, and swept a careless glance over the house, bowing to several, mostly well-known people either by profession or social standing, but had declined to see more than one fair one's invitation. Passing, as it were, a box on the left, his glance had rested on a face that instantly arrested it and caused him to exclaim. An elderly man sat with the vision of loveliness. In repose the girl's face lost some of its beauty and seemed care-worn; one felt impressed that girlhood's innocence had not remained untouched.

The lady was watching their box intently, and seeing herself discovered smiled a brilliant smile of recognition as she inclined her head in Sumner's direction holding his glance for one instant in a way that seemed to call him to her side. He bowed, then turned his head away with a feeling of confusion that annoyed him. He did not offer to go to her, however.

"Do you know her? Who is she, Cuthbert?" asked Jewel, intercepting both smile and bow.

"It is Miss Madison," he replied, lifting his glass nonchalantly. "I did not know she was in Washington. I have not seen her for three years. Looking remarkably well, is she not?"

"She is glorious! Her face somehow seems familiar to me. I must have met her. Have you seen much of her?"

"Can't say that I have. Met her at a ball at Cape May. But I found the place so dull I packed up and went home. After that I went abroad. Then I met a sweet little woman who has led me captive at her chariot wheels ever since."

Then followed some talk dear to the souls of lovers and the beauty opposite was forgotten. But throughout the next act Jewel felt her heart contract as the dusky eyes followed her movements with a restless, smouldering fire in their depths that pained her to see.

Amelia Madison watched the box opposite with hungry intensity. She was studying Jewel's face mentally saying: "There is not another woman in the house like her. She is like a strain of Mozart, a spray of lilies. My God! how he looks at her—he never looked at me like that! He respects her; he worships her—"

She sank back in breathless misery.

Aurelia Madison and Cuthbert Sumner had met one summer at Cape May. They had loved and been betrothed; had quarreled fiercely over a flirtation on her part and had separated in bitterness and pain; and yet the man was relieved way down in a corner of his heart for he had felt dimly, after the first rapture was over, that he was making a mistake, that she was not the woman to command the respect of his friends nor to bring him complete happiness. Yet after a fashion she fascinated him. Her grace, her beauty, thrilled his blood with rapture that he thought then was Love. Love came to him a later guest, and the purity and tenderness of Jewel's sweet face blotted out forever the summer splendor of Aurelia Madison's presence. Now it was all over; he knew he had never loved her, and that he was fortunate to have found it out in time.

No one knew of this episode in Aurelia Madison's life. Her father had been away on one of his periodical tours, and the girl was accountable to none but an old governess who acted as chaperone.

Since that time she had led a reckless life. Had lived at Monte Carlo two seasons, aiding her father in his games of chance, luring the gilded youth to lose their money without murmuring. Hers had been a precarious life and a dangerous one. Sometimes they were reduced to expedients. But through it all the girl held her peace, set her teeth hard, and waited for the day when she should again meet Cuthbert Sumner, trusting to the effect of her great beauty, and the fact that he had once loved her passionately, to re-establish her power over the man she worshipped. Once his wife, she told herself, she would shake off all her hideous past and become an honest matron. Honesty she viewed as a luxury for the wealthy to enjoy. Thank heaven, Cuthbert Sumner's wife could afford to be honest. They had met again, but how? All her hopes were dust.

New she saw Jewel lifted her eyes to his with devotion, love and faith in them; she saw him look down eagerly, with truest, tenderest love. The last act was on. She could bear it no longer, but rose impatiently, with rage and hatred in her heart, and attended by her father, left the house. When next Jewel stole a glance in the direction of the stranger her place was empty.

XIII

A Plot for Ten Millions

I t was near nine o'clock the next morning and General Benson was still invisible. His colored valet was moving about noiselessly, making ready for his master. Breakfast was on the table in its silver covers. A bell rang; Isaac disappeared.

General Benson's renown as a great social leader rested, not only on his lavish expenditure and luxurious style of living at Willard's Hotel, where he monopolized one of the most expensive suites, but upon his mental and physical attributes as well. The ladies all voted him a charming fellow. He had a remarkably sweet and caressing voice, which added to his attractions. The many women to whom he had vowed eternal fidelity at one moment, only to abandon heartlessly the next at the rise of a new star in the firmament of beauty, sighed and wept at his defection and voted him the most perfect lover imaginable. It was hinted that one girl had committed suicide solely on his account. But still the ladies believed in his professions.

The members of the various clubs that he affected acknowledged him to be an admirable card-player, a good horseman, an expert with sword or revolver, as well as an unusually agreeable companion in a search after pleasure; generous, too, with his money. But with all his popularity and increase of fame, his fortune declined, and he found himself at the present time embarrassed for money, his capital growing smaller each month in spite of a large salary. Debts of honor must be met, and to keep a good name one's opponent must sometimes win. Then, too, he was growing old; he carried his years well, but fifty was looming perilously near.

He and his friend Major Henry Clay Madison, President of the Arrow-Head Mining Company of Colorado, newly established in the city, had a mutual interest in the great scheme that was to make the fortunes of the different shareholders, but even the generous payments he received as his share of the profits made out of verdant men of means who became easy prey because of General Benson's sweet persuasive voice and exalted position in the political world, failed to assist him out of his financial dilemma. Within a month a new scheme had entered his mind,—one that dazzled him the possibilities were so great, a scheme which if successfully handled would put millions in the pockets of a trio of unscrupulous adventurers,—Major Madison and his daughter and himself.

As the clock chimed nine, General Benson entered the room and seated himself at the breakfast table. A moment later his valet informed him that Major and Miss Madison wished to see him.

"Very well; show them in, at once."

Presently the valet ushered them in. The major we have mentioned before; he was short, stout, more than fifty, with gray hair and ferret-like eyes, close-set, and a greenish-gray of peculiar ugliness; a close observer would take exception to them immediately. He was scrupulously attired in the height of fashion. He was accompanied by the strange beauty who had attended the theatre the night before.

"Well, General, you sent for us and here we are. How are you?" was the major's greeting as he shook hands with General Benson and then flung himself into an arm-chair.

"Very well, indeed, thanks, Madison. What, is it indeed you, Aurelia?" he exclaimed on beholding the girl. "How delightful to have you with us once again!"

The lady inclined her head slightly in answer to her host's warm greeting, ignored his offered hand, and subsided onto a chair with a preoccupied air, a slight frown puckering her forehead.

"Don't mind Aurelia, General; she's mooning as usual," laughed her father.

"You are looking very fit, Major," remarked Benson, recovering from the confusion caused by Aurelia's coolness. "Have a B. and S.?"

"Don't care if I do."

Benson poured a brandy-and-soda for his guest and another for himself; passed the cigars to him and the cigarettes to Miss Madison. She took one, lit it, and drew away in a manner that showed her keen enjoyment. A smile passed over Benson's face as he covertly watched her.

"Well, Madison," the General said, after a few moments' enjoyment of the weed, "I sent for you to come here this morning on a matter of business, because I shall not be able to call on you at any time today, for I may have to go out of town at any moment on some confounded office business. It's a nuisance, I say. The office interferes too much with a man's pleasure. If my plans succeed I'll cut the whole thing."

"Indeed! I imagine we are mutually interested when you speak of 'business.' You're not ruined I take it. Do you want to borrow money of me?" said the Major with a laugh as he drew his chair a trifle closer to his friend. The lady evinced no interest in the conversation.

"On the contrary, I wish to offer you a chance to make some."

"You are extremely kind, Benson; you could not have chosen a more opportune time for your offer. Will you believe it—I was compelled to part with a diamond pin this morning," replied Madison, touching his polished shirt-front. "But what can I do for you?"

"Since we joined forces, Madison, on the strictly respectable basis, we have gained fame and influence, and but little money. It takes money to maintain our position, and plenty of it. This you know. I have studied the situation and am convinced that our only surety for providing for the future lies in a coup that shall net us millions, on which we may retire."

"Yes, but how to get it," replied Madison with a mournful shake of the head. "Work is not in our line, unsafe expedients are dangerous and not to be thought of. I do not fancy running my head into a noose. One can't do much but go straight here, and money's a scarce article."

"Be patient. You need have no apprehension that I shall suggest anything dangerous, Madison; though the time was when you were the risky one and I the one to hesitate," with a significant uplifting of the eyebrows.

"True; but time has changed my ideas. I have a hankering for respectability that amounts to a passion."

"Remain as respectable as you wish, my friend; I have a legitimate scheme that will make us masters of ten millions! No risk; nothing necessary but judicious diplomacy."

Miss Madison had evinced no interest until now, but at the words "ten millions" uttered by this man whom she knew to be practical, astute in business and no dreamer, she seemed to awaken from her lethargy. She retained her self-possession, however, and maintained her unruffled calm, remarking carelessly, even sarcastically: "May I ask the nature of the plan, General, and where my usefulness comes in?"

"I was about to explain that point, my dear; but first permit me to ask a question,—has the idea of acquiring a fortune by a wealthy marriage ever occurred to you?"

"Yes, I admit it has. But you know too well my reasons for hesitating in such a course."

Benson moved uneasily in his seat, and for a moment his eyes dropped under the steady gaze that the girl bent upon him—eyes large, dreamy, melting, dazzling the senses, but at this moment baleful. A dull flush mounted to his brow.

"See here, Aurelia, have you tried to find an opportunity?"

"Possibly," she answered coldly.

"And you met with no success?"

"Evidently not, as I am single."

"Then your efforts were misdirected."

"Do you think so?" mockingly.

"Most assuredly I do. Your attention was bestowed upon men for whom you had conceived a real liking. That is not the way to bring success in such a venture."

"It is the wrong lead for a woman like me,—an adventuress, to forget her position for one instant and allow her heart to guide her head. What fool wrote 'Poverty is no crime?' I know of none greater. It is responsible for every crime committed under the sun. It is a foul curse!"

"Why, Aurelia, girl, what has come to you this morning? You talk like a man with the blue devils after losing all night at poker," said her father.

Her answer was a shrug of her handsome shoulders as she resumed her listless attitude.

"Listen to me; I will unfold a scheme that shall remove the curse of poverty, and give you for a husband a man who will fill the bill, heart and all."

He rose, approached the mantel, and turning his back upon it, rested both elbows on the marble—a position which brought him face to face with his guests, and asked: "Are you acquainted with Cuthbert Sumner?"

"Know him by sight and reputation. Clerk in your department," replied Madison. Aurelia did not speak, but a flush came into her face, a light to her eyes. One might have felt the thrill that passed over her form.

"What do you think of him?"

"He's all right; a genial fellow, but careful not to go too far; handsome, too, by Jove. No money, though?"

"O yes," nodded Benson. "Only in the department for experience in political life. His father's very wealthy. New England manufacturer."

"Indeed!"

"He's the one I've picked for our lady here."

"But he's engaged," broke in Aurelia.

"Exactly. And that brings me to the rest of the scheme. Sumner is about to marry Bowen's daughter. By the way, Aurelia, you got the cards for the ball, did you not?" Aurelia bowed in assent.

"Jewel Bowen is the Senator's only child, and his heiress. She will receive ten millions upon her wedding day. What I propose is that Aurelia fascinate the gentleman, thus leaving the field clear for me. I have taken a decided fancy to Miss Bowen and her fortune. If I succeed there is a million for you, Madison, and another for Aurelia. Sumner, too, has pots of money, and we shall all be able to settle down into quiet respectability. What do you think of my plan?"

"By Jove, Benson," blurted out Major Madison, fairly thunder-struck at the magnificence of the vista opened before him, "what a splendid idea! How admirably you have planned things!" Benson nodded and smiled:

"All remains with Aurelia, and certainly with her magnificent beauty to help us, we need fear no failure."

"Spare me your compliments. This is probably your last chance, General. So you think I can win this Mr. Sumner from his betrothed?" she said.

"Precisely."

"That is a droll idea. Do you think—"

"I think, I repeat, that you can easily make the person referred to sufficiently in love with you to do anything you ask."

"Suppose he proves obdurate? What then? You cannot judge all men alike."

"Break the engagement, if you can do nothing more. During a fit of insanity, if it lasts but a week, an hour even, you will have ample time to accomplish my desires."

"And then?"

"I will look after mademoiselle. It will make no difference to you. Your compensation will be my affair. It is only his money that you would want."

"Oh, I see!" There was a world of sarcasm in the three words uttered by a smiling mouth. "My dear General, you are indeed a marvel! No one knows better than you how to make love to a young girl."

"You are the cleverest woman I know, Aurelia. I knew you would comprehend the situation perfectly." After a moment's reflection the girl replied: "Yes, I think I'll try it. It will probably be announced before long that the marriage is broken off. I will earn my million, never fear. I shall, doubtless, find it an agreeable task."

"And a husband, too, my girl," added her father.

"Perhaps."

"Are we to be intimate friends or simply business acquaintances?" asked the Major of General Benson.

"Business friends will be best. Let us have no appearance of collusion."

"When shall we see you again?" asked the Major as they rose to go.

"Just as soon as you have something to tell me. How fortunate that Aurelia has never been introduced to Washington society. She will take the place by storm."

Then the friends separated.

XIV

Playing with Fire

About lunch time that same morning, as Sumner was leaving the office, a note was brought to him by a servant in plain livery:

"May we not be friends for the sake of the old days, when no other woman was dearer than I? Come to me just once."

Aurelia
New York Avenue

Sumner's brow was knit as he scanned the sheet of ivory paper in his hand, with its emblazoned monogram. He muttered an imprecation. Elise Bradford, the stenographer, glanced up from her work in surprise. Sumner was a gentleman in the office and a great favorite with all the employees; it was rare to hear an uncouth expression from the lips of this man, who honored all womanhood.

"I thought that was all over and done with," he muttered to himself. "What is the use of going through with it all again? Well, I suppose I must go once for decency's sake, but I'll take care to make short work of it. There shall be no misunderstanding."

Then softer thoughts came to him as he took from a pile of commonplace, business letters on his desk, a slim satiny envelope. It was from Jewel. He opened it and read the few lines it contained, reminding him of an appointment that he had with her for the evening.

"My little Blossom!" he said gently.

But his little Blossom did not keep him from going to see Aurelia Madison. She was less than nothing to him. He had never met her from the day he left Cape May until the night before. He never even thought of her. Yet he went to call upon her. Reluctantly and distastefully—but he went.

He was ushered into the drawing-room scented and flower-filled. A moment later Aurelia came into the room from the library. Ah, she stirred even his cold heart.

A white negligé clothed her from throat to foot, and her wonderful hair was caught in a mass low down on her neck. A deep light was in

PAULINE E. HOPKINS

the dusky eyes that bewildered a man and weakened his energies. In an instant she came swiftly to him—the white arms were about his throat, the warm lips against his.

"My love! my love!" she murmured softly, and Cuthbert Sumner (blind and foolish) was not the kind of man to let the memory of little Blossom prevent him from holding a beautiful, yielding form closely clasped in his arms, and returning clinging kisses with interest when such a rare opportunity offered.

I question if there are many men that would.

She was playing a part in a desperate game that meant everything to her. This was her first move toward the end she had vowed to accomplish. She would be victorious; she swore it. Her rôle was not a hard one for she worshipped this man so cold and unyielding to her arts. She would have preferred the lilies of virtuous winning; debarred from that she would take the torments of a love to which she had no right. By-and-by, she said:

"Bert, do you love her very much?"

He bowed with a long look in her face.

"And NOT as you loved ME!" she said passionately. "Tell me about her."

"My dear Aurelia, can a man sing the praises of one beautiful woman to another?"

"Tell me about her," she said again with the imperious gesture that Sumner remembered so well in that summer at the Cape. "I have not loved you for two long years, Bert Sumner, without learning every phase of your mind. When do you marry her?"

"At Easter," he replied proudly, disdaining further subterfuge.

"And you can sit there calmly and tell it to me—to me—," she bit her lip a moment; there was less time than she had thought.

"She is very wealthy?"

"Yes, as the world counts it, but I care not for that; if she had nothing it would be the same to me."

"I believe you. And I could see her beauty for myself; and she is good, not like me."

"She is an angel, my white angel of purity," he replied with a look of reverence on his face.

Aurelia was a gorgeous tropical flower; Jewel, a fair fragrant lily. Men have such an unfortunate weakness for tropical blooms, they cannot pass them by carelessly, even though a lily lies above their hearts.

Cuthbert could not ignore this splendid tropical flower; it caused his blood to flow faster, it gave new zest to living—for an hour. Jewel was his saint, his good angel; and he loved her truly with all the high love a man of the world can ever know. He trusted her for her womanly goodness and truth. And Jewel returned his love with an intensity that was her very life.

Aurelia looked at him and sighed heavily.

"May I know her?"

"I am sure, I cannot say. You may possibly meet her at some party."

"Then you do not object absolutely. I am glad, for we have invitations to Mrs. Bowen's ball. I want to go."

She looked at him keenly. "I think I have met Miss Bowen before. If I mistake not, we were at the Montreal convent at the same time. I am older than she, and left just after she entered. I remember her as a sweet cherub who resembled a pictured saint."

"Quite a coincidence," he replied with all his usual courtliness for womankind; but for all that he mentally anathematized the idiot who had sent the cards and the convent where the girls had met. He was vexed, and she felt it.

"Yes, I shall go—"

She caught her breath sharply and then fell at his feet in all her exquisite beauty.

"Can you never, Never love me again, Bert? My life, my soul is yours! Can you not give me a little love in return?"

He lifted her up gently.

"It is too late to ask that now, Aurelia. Try and forget that you have ever loved me. Believe me, you will be happier. No one can more bitterly regret than I the misery of our past. Let us begin anew."

She thrust him from her wildly, and bade him go if he did not wish to see her fall dead at his feet.

Cuthbert went away sadly.

He knew the full power of Aurelia Madison's siren charms. Nor was her emotion all feigned. She really felt all she had expressed. What was pride compared to the desolation that swept over her when she realized that his heart was hers no longer? Her great love obliterated even the thought of his wealth. She felt she should triumph, in spite of the coldness with which he had received her professions of love. Yes, she would be his wife, even thought it were a barren honor, since his heart was not hers.

PAULINE E. HOPKINS

"If his love is not for me, it shall be for no one else," she told herself, as she thought over her afternoon's work and prepared for the next move in the drama.

And so Cuthbert Sumner went back to his little Blossom, whose calm, pure face was continually before him.

XV

Renewing Old Acquaintance

The following afternoon Major Madison's carriage rolled up to the Bowen mansion on Sixteenth Street, and stopped. From it Aurelia stepped, clad richly and daintily in a becoming calling costume. She had determined to storm the citadel, as it were, and carry it by assault.

She rang the bell and asked the footman if Miss Bowen was at home.

"Yes, Miss—. What name please?"

She gave the man a card on which she had written, "Known to you as Aurelia Walker," and was shown into a morning-room to wait, Would Jewel recognize her, she wondered. Would she be pleased to meet her again?

Presently she heard the gentle frou-frou of silken skirts down the broad stairway and the next instant Jewel Bowen stood before her, holding out her hand in frankly-glad recognition—Jewel in a tea-gown that was a poem, a combination of palest rose-satin and cream lace. Surprise and pleasure mingled in her speaking face.

"The card said, 'Aurelia Walker.' Can it be possible that you are the same Aurelia whom I knew in Montreal? How delightful to meet you again."

Her greeting was most cordial, and put Aurelia instantly at her ease. After a time spent in recalling reminiscences of school life, and pleasant girlish chatter, Aurelia said:

"I must explain the change in name,—papa was embarrassed financially, and he placed me at school, calling himself Walker while he earned the money to satisfy his creditors; that saved him much annoyance, and as soon as he could satisfy their demands, we resumed our rightful name."

"Pray do not speak of it, Aurelia; such things are annoying, but cannot always be helped," replied Jewel with a smile. "Won't you come to the drawing-room and meet mamma?"

How beautiful everything was, thought the girl, as she passed up the broad marble stairs with velvet carpet in the centre, on which the foot fell noiselessly, and statues and flowers in niches and on landings, while the walls were hung with lovely frescoes that impelled one to pause and admire.

The drawing-room door was flung open, and they were in a spacious apartment with painted ceiling, and all things rich and harmonious in tone. In a moment she was standing before Mrs. Bowen, who greeted her warmly, as if truly glad to meet her daughter's school friend. No lovelier vision was ever seen than these two girls as they entered the Bowen drawing-room. Mrs. Bowen was a cultured lady and their grace and beauty gratified her taste.

She conversed freely and pleasantly with the unexpected guest, although after the first feeling of wonder and satisfaction at so much loveliness, she was surprised and puzzled at the vague feeling of distrust and dislike that personal contact with her young guest brought to her. It was intangible. She shook it off, however, the beautiful face and voice were so enchanting that she could not resist them, and felt ashamed of her distrust.

"Come and sit down by the fire and let us have a long chat before anyone else comes in. We never know how long we may be alone," said Jewel, indicating a seat near her own.

"This is very cosy and homelike," remarked Aurelia as she took the seat offered. "I have been so lonely since I came to the city."

"Poor child," remarked Mrs. Bowen in a sympathetic voice, "are you very much alone? How long since you lost your mother?"

"I cannot recall her at all, dear Mrs. Bowen," the girl answered, lifting a pair of dusky eyes, swimming in tears, for a moment to her face. "Papa is so intent on the fortunes of the mine, just at present, that he gives me very little attention. Indeed, I believe he forgets at times that he has a daughter," this last with a little sigh of martyrdom.

Mrs. Bowen melted more and more to her guest.

"Then stay and dine with us. Let me send away your carriage." She rang the bell and gave the order to the servant. "We have a few jolly people coming—not a dinner-party, you know, but just a few friends."

"I shall be delighted. How kind you are," replied Aurelia, feeling dizzy over her good luck.

"Thanks," said Jewel, pressing her hand. "Here comes tea, and with it papa."

Senator Bowen welcomed his guest with his usual Western heartiness.

"By Jove," he thought to himself, "she's a stunner! But my little girl doesn't lose a thing by contrast. What a sight for sore eyes the pair of them makes!"

Then he remarked aloud to the guest: "I know your father, my dear; I shall try and see more of him after this. My daughter's friends are my friends."

There were, beside Aurelia, four people to whom Mrs. Bowen introduced her. Two of them, the Secretary of the Treasury and his wife—she knew by sight, but Mr. Carroll West and a pretty widow, Mrs. Brewer, were total strangers. Lord Browning, the English Ambassador, and Lady Browning were shortly announced, and quickly following them came Cuthbert Sumner, completing the party.

"This is my dear friend, Aurelia Madison, Cuthbert; we were at school together. You remember that I told you at the theatre her face seemed very familiar to me."

"Delighted to meet you again, Miss Madison," he said as he bowed over her hand, suppressing a start of amazement at the sight of her. To himself he added:

"Confound the woman; what does she mean? Is she following me up? That won't help her any."

Aurelia thoroughly ingratiated herself with Lady Browning, paying her the greatest deference. Finding her ladyship much interested in religious topics and charitable projects, she affected an enthusiastic interest in them, and was rewarded by overhearing Lady Browning express herself as delighted with Miss Madison.

"Such a beautiful girl, and so intelligent to talk with."

She went down to dinner with Mr. West, who seemed much impressed with his lovely partner.

Cuthbert's attention would wander to the couple opposite him at table. West was talking to her with animation, while Aurelia smiled and sparkled, and looked irresistibly bewitching. West had but a small income for a wealthy man, and had always been incorrigible until now, but he seemed to have surrendered at last. Cuthbert watched her covertly, not at all deceived by the gaiety of her manner.

"So, the moth is still fluttering about the flame. Let her beware; I would sacrifice her without a moment's hesitation if I thought she meant Jewel harm."

He showed nothing of this outwardly, being as calm, smiling and well-bred as ever. But he was seriously annoyed by the inscrutable conduct of the woman opposite him. It was a vague feeling that he could not grasp—a shadow no larger than a man's hand.

PAULINE E. HOPKINS

Dinner over, the gentlemen did not linger long behind the ladies. Back in the drawing-room once more, Mrs. Bowen whispered to her husband:

"Do ask Miss Madison to play, Zenas."

"I will when I get a chance. West seems to have such a lot to say to her that it would be cruel to spoil sport."

Mrs. Bowen looked and laughed:

"I'll ask her myself then. Miss Madison, I am sure you are musical," she said to the girl, with a smile. "Will you not favor us?"

Aurelia signified her willingness and Mr. West, a minute later, had installed her at the piano, and stood by listening with delight to her playing. And she was worth listening to for she was a cultured amateur of no mean ability, and gave genuine pleasure by her performance. Mr. West was more and more infatuated each moment he spent in her society. Mrs. Bowen thanked her warmly as she rose from the instrument, followed by the plaudits of the company.

"Miss Madison," said the pretty widow, "you play beautifully."

"Do I?" gueried Aurelia, laughing, "but then I cannot sing, Jewel can, though—divinely, I hear."

"Flatterer!" said Jewel as she passed Aurelia's seat on her way to the piano, attended by Sumner.

"What is it to be?" he asked her as he turned over the contents of a folio.

"Will you choose, Cuthbert?"

A jealous pang shot through Aurelia's heart, as her ear caught the words, but she set her teeth hard.

Sumner took from the folio "Some Day," by Wellington.

"Always a favorite of mine, you know," he said.

She gave him a quick, trustful look, and smiled as she began the accompaniment.

Conversation was hushed; everyone listened while the rich, pure voice filled the room, giving the old song with the dramatic fire of a professional. There was a buzz of admiration when Jewel had finished. Cuthbert bent over with pride and delight shining in his face, and his softly-spoken "Thanks sweetheart," was heard distinctly by the woman sorely tried by jealous pain.

"Don't leave the piano; sing something else," came from all parts of the room.

"Very well," she said, and then gave with delicious pathos that sweet old song, "Dreaming Eyes."

The listeners were charmed. The singer rose, crossed the room and seated herself beside Aurelia. Their renewed acquaintance seemed destined to ripen into a close intimacy.

"Aurelia," the girl said as they sat there somewhat apart from the others, "Will you come with us to the—Theatre tomorrow night—we have a box?"

Surnames were dropped from that night. How did it happen? Circe alone knew. But after that these two were much together.

"Such a lovely morning, Jewel! You must come for a turn with me." or, "I shall be alone all day; do come and make the hours bright for me."

Sumner's first undefined fears gradually subsided. Time, rolling on springs of pleasure, passed swiftly bringing the night of the ball.

XVI

The Ball

The Bowen mansion was ablaze with light. Servants in livery hurried about attending the arrival of guests. Outside the house a continuous stream of carriages deposited the fortunate ones bidden to the feast.

The ball-room was a vast apartment arched, with a gallery of carved oak, in which the orchestra was seated. The rooms were filling fast, yet at no time, even when the crowd was densest, was there a pressure for room. Flowers wreathed the gallery, the national colors hung in the angles, banks of roses were everywhere. Mrs. Bowen, in white velvet, old lace and diamonds, stood near the entrance, supported by her husband, her daughter and Cuthbert Sumner. The house party was enforced by several gentlemen of political importance and their wives.

> *"In glass of satin,*
> *And shimmer of pearls."*

Jewel Bowen stood, a flush on her cheeks, her hair falling in waving masses, pearls clasping her white throat and arms, her large gray eyes like wells of light. An only child and heiress of many millions, she would have been the bright star of fortune to the gilded youth of Washington had not Cuthbert Sumner stood first in the field; albeit, a man might be pardoned for losing his head had she possessed only her youth and beauty.

A band hidden away in the great mansion discoursed Rossini's dreamy music in a concert during the arrival of guests. Fashionable Washington greeted its world and congratulated itself on being there, discussed the host and hostess, admired the arrangements for dancing just as the dear five hundred always have done and always will do. It was evident that the Bowen ball was to be the hit of the season. The Senator was voted charmingly original, and his wife attracted as much comment and attention as the debutantes who graced the occasion.

"I hear that we are to have a new beauty introduced tonight. A girl who is fairly startling," remarked one man to another. The rumor was started by Mrs. Bowen saying to a number of dancing men, with a roguish smile:

"Don't fill up all your dances, for there is another beauty coming. Nobody you know, either. A stranger in the city."

"We have heard something of her charms through West, I think, Madam Bowen. You mean Miss Madison. West is fairly a drivelling idiot over her at present. I'm worried over the poor chappie."

"Tiresome man, why couldn't he allow me the pleasure of trapping society. Have either of you met her?"

"Alas, for your intended surprise, dear Mrs. Bowen, I have seen her on the boulevard once or twice," replied the one who had not yet spoken. "What a perfect pair Miss Jewel and she will make, and puzzle anyone to award the palm."

"Mrs. Bowen is certainly a charming hostess," remarked one to the other as they walked away, displaced by fresh relays of guests.

"She is really a beautiful woman, but too cold to please me," was the reply.

"She has a throat and shoulders of alabaster, a superb head and a flower-like face."

"Hear, hear! Wasting compliments on a passé elderly matron—it isn't like you, Rollins."

"A pretty woman is never passé; you fellows who are new in society have something to learn, let me tell you."

"Granted. But we don't waste ammunition on elderly females who have had their day."

"Has a woman, once a beauty, ever had her day?"

"What a queer fellow you are tonight, making flowery speeches about old folks."

"There is no denying the truth of what I said, though. It is human nature. With a woman it is her good looks—with a man his strength, which at no age will he ever admit to be materially lessened any more than a woman will allow her good looks quite gone into the past, or if they do admit a decay of their charms or strength there is still a feeling of pride in what they were once."

"Here endeth the first lesson," laughed his companion as they separated to find partners for the opening number.

Other men, older than the two recorded, remarked the nobleness and charm of the hostess.

"There is a story written on her face, if I mistake not; I would give much for the power to read it," said a famous student of psychology to a celebrated physician, as they stood together surveying the brilliant scene.

"Granted she is beautiful, but she looks a creature of snow and ice. The daughter is more to my liking."

"Yes, but you must confess that they are alike."

"Alike, yet unlike; in the daughter there is fire and life, and a little diablerie, if I mistake not."

"Ah! but the beautiful Mrs. Bowen is only step-mother to the lovely Jewel."

"Is it possible? I should have thought them of one blood. Who was madam before her marriage?"

"No one knows," was the reply, accompanied by a suggestive shrug of the shoulders. "We do not inquire too closely into one's antecedents in Washington, you know; be beautiful and rich and you will be happy here."

Meantime the room was filling fast. Directly the butler announced "General Benson," Senator Bowen moved forward a pace and shook him warmly by the hand and then presented him to his wife and daughter. A puzzled look swept over his face as he bent for an instant above Mrs. Bowen's hand. Then he stole a furtive glance at her white impassive countenance, started slightly—looked again with a quick indrawn breath. There was now a questioning look in her eyes of seeming surprise at the evident interest—a quick contraction of the straight brows, the next second the dark eyes drooped, but he felt conscious that under those long lashes they still watched him. It passed in a second of time, there was no change in the beautiful cold face of the elegant woman of the world save that one might have imagined that she grew whiter, if possible. Then he recovered himself and turned with easy self-complacency to Jewel:

"Am I too late for the first dance?" he asked in his most courtly style.

"The first is gone certainly," smiled Jewel.

"Well, never mind; the first waltz, then."

"So sorry, General, but it is promised," with an arch glance at Sumner, who was standing back of her.

"Oh! I see. You unprincipled fellow, to steal the march on the world of us who are in darkness. We must all give first place to your claim, Sumner, lucky boy," he said with a genial laugh. "The fourth then? I shan't get another chance, so I must secure my luck while I can."

"With pleasure."

"And the one right after supper, dare I ask?"

"Very well," she replied again, smiling at his persistency.

The General took her card and inscribed his name against two members, and as the opening bars of the first dance sounded, and her partner came to claim her, bowed and moved away.

There was a movement near the door, and "Major Madison and Miss Madison" were announced. There was a moment's hush as they entered the ball-room, and every man present mentally uttered an exclamation of surprise and admiration. For once rumor had not lied. This woman was quite the loveliest thing they had ever seen, startling and somewhat bizarre, perhaps, but still marvellously, undeniably lovely. Her gown was a splendid creation of scarlet and gold. It was a magnificent and daring combination. Her hair was piled high and crowned with diamonds. A single row of the same precious stones encircled her slim white throat. She looked superbly, wondrously beautiful.

Truly this girl was an exquisite picture, but it bewildered one so that the eye rested on Jewel's slender, white-robed figure with pleasure, and intense relief.

Sumner was talking with Mrs. Vanderpool, the wife of a New York millionaire, as the Madisons entered, and turned at her exclamation:

"What a lovely girl! Who is she, Mr. Sumner?"

"She is the daughter of Major Madison, President of the Arrow-Head gold mines, so much talked about at present. You admire that vivid style?"

"Do introduce me, Mr. Sumner, I adore pretty girls." He was greeted by a flash from Aurelia's dark eyes, and a brilliant smile as he came up to give the desired introduction. Already she was surrounded and her ball card besieged.

"Miss Madison, Mrs. Vanderpool."

Both ladies bowed and immediately opened an animated conversation that ended in Aurelia's promising to grace Mrs. Vanderpool's german with her presence. Then Sumner gave the elder lady his arm across the room to join Mrs. Bowen. He passed Aurelia again on his way to the card-tables, in an adjoining room.

"You are going to ask me to dance, Mr. Sumner, of course?" she said to him as he paused an instant beside her chair. Her manner gave the bystanders the idea that they were old and intimate acquaintances. Her words and way jarred on Cuthbert. He took her card, and after consulting her, scribbled his name down for the after-supper dance, bowed and passed on.

PAULINE E. HOPKINS

He drew a deep breath of relief as he saw Jewel talking to the Russian ambassador, an old man in gorgeous dress and orders blazing on his breast.

"You are lucky, Excellency, to have a moment of Miss Bowen's time bestowed on you."

His Excellency bowed his head.

"I was just telling this lovely little lady that I must not be selfish, that I must give way for others who have a better right to her company than an old man like me."

"I have enjoyed talking with you so much," Jewel said simply.

"Thank you, my child. I see a friend of mine over in the corner. I can leave you in safe hand, now Sumner has come. By-and-by, perhaps, you will let me return and have a few more pleasant moments."

Sumner felt his vague sense of repulsion, which his encounter with Aurelia had aroused, fade, as he came in contact with the pure fascination of his betrothed. He smiled down at her tenderly. How inexpressibly sweet and lovely she was!

The band was playing a delicious waltz. Aurelia, flashing in her jewels, was flying round in the arms of West, who was her shadow. Sumner's brows met in a frown.

"How lovely Aurelia is!" cried Jewel with eager enthusiasm. "She is the most beautiful woman in the rooms."

"Bar one," said Cuthbert, smiling.

"Oh, you; you don't count. You are prejudiced," replied Jewel, laughing. "She seems to get on very well with Mr. West. I wonder—"

"Little matchmaker! I imagine West stands no chance in that quarter. He has nothing but his salary."

"Would that make a difference with her?" in a surprised, regretful tone.

"I imagine that they are not wealthy. Miss Madison, if I read her correctly, will marry for money."

The next instant his arm encircled Jewel's waist, he held her form pressed closely to his throbbing heart, and they glided away from earth to a short period of heaven.

As an intimate friend of the family, and soon to be a son of the house, Cuthbert Sumner had shared the dispensing of hospitality with Senator Bowen.

"My boy," said the older man, "just fix the thing up when you see 'em laggin. I'm going into the card-room and have a game with Madison.

He's an old duffer like myself. You understand all this sort of thing, but I'll be hanged if I ain't sick of it before I begin."

So Sumner had found himself pretty busy. After that waltz, however, which came just before supper, he and Jewel had a few precious moments together in the conservatory, sitting out the remainder of their dance. Then came supper, at which Sumner insisted upon being her escort. "I will not waive every enjoyment for the pleasure of others," he declared firmly.

XVII

The Spider's Web

The first dance after supper Jewel had given to General Benson.

"A short Elysium at last for me," whispered the gallant General as he passed his arm about her slight form. Jewel was a Western girl with all the independence that the term implies. She glanced up at her partner, as they whirled away, with a little amused smile slightly sarcastic; "I expected something different from you. Something at least original."

"Well, it is Elysium to find one's step perfectly duplicated."

"Oh, that is easy where one's partner is master of the art as you are. I imagine that you are one of the best dancers here."

"You are fond of dancing?" asked the General, after a silence.

"Yes; that weakness was born with me."

"In the tremendous crowd, I could not judge. But I can speak from this waltz—you dance like a fairy. Are you pleased with Washington?"

"Oh, yes; but I miss the freedom of the ranch, the wild flight at dawn over the prairie in the saddle, and many other things."

He looked at her with glowing eyes: "There we have congenial tastes. I am never so happy as when in the saddle."

The ball-room was a whirl of fair faces and dazzling toilets—the light, the heat, the perfume almost oppressive.

Knowing himself to be a fascinating conversationalist, he took advantage of a pause in the music to speak of the heat and suggest a turn in the conservatory where he knew that he could exert this power of enchantment. Jewel was nothing loth.

They stood a moment, before taking seats, at an open glass door gazing out on the gardens sered and withered and covered in places with patches of snow, but bathed in moonlight. There was something solemn in the scene, merriment seemed out of place; even soft laughter jarred on the nerves. See looked up to the heavens, where the Southern cross shone in all its brilliancy surrounded by myriads of other stars. The glorious Southern moon rode high in the sky. The flutes and viols were pouring out their maddest music.

"How glorious," Jewel said softly.

"Ay glorious indeed!"

"I mean the moon," she said.

"I mean your eyes, fair lady."

"You will persist in saying pretty things, General," she replied, turning away indifferently.

The General bit his lip in vexation. It was not to be easy work, that was plain.

There was a subdued murmur of voices and sometimes a ripple of laughter, for many couples stood, or strolled about the extensive greenhouses. They were lighted softly, from the arched dome, by silvery lamps; fountains flashed scented waters into marble basins where aquatic plants of strange beauty had found a home. Leading from the main conservatory were many arbors and grottoes, transformed for the time being by draperies of asparagus vines and roses into a charming solitude for two. The cool stillness was refreshing after the head of the ball-room.

"Really, this is well done," remarked the General, stopping to admire the effect. "None of the balls I have attended in Washington was so beautiful."

"Another compliment, General?"

"It is not flattery to speak the truth."

They seated themselves on a rustic chair for two, and the General entertained her with tales of his travels in Italy and India, and cyclone and typhoon, all very fascinating to the girl before whom life was just opening.

"Were you long out of the United States, General?"

"About ten years," he replied, looking down. "It was this way, Miss Jewel, I was a hot-blooded young fellow who could see no wrong in the decision of his section to secede from the union of states; and so, when it all ended disastrously, I gathered together what remained of my shattered fortunes, and went abroad until the pain of recollection should be somewhat dimmed. I returned almost a foreigner."

"Ah!" she said, with a gentle sigh of pity, "how dreadful that time must have been. Thank heaven, ours is a united country once more. And you are mistaken, too, in your judgment: we have no foreigners here. We have effaced the word by assimilation; so, too, we have no Southerners—we are Americans."

The General accented her remark by a courtly bow, and then he drifted into an animated description of a sail down the Mediterranean

PAULINE E. HOPKINS

Sea. Jewel could imagine that she inhaled the odor from boatloads of violets, brought to her senses by his wonderful descriptive powers.

At this moment their enjoyable tête-á-tête was interrupted by the sound of a woman's voice in passionate pleading.

EARLY IN THE EVENING AURELIA Madison had whispered to General Benson:

"If you can, take Jewel into the conservatory after supper. I shall have something interesting for her to hear."

"How are you getting on? Any progress?"

"Wait," was her answer.

After supper Sumner went to her to claim his dance. It was a duty-dance and a painful one he found it. As they floated down the long room, Aurelia gazed up at him with flushed cheeks and glittering eyes.

She had taken a great fancy to Jewel Bowen, not only because the latter was very kind to her—kinder than anyone had ever been to her in her lonely, reckless life, but because she really carried in her heart a spark of what passed for love and which would have developed but for Sumner. She could even admire Jewel's beauty without jealousy; she did not envy her her wealth although so pinched herself in money matters, and yet—strange nature of women, or of some women—for that reason she was the more determined to triumph over her as a woman, and, if she could, stab her. She had forced the friendship with that intention.

She felt instinctively that Cuthbert shrank from allowing a continuance of the intimacy between them, and she resented it. Yes, she would have her fling, her triumph; Jewel should know, beyond a doubt, that Cuthbert Sumner and his fortune was hers, belonged to her—Aurelia Madison.

Now she watched his face and resented his cold, preoccupied air.

"How quiet you are; aren't you well?"

"Never better," he replied, with an apology for his seeming indifference. After all she was a woman, and a beautiful one. Why should he try to mar her favorable reception among the élite.

"Only, I am not Jewel; is that it?"

"Pardon. Let us speak of something else. Shall I take you to have some refreshment?" he said coldly.

"Oh, let us go to the conservatory. I want air and rest," she said, slipping her hand through his arm. "I have seen nothing of you all the evening. Now you must devote a short time to me." Her air was bolder than Sumner had ever noticed before. He bowed low in acquiescence, though he would willingly have left her there.

She bit her lip and a dogged look came into her face that was not pleasant to see, and in her heart she felt that she could take the strong, handsome man and dash him senseless at her feet. She hid her feelings well, and glanced up at him with a pretty pleading look.

"Oh! Bert, I keep forgetting—of course—," then she broke suddenly, "I wish you loved her less!"

"A useless wish," said Sumner coldly. "Happen what may, Jewel must always be my first thought."

"Aye, your best and truest love," she said through her teeth.

They were in the deserted conservatory where all was coolness and shadow; Sumner walked by her side until they reached one of the grottoes, where from between the folds of the rose-curtain drapery a rustic seat held its inviting arms toward them. Aurelia dropped upon it:

"I am afraid I can't give you many minutes," he said with a cool smile. "Senator Bowen naturally expects me to assist him in looking after the guests."

The band was playing divinely and the notes came to them in waves of undulating melody. Sumner never forgot that night, and the music of the band haunted him ever after.

She sat there in sad languor that would have touched any heart but his. They talked a moment of indifferent subjects, then he arose and offered his arm with a motion that indicated a return to the ball-room. But with a low and exceedingly bitter cry she stood up.

"Must we part like this? My God! I cannot bear it! Have you no mercy, no pity?"

The tears were streaming down her cheeks, she held out her hands imploringly.

With deepest sympathy and pity he took them in his.

"Aurelia, you will forget. Believe me, dear, you will forget all this in a very little while. What good would my love do you now. It could bring you nothing but sorrow. We must forget each other. I hope—I know you will be happy yet. God be with you, dear girl." He bent down and pressed his lips to her trembling hands, feeling himself a wretch for bringing sorrow to this beautiful woman who loved him so.

But she flung her arms about him, and clung to him in desperation and the abandonment of grief, sobbing hysterically, with low, quivering moans, that cut him to the heart.

"Aurelia, do not weep so. It is torture for me to hear you."

"I hope I may die! Oh, if I only could!" she sobbed faltering and shivering, and clinging to him, and he put his arms about her and kissed her twice on the brow. Her lovely wet face was pressed close against his cheek.

A deep sigh startled him. He lifted his head. Standing in the doorway of the curtained recess, pallid as a ghost, all the graceful beauty gone from her wan face, with frightened woful eyes and despair in every feature, stood Jewel. With a loud exclamation, with rage and impatience and disgust, he shook the exquisite form from his bosom.

XVIII

It was long after midnight and the guests were leaving, when Sumner, with white, set face, sought Mrs. Bowen and asked for Jewel. She was much concerned over her daughter.

"I do not understand it," was her reply to his eager questions; "Jewel sent word by General Benson that she was not well, and had gone to her rooms. She was all right, and as gay as possible all day. I thought you would know."

Finding that he could not explain matters that night, and would accomplish nothing by waiting, Sumner left the scene of revelry, desiring to be alone. How it had all happened he could not tell. But what a sentimental fool he felt himself to be, for allowing himself to be betrayed into acting such a scene in so public a place. Still, he felt that he could blame no one but himself. Aurelia was free from any intention of scheming for how could she know of Jewel's presence at just that moment? So he argued, lulling his suspicions to rest.

At eight o'clock, while breakfasting, there came a letter from Jewel with his ring enclosed. Then, indeed, it seemed to him that life was over. With mad and bitter wrath, he cursed Aurelia Madison; then he started for Jewel's home. The servant who answered the summons was wont to have a welcoming smile for the familiar visitor. There was no expression in his well-trained face when he informed Sumner that the ladies were not at home. Night found him again at the Bowen mansion. Mrs. Bowen was coldness itself; Jewel begged to be excused.

Despair seized him. Everything, every one, was repulsive to him. Days of insane recklessness followed. A month went by in this manner—working furiously days, spending his nights in search of the excitement that is supposed to drown care. Then he grew calmer. He would seek Jewel again; he would force her trust; she should believe in him. Life was not worth living without her. For one touch of her cool hand, one glance from her calm eyes, one smile on the sweet, earnest lips, he would barter wealth and fame, and all the world had to offer—aye life itself!

They had met frequently in society during this memorable month, but Jewel passed her lover without a sign of recognition or with a slight bend of the head in acknowledgment of his reverential uncovering. General Benson was always in close attendance, and Aurelia Madison also, was often her companion.

After the usual nine days of wonderment and surmises as to the cause of the estrangement between lovers, public curiosity turned to speculating on the middle-aged general's chances with the fair heiress.

At seven o'clock one evening, Cuthbert sat at his desk in his rooms lost in sombre thoughts. He had determined to devote himself to the hardest of tasks, heavy brain work, when his heart and soul were racked with agony. He was busy on a political treatise. He was considered a brilliant writer. If he could make a stir in the literary world, it would please his father, and he had no one else to think of now.

Work! Could he work? He flung out his arms over the papers on the desk before him, and bowed his head upon them.

"If I knew that the suffering was for myself alone, my Blossom, I could bear it better."

He lifted himself at last haggard and weary as with weeks of sleepless toil, resolved to devote himself to his chosen work.

"What I am I will live on to the end—Ambition my only bride." He was striving with all his young courageous heart to kill the memory of the girl he loved. It was a bitter task, and an impossible one.

Modern pessimists are fond of crying that love, as well as chivalry, has died out of our practical world. If this were true, then Sumner lived after his century, for his belief in higher and better things was intense. He had a desire to worship purity in any shape, to champion the weak, and carve a pathway to honor that was characteristic of the chivalrous days of old.

The minutes passed, half-past seven ticked away, and then eight, and he never moved. He sat with his face on his two hands, his elbows planted on the table.

"I will not think more about her," he said to himself, doggedly. "I will not—I will not."

John, his servant, a New England colored man who had known him from his youth, had put his evening clothes out in the dressing-room, and now entered the room to remind his master of an engagement to dine.

"It's time you was dressed, Mr. Cuthbert," he said in his quiet way. John was eager for his master to leave Washington and return to Massachusetts and the family home.

"'Deed," he argued to himself, "this Washington's no city for me. Give me old New England every time; it's God's own country. They's nuthin' human about the South for chocolate complected gents like me, no matter how you fix it. The pint of the argument is in the scorpion's tail. Jes' so; and this here Southern idea of colored Americans ain't good fer black nor white when you's done had a New England raisin'."

"Mr. Cuthbert's an altered man sense the night of that there Bowen ball," he told himself again and again, "if he ain't twenty years older in his looks then I'm blind in one eye and can't see out of 'tother. He'll be best off if he gets back home to the old gentleman. Dog my cats but there's something strange in this whole kickup or my name ain't John Robinson."

Sumner roused himself at last: "What's the time, John?" he was asking as the bell of the suite rang shrilly.

"If that's Mr. Badger, show him in," he said as John went out of the room.

Cuthbert stood gazing down into the fire. He heard voices outside, but he gave them no heed; there was always a good-natured controversy between his friend and his servant.

A slap on the back, and "Holloa, Sumner, old man!" made him start round and put his gloomy thoughts behind him, and greet his friends, Will Badger and Carroll West.

"Ah! How are you, Will? How are you, West? How goes it?" he said, holding out his hand in greeting to his guests.

"Thought I'd bring West with me, and after we dine at the club, take a look in at the Madisons, this is their at home night. West's agreeable," with a laugh and a meaning look in the latter's direction.

Sumner hesitated. Aurelia had written him again and again, but he had not answered her impassioned letters. She had begged him to call and let her help set matters right, but as yet, he had not been able to bring himself to comply with her request.

"Well," he replied to Will Badger after a moment, "I don't mind. Have a glass of wine while I change."

"Thanks—we don't mind," said West.

West never did mind. He was fond of a social glass, and Sumner was noted for his fine wine and excellent brand of cigars.

"Yes, we'll have a little game with the Major," he remarked, as he helped himself from the side-board. "Great fun, the Major knows a thing or two about life does the old man."

"He knows enough to win your money, I suppose, you foolish boy," replied Sumner.

"It's very little I've lost there. He always insists on returning me my money."

"Have others been as fortunate?"

"That's their own fault; the Major wins fair every time," replied West hotly.

"Oh, West, you're prejudiced in his favor," broke in Badger.

"A pretty daughter is a trump card."

"She can't help being charming and attracting men to the house," stoutly maintained West.

"Charming, but dangerous, my dear fellow."

"She's my friend. I would be more to her if it were not for my poverty. Don't malign her, Badger, I won't stand it."

"My dear boy," broke in Sumner, soothingly, "Badger and I are your friends. Don't be angry with us; we mean it for your good. Aurelia Madison is one of those women with whom mere friendship is impossible. Men must always be half her lovers and therein lies the secret of her power—of any woman's power over our sex, if she is inclined to use that power to our detriment. Oh! she's circumspect," he continued as West attempted a vehement interruption. "I believe that it is not in her to care enough for any one to kick over the advantages of respectability for his sake, but she'll sail close to the wind."

West laughed bitterly: "You speak from experience I suppose; the city is ringing with your broken engagement and its cause."

Sumner stood silent. The blow was a keen one because the wound was so recent.

"Oh, come, fellows; drop it," hastily exclaimed Badger. "What do we care for Miss Madison except as any man admires a handsome woman. She'll bowl you over, Carrie, my son; she's using you just now to suit her own purposes. You're young yet," he continued affectionately, "but when you've had two or three seasons of this sort of thing, you'll hold your own with the deepest of them."

"Yes, West," rejoined Sumner who had regained his self-possession, "there are scores of just such women in the world: I will own that once I thought Aurelia Madison divine, but," shrugging his shoulders, "I have changed my opinion, and I am not sorry to have escaped from her toils. If you enjoy her society, continue to do so, but be careful; don't let her snare you."

"You ought to do some of your preaching to old Bowen. Dogged if he ain't gone on her worse than I am; any way, it looks so; he's there every night."

"What!" exclaimed Sumner.

"Let up, West, why don't you?" said Will Badger giving him a meaning look. "It's my idea, Cuthbert, that Senator Bowen is putting money into the mine. That's what I think is the attraction. I intended to speak to you about it some days ago."

Sumner made no reply, and in a few moments the trio left the house.

Washington society, with its proneness to overlook small trespasses, was beginning to talk about the Madisons. Some declared the beautiful daughter but a bait to snare theunwary, and openly voted the Major "shady." A good deal of money changed hands in the salon of the unpretentious house on New York Avenue: it was whispered also that the mine was a gigantic swindle. As yet these reports were but floating rumors; no one had made open complaint.

Meanwhile, the evenings were gay in the drawing-room where Aurelia smiled and flirted with the greatest intellects of the great Republic. There was an excellent buffet, obsequious servants, the soft shuffle of cards, and in the billiard room room at the rear of the house, a chosen few rattled dice or gave themselves up to the fascination of rouge-et-noir.

It was past eleven when the servant opened the door of Major Madison's salon and the three friends entered. Sumner found himself in a fair-sized and well-furnished room, containing a semi-grand piano; it was the one he had entered on his formal visit. Aurelia was the only woman present. The Major came forward from a group near the fire-place to receive them.

"So pleased to see you," he said, shaking hands in his cordial fashion. "Aurelia, my dear, here is Mr. Sumner." West was already standing by the beauty's chair, and Badger had passed on to a group of men in another part of the room.

Aurelia was exquisitely dressed in her favorite colors, cream and terra-cotta, combined in a wonderful gown.

"Well, Mr. Sumner, have you honored us at last?" she queried as she laid her hand lightly in his. Then as her father moved away she said with a bitter smile:

"The fault was not mine. I would have died rather than Jewel should have heard my foolish words."

Her manner more than her words, broke down all Sumner's lingering suspicions, and he warmed perceptibly toward her. She was but a girl, impassioned, impressionable. What right had he to accuse her of perfidy. Some one came up to them and interrupted her.

PAULINE E. HOPKINS

Yes, she would give them music. She went to the piano and Sumner followed her. She played popular selections from the latest opera bouffe, and then a morcean in a style that satisfied the most critical taste.

Senator Bowen had just entered the house and paused for the music to cease before speaking to Miss Madison, then he went up to her passing Sumner with a cold nod. Presently Major Madison and he disappeared, and Sumner felt they had gone to the card room. He wandered about for a while seeing enough to alarm him at the ascendency Major Madison had evidently gained over the Senator. As he stood at the door of the room watching the party where Senator Bowen sat staking large sums of rouge-et-noir and losing at every turn of the wheel, he felt dejected at his own helplessness. Gaming was Senator Bowen's only vice, a legacy from the old days when as mate he played every night for weeks as the cotton steamer made her trips up and down the river highways in the ante-bellum days. Sumner determined to rescue the honest old man from the toils of these sharpers. Just then Aurelia came up to him and touched his arm.

"I wish to speak with you, Bert, come with me."

He gave her his arm and they went to the vacant library. As they passed from view one man standing back of Senator Bowen's chair watching the game said to another:

"Sumner rich?"

"Very."

"It would be a fine thing for Miss Madison to catch him in the rebound. He seems fascinated."

"Indeed it would. And why not? She is of good blood, and he does not need money."

"Ah, no! only beauty and love. She is worthy of a coronet."

The soft light of tender sympathy was on Aurelia's face. Sumner clasped both her hands in his and begged her to tell him all she knew of Jewel.

"That is why I brought you here," was her serious reply. "I mean to undo this tangled web which I have unwittingly woven."

"Is she well? does she hate me? Dare I go to her?" he asked with passionate earnestness.

Disengaging one of her hands, Aurelia laid it on his shoulder, while she answered in soothing tones:

"Jewel is quite well, Bert dear, but she is allowing General Benson to monopolize her attention; in fact, I sometimes fear that the mischief is beyond repair and that she is pledged to him. But I am sure she loves you still. Trust a woman's intuitive powers. She cannot deceive me. Whatever she has done has been in a spirit of pique which needs but your presence to overcome. We will save her if it is not too late."

"Bless you for those words," he said, "your sympathy is very sweet to me."

"Be patient, and leave it all to me; I will bring you together again."

"You have filled my mind with forbodings," he said dejectedly, "I fear it is too late."

"Not too late, Bert; leave me the hope, at least, of redeeming myself in the eyes of Jewel. I have arranged for a meeting between you on Tuesday. On that day the Senator and Mrs. Bowen go to the President's reception. Jewel has a cold and will not be able to accompany them. She expects me to spend the evening with her. I waive my engagement in your favor, Bert; see that you improve your opportunity."

Tears filled her eyes, her voice broke, she was pale with emotion. She was proud of the intense feeling she displayed, and felt that she was acting her part splendidly. For a moment Sumner was speechless, then he kissed her hand and said in a broken voice, as he turned to go:

"God bless you, Aurelia."

AT FOUR A.M., GENERAL BENSON, Major Madison and Aurelia stood alone in the deserted drawing-room.

The Major waved in triumph two checks for large amounts, bearing Senator Bowen's signature.

"That's all right, Madison, but it is slow work—too slow for me. How are you getting on, Aurelia?"

She looked at him with an evil smile on her face that destroyed all its marvelous beauty: "I have told Cuthbert Sumner to call on Jewel, Tuesday evening. The Senator and his wife will be out, the girl alone. I think, General, you can do the rest, and settle the matter once for all."

"By jove, Aurelia, I will convince him of my triumph against all odds. You've earned your husband and your million."

PAULINE E. HOPKINS

XIX

The burst of gaiety which the ball brought into Jewel's life, made the succeeding days of gloom more depressing. Her high spirits had received a severe shock in her supposed discovery of Cuthbert's treachery, from which they rallied with difficulty.

"Don't stand there, my darling, those large windows are always draughty."

"I feel nothing of the sort, mama; don't libel this beautiful house, if you please."

"Beautiful house indeed; I shall be glad when June is come. I long for the breeze of the ranch."

"There will be more snow by tomorrow, mama."

"Of course! It seems to me that everything is out of joint. Think of snow in Washington in March!"

Jewel left the window where the light was darkening. She smiled at Mrs. Bowen and one could see how wan and delicate she looked.

"Mama, you are pessimistic to-day," she said kneeling beside the fire and stretching out her hands to the blaze.

Mrs. Bowen made to reply. In truth, her heart was bitter within her breast. She made an effort to appear cheerful before Jewel, not altogether successful.

The two ladies were in the favorite lounging room of the family— the small reception room. Jewel's great mass of bright hair rolled at the back of her small head, seemed too heavy a weight for it, while the hand that held the fleecy shawl about her was so shadowy as to fill one with apprehension. Yet she did not complain, only her parents noted the change in her since the night of the great ball, with feelings of uneasiness.

"My dear," said the Senator to his wife in one of their conversations about the best course in the matter, "My dear, if it were left to me, I'd shoot Sumner on sight. Out in 'Frisco his life wouldn't be worth a cuss. I've as much as I can do to keep decent and not put a ball into his miserable carcass. Think of a feller philandering after two women to once, either of them handsome enough to satisfy any reasonable man even if he is dead sot on looks in a female. Blast my eyes, Mrs. Senator, it's lucky we start for 'Frisco as soon as the session closes. I'd not answer for holding in much longer.

"Who'd have believed it possible! Sumner seems such a decent feller. Talk about deceit in women! Women ain't in it compared with these Eastern raised gents they call men!"

Then Senator Bowen retired to his club to vent his rage in pushing billiard balls about. It was during one of his fits of impotent wrath that he fell into Major Madison's toils and became an easy victim.

"Oh! my dove," murmured Mrs. Bowen to herself, as she had murmured many a time during the past few weeks; "my gentle, proud, suffering flower, how I wish I could take the pain out of your young heart and bear it for you; it is so hard to see that look on your child face, and feel that the sunshine is gone for you, and then realize that with all my love I can do nothing—nothing, nothing. A woman's life is hard, hard, from the cradle to the grave. O, God! why were we made to bear all the punishment for Adam's fall! Why are men so cruel? Why did he win her heart to throw it one side as a worthless bauble?"

Mrs. Bowen was crocheting an afghan and the needle dropped from her long white fingers and a settled look of pain crept like a veil over the beautiful proud face as she gazed into the fire.

Aurelia had been to see Jewel, had told her with many tears and sobs, of the broken engagement between herself and Cuthbert, that they still loved each other, that Sumner blamed himself for believing that he had forgotten her (Aurelia) and had engaged himself to Jewel without realizing the true state of his feelings, and now he would never marry—neither of them felt that they could know happiness without the thought of Jewel's wrongs before them. Could they not be friends still, she and Jewel? She was so lonely and miserable feeling that she had brought so much suffering on her dear friend. Mrs. Bowen heard it all but deep in her heart was a doubt of the specious pleader.

"I wish we had not been so hasty, and had given Cuthbert a chance to explain," she remarked to Jewel one day.

"There is nothing to explain," replied Jewel lifting her head proudly. "I saw and heard it all for myself. He told me he had only met Aurelia casually at the Cape, leaving almost immediately; now I find beyond a doubt, that they were actually engaged. Nothing can alter the fact that he had something to conceal and for that reason deceived me. Then, too, papa has met him at the Major's, and has heard the gossip of the clubs. It proves itself, mama; there is nothing more to be said. I—I have learnt my lesson—I shall never be so foolish again. I have to thank Mr. Sumner for teaching me worldly wisdom."

"I had thought better things of Cuthbert. I would never have believed him to be the cruel, selfish man he has proved. Well, may he have some peace before he marries Aurelia, for I suppose it will end that way. He will be punished if he marries her or I greatly mistake her nature."

Jewel knelt on, gazing into the fire. She was silent for a time, and then she said gently:

"You dislike Aurelia, mama, simply for my sake. It is not like you to be unjust."

Mrs. Bowen glanced at her sharply.

"It is not that alone, Jewel, but I believe her false. I have a presentiment that there is something wrong. O, my darling, do be careful. I think it would kill your father if anything happened to you," exclaimed Mrs. Bowen as she folded her daughter in her loving arms.

Jewel answered her tender embrace with warm kisses.

"Dear mama, the sting is taken out of all the pain when I remember that no matter what comes my own darling father and mother see no fault in their dear girl."

Ah! children who have not needed it yet, believe that the wound must be mortal that cannot be soothed by a parental balm and oil. Those dear ones have the power to restore self-respect though they may be powerless to restore happiness. Mrs. Bowen put the girl from her and left the room.

"Yes, I, too, shall be glad to return to the ranch. It will be quiet and peaceful there. I shall forget."

She shivered. "Forget," she repeated, pressing her hands to her breast, and moving to and fro in agitation, "no, no! I shall never forget—I shall remember as long as I live."

She rose to her feet and began walking the length of the room. The opening of the door aroused her, and turning with a slight frown, she saw General Benson.

The frown deepened as she saw him place a basket of lovely flowers on a table. She did not desire him to bring her gifts; but this did not cause her pain. It was the vision of a by-gone-day, when some one else was wont to come softly into the room with beautiful flowers.

Her face flushed for a moment, then became paler than ever. She gave General Benson her hand silently, he bit his lip when he saw how quickly she withdrew it.

"Sam told me I should find Mrs. Bowen here," he said courteously.

"Mama is in her room. I will ring and let her know you are here."

"Wait one moment," he pleaded. "I have brought you some flowers, Miss Jewel."

"They are very beautiful," she answered coldly; "and you are very kind, General Benson."

"Flowers suit you," he said in his soft caressing voice, that had never failed him with other women, but which was wasted on Jewel. "You should always be surrounded with them, Miss Jewel."

She did not smile. This man's admiration jarred on her. Her father liked his pleasant ways and found him a good companion to wile away the hours, but somehow she could not assume the easy familiarity of friendship with him.

She took herself to talk for her growing dislike of him. Why should she be so ungenerous to one so kind? Why should she shrink from him with a loathing she could not repress? She had never voiced her feelings but she knew that her mother felt with her toward this suave, diplomatic gentleman. She had once seem him kick the dog that followed him, cowed and faithful only through fear, and she disliked him for the cowardly act. She spoke to him about it.

"Oh, one must be in the fashion!" he replied, never dreaming of the anger and disgust beneath the girl's cold exterior. "And dogs were made to kick. People talk a lot of rubbish about the faithfulness of dogs. It's all bosh! Their devotion means dread of the whip, or a strong boot, Miss Jewel."

Jewel's disgust was so great that for the moment she lost all other feeling, every remnant of respect and liking fled. He had forgotten the incident; and though resenting the girl's coldness, he did not associate his own cruelty with it. In fact, he put it down to coquetry, and it only inflamed his admiration and strengthened his determination to make this girl his wife. He wondered if Senator and Mrs. Bowen would oppose him?

Jewel's stepmother was a woman of the world, and between General Benson and herself there was no great liking. He felt uneasy in her presence, that under her rather haughty manner a keen sight was hidden that read his motives. Senator Bowen was more to his liking. In reply to Mrs. Bowen's cautious questioning concerning General Benson, the Senator's answer was:

"The government, my dear, gives him its confidence by placing him in a responsible position. That is enough for me. Uncle Sam never employs rascals to transact his business."

Opposition or not, General Benson meant to win in the end. Aurelia might fail with Cuthbert, but he would win with Jewel. He was irritated by the delay; apart from his vanity which was injured by Jewel's indifference, it was time the engagement was announced. His creditors were unpleasantly pressing. His property in Baltimore was mortgaged up to its full value. There was nothing for it but this marriage with the California millionaire's heiress.

Heiresses were not easily found. It was only a question of time and management, and Jewel must be his wife.

"Yes, you are one of those beings for whom it seems flowers were especially created. I always think of you as a delicate lily or a white rose."

The girl's face flushed, but not with pleasure.

"Mama must see them. She will admire them," she said as she rang the bell, and sent a message to Mrs. Bowen.

General Benson bit his lip. He had intended speaking to her today, but it was not an easy thing to do. She kept him at bay.

"Have you seen Miss Madison lately?" he asked sauntering up to the fire. Jewel shook her head.

"Not this week," and the troubled look returned to her eyes.

"She is a great girl," Benson said with a laugh—he leaned against the over-mantel and stroked his moustache. "She and Sumner are going the pace. I suppose we cannot expect lovebirds to remember anything outside their paradise." Jewel shivered.

"She loves him still," he said to himself between his teeth. "Well, it is no matter; she may love him now, but I shall alter that when she is my wife."

Then with the innate cruelty of his nature he continued:

"Sumner is to be congratulated, if what I hear is true; the Madisons are a fine old Southern family, and Miss Aurelia is worthy of her race." He hid a smile behind his hand.

"It is quite refreshing in these matter-of-fact days to come upon a real genuine romance. Love, they say, is out of fashion, if so, I am afraid Sumner is a long way behind the times, for I am told he is madly in love. That I guessed the first time I saw them together. One could read his infatuation in his eyes. Miss Madison's magnificent beauty easily accounts for it. Her face is her fortune, most assuredly." Jewel drew herself away a few steps. The pain he hoped to give her was not there. She had schooled herself to bear hearing the news of the engagement at any time. He could arouse her indignation—pride; this he did successfully.

"Then it is settled. Aurelia is very beautiful," she said quietly. "She is my friend, and I think her one of the most beautiful women I have ever seen."

He smiled.

"Ah, pardon, Miss Jewel; I had forgotten while speaking that you were more than ordinarily interested. Always sweet and generous, Miss Jewel, most rarely so, for one beautiful woman seldom acknowledges another."

"Here is mama." Jewel turned to the door with a faint sigh of relief. "Will you excuse me, General Benson, I want to catch the next mail?"

General Benson did not stay much longer. He was not at his ease with Mrs. Bowen. He was furious with Jewel for retiring and leaving him with her mother. He set it down against her in his book of reckoning to be settled in a future not far-distant.

Mrs. Bowen went to Jewel after he was gone. "You have not looked at your flowers, Blossom," she said gently. Her daughter colored.

"They are very beautiful, but—"

"They give you no pleasure?"

"I do not like presents from General Benson."

"You do not like him?" queried her mother, stroking the wonderful coils of shining hair.

The girl shivered.

"No—no. I do not like him at all; he is very kind, but I cannot bring myself to like him, mama, dear."

Mrs. Bowen kissed her brow.

"Nor do I; he is a bad man and I shall find a way to stop his calling here." She paused a moment lost in deep thought. "Perhaps it is well that we do not return to Washington next fall. I am glad your father has so decided."

The small hours of the morning found Jewel still sitting before her bedroom fire. She had returned from a reception, and had dismissed her maid, telling Venus that she would manage without her.

She was thinking of words she had heard that confirmed the report that Sumner and Aurelia were engaged. She had not seen the latter for a number of days, but she felt that she might expect her at any moment to confirm the report. What is first love? Some say first love is "calf love," a silly infatuation for an insipid hero or heroine.

Others will tell you first love is the only true passion; that it comes but once to every human being; that the intense yearning for the sound

PAULINE E. HOPKINS

of a beloved voice, the sight of an adored face, the clasp of a hand, only fills the heart once in a lifetime. The question as to whether it is the deepest love must be answered by each individual.

"The heart knoweth its own bitterness," says Holy writ. So also it knoweth its own joy. Jewel was a firm believer in the strength of first love. And now she found herself suffering the pangs of love despised, the anguish of disappointment, the humiliation of neglect. Ever before her inner sight was the merry dancing, daring, the glancing fun in those dark eyes so recently her sun. How little she had been to him that he could so soon forget.

Oh, they were beautiful eyes, she thought, with a stirring of the old rapture at her heart. What a noble face he has! high-bred, refined, and manly, too! There was not another man to compare with him; and—he belonged to another. A bitter pang smote upon her, a keen memory of the events of the past weeks. She wept over her baseless dreams, and prayed for strength to solve the problem of her life.

"How shall I meet him?" she asked herself. "How shall I be calm, conventional to Mr. and Mrs. Cuthbert Sumner?" Long she sat there pondering many things.

XX

The last of March came, but winter still lingered in the lap of spring. Jewel's couch was drawn up before the blazing fire; the parlor was snug and comfortable, just cosey enough for a semi-invalid. The room was half-panelled with oak, and the furniture was of the same material covered with bright silk and embroidered cushions.

Jewel was not well and had excused herself from attendance at the President's reception. Her mother had ensconced her in the small reception parlor promising to return early, and bidding her doze away the time until then. She was not asleep. Her eyes were open, and fixed upon the fire; they were filled with intense pain, and her hands were clenched, while now and then a shiver ran through her frame, as she turned restlessly from side to side.

She sought solitude that evening, and yet the sound of Sam's voice in the hall admitting a visitor whose tones betrayed Gen. Benson, was not distasteful to her.

He was very much at home now, and drew a low chair round between her and the fire, after bidding her good evening, took his place there, and gazed steadfastly into her face a few moments without speaking.

"Of what are you thinking?" he asked gently.

"I am thinking what a horrible thing it is that we women are always loving the wrong men—worthless, heartless men, who cannot appreciate in even a small degree the love we waste upon them."

He took one of her hands in his.

"Look at me," he said. "You are very young—you will get over this happening—this episode in the life of every young girl. Don't start. How can anyone who cares for you, help knowing that you have suffered through loving the wrong man? But time is a great healer. Now don't try to free your hand. It must belong to me some day, so why not let it rest in mine now?"

She shivered as she turned from him.

"You don't understand," she said speaking very low. "My heart is dead, or only so much alive that I can feel it ache. I can never love—never marry. I must go on living—expiating my wilful blindness in being so reckless as to love a—a villain with all my heart and soul."

The tears rolled slowly down her face.

"Won't you let me try to comfort you?" he asked.

PAULINE E. HOPKINS

She shook her head. "You cannot give me back the man I believed in," she replied.

Benson rose, frowning heavily.

"Can't I horsewhip him or do something to punish the scoundrel?"

"No, no!"

"You don't love him still?"

"No," she answered. "But I can never hate him. Don't let's talk about it any more," she continued wearily. "Dead loves are like dead people—talking will not bring them back."

"I will make you forget him some day," he said, kissing her hand.

"I wish you could," she replied with a sigh.

Benson felt encouraged, and determined to follow up his advantage.

"What has put you in this state?" he asked tenderly.

"Why are you not at the reception?" she laughed evasively.

"That is not answering my question?" he retorted. "Either you need a doctor or your distress of mind calls for an adviser. Shall I hold your hand, and see if I can mesmerize you into telling me all your thoughts?" he continued half-laughing. Jewel drew back in alarm. She raised herself on her arm and looked away from him into the fire.

"You have no right to question me as you know."

"Why won't you give me the right?" he asked earnestly. "Look, Jewel, I love you and trust you so much, I am ready to take you on any terms. I should be glad and proud to marry you tomorrow, and wait for time to bring me love."

"Why will you tease me?" she asked desperately. "Be my friend without asking reward, but never hope to be anything else."

The girl was sitting now on the couch that had served her for a resting place. She bowed her head; the long silken lashes lay on her cheeks.

He still held her hand; and as he gazed down upon her face, so pale and sorrowing, his pulses throbbed with greater passion.

"Jewel you are an angel! Be one to me. You have many years to live; you could not, would not pass them alone. Be merciful then to one who worships the ground you tread! I know my heart. It is yours. None other can, shall ever share it. Accept my love and me, my darling!"

He was bending over her, his breath ruffled the soft rings of her hair. His feverish earnestness moved her. She felt a great pity for him. For the time she forgot her repugnance.

"He feels as I feel," she thought.

What would she not have done for him in her compassion! Anything but what his lips pleaded for; that was impossible.

"I am so sorry—so very sorry!" she said, and the light of her eyes, even the touch of her fingers confirmed her words. "But you see I have no love to give."

"Jewel," lightly he placed his arm about her, "I give you my love; I ask but, in return, you. Let me have the right of loving you through life. I will be content; for I shall live in hope that my affection shall one day win yours. If you must think your whole first love given, let me hold the second place in your heart."

"Is second love possible?" she asked.

"Most surely. Give me that; I will be satisfied." Her lips moved; assent seemed to quiver on them, when looking up, she gazed directly into Cuthbert Sumner's eyes. He had been waited upon to the room by Sam, and had stood there looking at them without being noticed so absorbed had they been in their conversation.

With a cry Jewel staggered to her feet.

"Jewel, Jewel, hear me," cried Sumner in desperation, "I pray you, before you part us forever. Do not be rash; for God's sake, let me speak, hear me!" She waved him back as he stepped toward her.

General Benson was bewildered; his active mind comprehended instantly the peril of the moment—the frustration of his plans if he hesitated an instant—and his ready wit saved him. It was the time for decisive action. With a swift movement he placed himself at Jewel's side, took her hand in his, and thus faced Sumner.

"Mr. Sumner, this intrusion is unwarrantable. Miss Bowen is my promised wife."

Cuthbert bowed his head, and turning, rushed from the room and from the house.

XXI

Cuthbert Sumner tendered his resignation to General Benson to take effect at the close of the official year, and it was accepted. "I have no feeling but friendship for you, Mr. Sumner," said the General after he had folded the document away. "I hope and trust that whatever happens we shall remember each other without enmity," he continued in his sweet voice so effective with most people. "Still, feeling that it must be unpleasant for you to serve under me, when we consider existing circumstances, without doubt what you propose is the best course."

It was ten o'clock the next day and Sumner sat at his desk looking out occasionally at the gathering storm that threatened to send March out with tumultuous blustering winds and heavy rain. The secretary and the stenographer occupied the same apartment with the chief. The ceiling of the apartment was lofty, there were elegant paintings on the walls, and the furniture was luxurious. There were rich hangings at the windows, carpets and rugs on the floor, lounges were grouped about the spacious room giving it more the appearance of a boudoir than a public office. The style of the wardrobes ranged about the walls would lead one to infer that all the conveniences for dining or longing could be easily found within its four walls. Nor would one have been mistaken in inferring such to be the case; indeed, the chief's lunch was generally served in this room in sumptuous style by his valet. It was rumored, too, that here gay spreads and bachelor parties were not unknown; happenings at which grave questions of state were sometimes decided.

A warm fire burned in the grate for there was a chill in the air that furnace heat did not entirely remove, and the large pile of blazing coals shed a glowing radiance of cheerfulness on all around.

General Benson, it was evident, though a servant of the people, was using their resources freely to gratify an extravagant taste. His was the life of a popular official floating at the ease of his own sweet will.

The only other occupant beside Cuthbert and Benson was Elise Bradford the stenographer. This woman was elegantly attired, and here again one noticed how utterly out of keeping her dress was with the work supposed to be performed by a simple government clerk. She was tall, fair and pale, with a countenance that impressed one with its resigned expression and sad dignity.

General Benson sat before his splendidly covered table where cut-glass bottles of eau de cologne gleamed, vases of fragrant flowers charmed the eye, and ornamental easels of costly style held pictures of fashionable ladies. He was looking over some papers which had just been submitted by Cuthbert. This morning he was abstracted and silent. Finally he called Sumner to him in a recess of a curtained window and said:

"Sumner, I have a favor to ask of you."

"I shall be happy to grant it if it is in my power, General."

"Thanks, I felt sure such would be your answer. I shall have to ask you and Miss Bradford to work overtime tomorrow and Sunday. This work must have our special attention. It is of such a nature that I can not confide it to an ordinary clerk. I cannot superintend to work myself because a party is to leave here on Saturday, myself among the number, for New York, on official business—two or three Senators and a Cabinet official to represent the President. We shall not return for ten days and I shall depend upon you to keep the office business in hand."

"I will do all that I can willingly," replied Sumner.

"And I think I'll go off now. The time is short until five tomorrow. I have some preparations to make. You may as well take charge at once."

Leaving Sumner he stepped to the side of Miss Bradford and engaged in a whispered conversation. Cuthbert was a discreet person and gave no heed to the couple. He was used to the manners of many high officials with their female clerks, and paid no attention to what did not concern him. He had observed that an apparent intimacy existed between his chief and Miss Bradford. If they knew that he had noticed them they gave no sign that his knowledge was an annoyance. His presence was treated with the utmost decorum.

The whispered talk kept on for some time. Finally, whatever subject had been under discussion seemed to have been satisfactorially arranged, and the chief arose from the seat he had occupied beside the lady and shook her hand warmly, with the words:

"At Easter then without fail."

"Poor Jewel," thought Cuthbert, "what will be her fate when she is the wife of this man who is but a reformed rake seeking to re-instate himself in society by a high political position and a rich marriage."

As the thought lingered in his mind, General Benson paused beside his desk. Sumner could not refrain from giving him an admiring glance nor could he wonder at the infatuation of most women for the handsome chief who stood there drawing on his gloves, his costly fur-lined coat unbuttoned and nearly sweeping the carpet giving an added charm to this handsome face, elegant figure and gracious manner.

"I have intrusted you with a delicate piece of business, Mr. Sumner." His voice was impressive. "The official relations between us have always been coordinate in character. I am confiding in you now as I would in a personal friend. You will find some additional papers to be collated in my desk," he continued drawing him behind the rich folds of the curtains back of the official desk. He gaze was fixed full in Sumner's face with such earnestness and anxiety that at once appealed to the secretary's sympathy. Sumner's face was like an open book in its candor and innocence of guile, as he replied quietly:

"You may trust me, General Benson, to respect your confidence. Personal matters have no entrance where they would interfere with obedience to my superiors."

"And, see here, Sumner, you may be detained later tomorrow night than tonight. Your work will probably keep you until sharp midnight, perhaps past. I have given the watchman notice of your being here by my orders. Here is my private entrance key and you can let yourself and Miss Bradford out without trouble. See that everything is safely closed up. You shall be handsomely compensated for your extra labor, although I know that you have no thought of the money," he added in answer to Sumner's deprecating wave of the hand. "Good-bye," and giving him his hand, the chief shook his warmly, and left the room."

They heard him descending the stairs, talking and laughing with messengers and others employed about the building, in the genial way for which he was noted among government employees.

XXII

Time and tide wait for no man; brains may throb, and hearts may ache or break, but the world rolls on just the same, for weal and woe, whether the grim skeleton that comes an unbidden guest on so many a man's hearth is shrouded in elegance or bare in all its appalling hideousness.

It was not until two P.M. of Sunday that the secretary and stenographer had time to rest as they neared the close of their labors. Sumner felt a weariness of spirit and a dull aching of the heart that was not due to overwork. Worriment had removed the fresh heartful bloom from his face, but the paleness and thinness added to its refinement and intellectuality; while the restless feverish dilation of his dark eyes rendered them singularly striking and brilliant. More than once during this wretched time he had been possessed with a longing to be back with his father in their quiet New England home.

"Yes, this shall be my last year in politics. I'll go home and take up the business for which I was born; it will please my father."

As he turned to resume his work with a sigh, he became conscious that Miss Bradford was watching him. There had been a time when he had felt a passing admiration for the good-looking stenographer, and had paid her some attention, but after he met Jewel he had never pretended to give her a second thought.

She, on her side, had not resented his dessertion but always seemed to retain a genuine regard for him which had shown itself in many neighborly acts of kindness which the close intimacy of office life often brings about between women and men. She had been rattling the keys of her typewriter at a furious rate of speed all day, and now, with a final pull of the carriage, finished her work. Then she rose with a sigh, crossed the room and flung herself down on one of the couches opposite Sumner's desk, evidently bent on conversation.

"Mr. Sumner, you look—oh, I don't know how you look, but I should say a rest would do you good."

"I shall have one when the vacation comes. I am going home and I shall not return to Washington."

"Are you going for good?" she asked in a surprised tone.

"Yes," he answered as he adjusted a pile of manuscript, and began folding up the papers scattered over his desk. "Washington holds no charm for me."

She was silent for a time and as she sat buried in deep thought she tapped the floor with one foot in restless fashion. At length she said:

"Don't think me intrusive, or that I seek to harrow your feelings, but isn't this sudden resolve the result of the misunderstanding between you and Miss Bowen?"

"I will answer you as frankly as you have asked, Miss Bradford; it is so."

There followed another pause, a silence so long that the young man thought that she had forgotten his presence. Suddenly she spoke again.

"Mr. Sumner, I like you; I trust you; why I know not, for my experience in life has not been of so pleasant a nature as to cause me to trust anyone; not a man, surely. But today I feel a desire to talk on forbidden subjects, to take someone into my confidence.

Sumner looked at her keenly as he said significantly:

"It is a safe rule, Miss Bradford, to keep one's own counsel."

"I feel impelled to tell you what I am about to disclose, by an unseen power. Do you not believe in unseen forces influencing our acts?" she asked wistfully.

"I cannot deny that I have sometimes felt the same influence of supernatural powers that you speak of, and I do firmly trust that the world of shadows and mystery to which we are all bound may be one of infinite love, infinite calm and rest."

"For those who have been upright here," while a look of pain crossed her face. "But what of those among us who have been guilty of many sins? That is the thought that haunts me tonight." She pushed her hair from her face with one hand as she looked up at him.

"Why trouble ourselves with such questions, Miss Bradford? Why not simply trust the judgment that sees not as man sees?"

She felt calmed as she looked into the true, earnest face opposite her. "Thank you," she said at last, simply. Then—

"May I tell you?"

"Whatever confidence you honor me by giving shall be sacredly respected."

"I know that. Did I not tell you that I trusted you? But you have my permission to tell Jewel Bowen as much as you think fit, for it is her due."

Sumner colored as he said:

"I am not on terms of intimacy with Miss Bowen."

"I know that, too," she replied impatiently, "but you probably will be after you hear what I have to tell you. I, too, am about to leave

Washington. When I leave the office tonight I shall never return. Easter is two weeks off, and at Easter I am to be married to General Benson."

"Married—General Benson! Impossible! You jest!" exclaimed the startled man.

"To General Benson," she repeated emphatically.

"But—Miss Bowen—"

"Will have a welcome release," she broke in. "It is a long-delayed ceremony that should have been performed five years ago. I have a son four years old, Mr. Sumner!"

Sumner could not answer her. He stared at the woman before him with unseeing eyes. He could not believe that he had heard aright.

"A son four years of age!" he repeated mechanically in shocked surprise. "This is most extraordinary! How can it be possible?" No wonder you are incredulous.

"Wait, wait!" she went on, "give me time. I will tell you all; it is your right to know. It has all been arranged so suddenly that my brain is in a whirl—I cannot think!"

She flung herself down against the cushions of the couch, and endeavored to grow calm. Sumner waited, disturbed, unhappy, heartsick, over this scene, fearing he knew not what. He watched her labored breathing, her clenched hands, and there was a long pause.

Sumner cast anxious glances over at the bowed head opposite him supported on its owner's hand. The fire blazed cheerily, and outside the wind rose, whirling the rain in great sheets against the window panes. It was a wild night.

Finally Elsie Bradford sat up pushing her hair back restlessly from her temples, and faced him white and agitated.

"All this misery that you have endured for the past month," she began slowly,—"all the sorrow, you owe to one man. He has tortured you, fooled you, deceived you—Yes, it is true; but I—God help me—I love him."

"I do not comprehend your meaning, Miss Bradford, to whom do you refer?" he asked soothingly, for there was the glitter of fever in her eyes.

"Silence!" she interrupted sternly. "I must tell you certain things for your own welfare and the welfare of the girl you love. I dare not hide them. Perhaps—who knows—it may be put down to my credit in that great future life toward which we are all journeying. In the years that are coming, when you are both happy and forgetful of this present miserable time, remember me and my misery with pity."

PAULINE E. HOPKINS

Sumner could only wait in pained surprise for her to continue. She pressed her hands convulsively to her heart, as she sat there white as death, and trembling all over.

"Did it ever occur to you, Cuthbert Sumner, that you are the victim of a plot?"

"You will speak in riddles, Miss Bradford. I must confess that I do not understand you."

"And yet you are a man of remarkable intelligence, and not a child in the world's ways. I cannot swear to it, but I believe that you have fallen into the net of two adventurers and a daring adventuress. Have you noticed any intimacy between General Benson and the Madisons?"

"No; they seem to be merely chance acquaintances."

"And yet, they are partners in crime, and I believe that General Benson introduced the Bowens to the Madisons."

"Great heavens! No!" cried Sumner a great light breaking in upon him at the bare possibility of such a thing being true. "Miss Bradford, are you sure?" he asked hurriedly.

"I am almost certain of the truth of what I say; you can easily ascertain if I am correct in my suspicions. I believe the intention was, your fortune for Aurelia Madison, Miss Bowen's for the General."

"But where do you get your information? Upon what are your suspicions based? Surely you have something to go upon," cried Sumner recovering from his first bewilderment.

"How can I tell you? Oh! the shame of it all will kill me," she said as she drew a long shuddering breath.

"Your distress pains me, Miss Bradford," said Cuthbert gently as he watched the wretched girl; he was moved more than he cared to show—indignant—furious over the conduct of this scoundrel in a high place. He went to one of the wardrobes and opened the door disclosing a compartment used as a wine closet. He quickly filled a glass from a costly cut-glass decanter, and carried it to the half-fainting woman urging her to drink it.

She took it eagerly from his hand and drained the glass.

"Yes, yes, I must go on. It is part of my punishment—my atonement! It is such misery, shame!" she sobbed brokenly. "I heard he was about to marry Miss Bowen. I accused him of treachery toward you in the matter. I threatened him with exposure. I told him that he must make atonement to me and the child at once. He must do it or I would speak; I would go to Miss Bowen with the whole miserable story."

"And he?" questioned Sumner gently, yet sternly, stifling his own feelings for the sake of the heart-broken woman before him, giving out strength and protection with womanly tenderness to soothe. "Tell me all, and be sure that I will speak of nothing that you desire kept secret."

"To have you understand the man known as General Benson, I must tell you a portion of my history."

"Excuse me," broke in Sumner, "you say 'known as General Benson,' is not that his true name?"

"No, it is not. And I cannot give you the true one. I have my own thoughts about it, however, When I was eighteen years of age, I came from Kentucky, where I was born, to Washington seeking employment.

I was left an orphan while an infant, and brought up by my aunt who was too poor to support me after I entered womanhood. She did the best for me that she could, however, and I started out with high hopes, telling her that I should soon be able to repay her for her kindness and care. I had heard much of the large salaries paid to government clerks, and determined to seek employment here.

Arriving in the city, I went to call upon the congressman from our district to whom I brought letters of introduction. He received me kindly, and said that he would do his best to have me appointed. After a week he sent me word to call at the Treasury Building. There he introduced me to General Benson who wanted a clerk. The General immediately engaged me, and it is needless for me to say that I was overjoyed at my good fortune. I was able to send my aunt money, and for a time I was perfectly happy. It is useless to dwell on the details—I wish to hurry over this part of my life—suffice it that in six months time I had become the chief's victim.

I am abhorrent to you, no doubt. You who have been rich all your life may despise me; but I had tasted poverty, I appreciated its effect on my future welfare, and I sickened at the thought."

She paused a moment to take breath, for she had spoken rapidly, as if eager to have done with the shameful and painful details. "Official wealth, power and opportunity were my ruin. I was led to confide in the chief by his high position; and he, like others in such places, deceived me and betrayed that confidence. He was my first lover, for I was but eighteen, and I loved him as we always love the first man who teaches us what love is. I admired his genial ways, his distinguished air, and even his success in his vices was a source of pride to me. He took advantage of my youth to mold me to his fancy, and make me like himself. Oh, I can never make you realize the depravity of our elegant chief.

For a long time he was content with my love. I was young enough and pretty enough to satisfy even him. But after a while he met Aurelia Madison, and then my agony began."

"What!" exclaimed Sumner, "do you know what you say? Aurelia Madison one of General Benson's mistresses?"

"That is not the worst thing about her," replied the woman with a bitter smile. "Will you believe me when I tell you that she is a quadroon?"

"Impossible! you rave!" almost shouted the young man.

"I would it were not true. Yes, she is a quadroon, the child of Major Madison's slave, born about the time the war broke out. That is why the two men find in her a willing tool."

"My God!" exclaimed Sumner as he wiped the perspiration from his face, "a negress! this is too horrible." Repeated shocks had unnerved him, and he felt weak and bewildered.

"Do not blame her. Fate is against her. She is helpless. The education of generations of her foreparents has entered into her blood. I should feel sorry for her if I could, but I feel only my own misery and degredation. I am selfish in my despair. Happy, prosperous people sympathize with the woes of others, but sometimes I feel like laughing at their mimic woes, my own are so much greater in comparison.

Yet Aurelia in a measure deserves our pity. The loveliness of Negro women of mixed blood is very often marvellous, and their condition deplorable. Beautiful almost beyond description, many of them educated and refined, with the best white blood of the South in their veins, they refuse to mate themselves with the ignorant of their own race. Socially, they are not recognized by the whites; they are often without money enough for but the barest necessities of life; honorably, they cannot procure sufficient means to gratify their luxurious tastes; their mothers were like themselves; their fathers they never knew; debauched whitemen are ever ready to take advantage of their destitution, and after living a short life of shame, they sink into early graves. Living, they were despised by whites and blacks alike; dead, they are mourned by none. You know yourself Mr. Sumner, that caste as found at the North is a terrible thing. It is killing the black man's hope there in every avenue; it is centered against his advancement. We in the South are flagrant in our abuse of the Negro but we do not descend to the pettiness that your section practices. We shut our eyes to many things in the South because of our near relationship to many of these despised people. But black blood is everywhere—in society and out, and in our families even; we cannot feel assured that it has not filtered into the most exclusive families. We try to stem the tide but I believe it is a hopeless task."

Sumner listened to her bound by the horrible fascination of her words. At last he said:

"But a white man may be betrayed into marrying her. I certainly came near to it myself."

"Very true; and if she had been a different woman, she would have succeeded, you would have been proud of your handsome wife because of your ignorance of her origin. As life, real life, has unfolded to my view, I have come to think that there is nothing in this prejudice but a relic of barbarism."

"Perhaps your reasoning is true; I will not attempt a denial. But I am thankful for my deliverance."

"Your feeling is natural; certainly, I do not blame you," she said, and after a slight pause resumed her narrative.

"One day the General came to me and told me that we must part. I owe you many obligations for your kindness. You have made the past few months very pleasant; of course you knew it was only for awhile, and that it must end some day. It is past now, and we will each go our way just as if we had never met. You must know that with men of the world these things are very natural and very pleasant. Here is some money;" and he thrust a well-filled purse in my hands.

My heart was filled with terror and agony. 'But you said that you loved me.' I managed to falter in a dazed way. 'Well, perhaps, for the moment. But—can't you understand these things? I will spare you as much as I can; if I am harsh you press me to it.' He spoke lightly, carelessly, to me as I stood before him crushed for all eternity—to me, who had fallen, without a thought of resistance, under the charm of his manner and beauty, that have ruined more than one woman among those who are above me in wealth and position. It is left for men to change quickly. He seemed dumb, frozen, dead to all feeling. His heart and mind were filled with the dazzling beauty of his new love—the Negress Aurelia Madison. He had nothing left for me—not even pity. Then he continued,—

'Elise, it is particularly necessary for my future plans that this affair of ours be kept secret. If you bury it in your heart, and seal your lips upon it, you shall be recompensed finally, I will never lose sight of you and the boy, but direct that a large sum shall be paid to you yearly. If not—people have died for a less offense than that.'

While he was talking I was thinking deeply and rapidly. I felt that my only chance lay in matching his cunning with diplomacy. I made up my mind to compromise the matter. He was stronger than I; I could do nothing at present. Finally I told him that I would agree to all he asked if he would allow me to retain my position in the office with him, and would provide for the boy and educate him.

This he agreed to do, and there has been a sort of armed neutrality between us ever since. I have learned much by being here. I know enough to ruin him. I planned for it and I have succeeded. He dares not go against me now, and so he has promised marriage, and I shall once more hold my head up among honest women."

Sumner felt a great wave of pity sweep over him at the thought of this delicate woman hoping to cope with the cunning deviltry of the man she had unmasked; but he could not find it in his heart to speak one discouraging word. His eyes filled with tears which were no shame to his manhood.

"Where is the child?" he asked when he could collect his scattered thoughts enough to speak.

"In Kentucky with my aunt," she replied naming a town.

"If what you tell me is true, and knowing what I do, I cannot doubt your story, General Benson is a consummate villain, a dangerous man," said Sumner as he paced the floor in excitement and wrath. "It is not possible that such things can be and go unpunished."

"You know now why I think it all a plot against you. Cannot you see for yourself?"

"Yes; I can never repay you for what you have done."

"Do not mention it. I shall be repaid if only you circumvent that woman, and all is made right between you and Miss Bowen."

It had grown very dark and Sumner lighted the gas.

"I will call a herdic and see you home," he said, "if you will come now. It is long past the dinner hour. We have been here long enough. I feel it impossible to stop here longer, the place stifles me."

"I cannot go yet," she replied, "I have papers to sort and many articles to destroy as well as to gather up. I never wish to see the place again."

"I will stay then until you are ready to go."

"No; that is not necessary, thank you. Give me the key. I will lock up and leave it with the watchman."

"Well, then, if you are not afraid," he said reluctantly. He was dazed by all he had heard and wished to be alone. When he was ready to leave, he took her hand in his and shook it warmly.

"Good-bye, my friend; you have given me renewed hope."

In after years, Cuthbert remembered her face with its varying, changing tints—hope and despair—each struggling for the mastery.

"Yes," she said softly, "I am your friend, but friendships are short—made to be severed. Still, I am sure we shall meet again. How strange it is that lives are touching thus all the time—strangers yesterday, today helping each other—let us hope so at least—touching—parting—but not forgotten—not utterly forgotten."

There was a new dignity in her manner that he had never noticed in the silent stenographer. But there was still a weary, listless tone in her voice.

He pressed her white fingers with his strong eager hand, feeling his heart throb with suppressed excitement—the joy of living once more. He lifted her cold hand and touched it with his lips.

"Good-bye, then, once more; someone said once that meant 'God bless you'; I could say no more if I knew that our parting would be eternal which it is not. I want you to know Jewel."

She looked at him steadily a moment, then her face fell; a slight tremor passed over her face; she was unaccustomed to the chivalrous treatment that men give to women whom they respect. The hand he had kissed fell to her side. As he turned to close the door of the apartment, she was still standing where he had left her, with listless hands and bent head.

XXIII

C uthbert's mind was in a tumult as he walked down the stairs and through the corridors of the great building. His strained nerves relaxed; he felt the intense relief of a man who throws a heavy load from his shoulders.

He accepted without question the story told him by Miss Bradford and her suggestion of a vile plot by these arch-conspirators to gain possession of a fortune. The story was feasible whichever way he viewed it. "Yes, it must be so." The more the thought of it, the more he wondered at his own blindness in not solving the problem before. His eyes flashed, and he clenched his hands in anger. His mood boded ill for his enemies. Already his mind was filled with plans to disconcert the plotters.

He hailed a passing herdic and was driven to his rooms. He felt sick, giddy, his hands trembled. This unexpected revelation, while it caused him intense happiness, nearly overcame him. He longed to be alone in his rooms where he could think over what he had heard. But in the midst of his joy and his plans to see Jewel and explain this great wrong and mystery to her, came thoughts—sorrowful thoughts of the woman who had befriended him. What would be her fate? he asked himself. Surely it was but a question of time before the chief, with his method of living, would disappear beneath the maelstrom of his own unprincipled acts.

It was nine o'clock when he arrived at home thoroughly worn out. A splendid fire in the grate bade him a cordial welcome. John served him a good dinner. After making a pretense of eating, Sumner sat with his wine untasted on the table before him, smoking and staring into the fire. He sat there for hours smoking and thinking. Troubled thoughts disturbed him, shadows lingered on his face which the pleasant surroundings had not the power to dispel. He was deeply impressed by the insignificant trifles that had solved the secret of this wicked plot, in a skillful woman's hands, and more than thankful to know that through her he held the threads of the labyrinth in his own strong hands. He retired to rest worn out in mind and body. Physical and mental exhaustion brought some degree of calm, and he slept, but his slumber was fitful and broken, and he could still hear the moaning of the wind and the beating of the rain against the window panes. Mingled with these sounds were distorted dreams—bearing a shadowy relation to the scenes through which he had just passed.

In those uneasy slumbers he dreamed that he was in a deep, dark pit. Darkness blacker than the blackest night was all about him; but as he lay there, for he dreamed that he was reclining on the floor of the pit, suddenly beneath his body he felt a movement as of a monstrous body—a regular undulating movement. Then it seemed borne in upon his mind that the pit was a snake's den; the monsters—three in number—pythons of immense size to whom human victims were offered as sacrifices. He had been thrown to these sacred reptiles as their next victim. In his dream, horror and terror paralyzed both thought and action for a time. Then he realized that he must act quickly. As he looked into the dense darkness a tremulous ray of light pierced the gloom of the pit and for an instant Jewel's face smiled upon him, then disappeared. In that instant of light he discerned a ladder leading to an opening at the top of the pit, through which he must have been thrown into the horrible dungeon. As he calculated his chances of escape, he heard the dragging and sweeping of a long ponderous body in motion moving toward him. With a determined wrench he broke the spell that bound him, sprang up the ladder and reached the blessed light of day.

He awoke bathed in perspiration, shivering with horror, his heart beating with fear. He lay there a while trying to shake off the effects of his dream, but for a time it seemed impossible; it would not slip away as dreams do; it was too vivid not to leave unpleasant thoughts behind.

Finally he sprang up. It was very early but he rang for John, and took time to make a careful and refreshing toilet. By half-past eight he was ready for the excellent breakfast brought by the delighted John who had not seen his master so cheerful for many weeks.

He wrote a note and despatched it by messenger to the department saying he would be late, and to refer all matters to the assistant secretary until he came.

He wandered aimlessly about the rooms wondering how he could possibly content himself while he waited for a conventional hour to come for a call on Jewel. At length he resolved to go for a walk, and was just getting into his street garments when there was a loud ring at the outer door of the suite. John answered it. He herd a question in a man's voice:

"Is Mr. Sumner at home?"

Then as he turned from the window to answer John's call, he saw his servant's frightened face, and close behind him an officer. Sumner stood still in amazement.

"Mr. Cuthbert Sumner?" asked the officer.

"I am Mr. Sumner. What is your business with me?"

"Well, sir," said the man laboriously, "there's been a murder up at the Treasury building there. Young woman found this morning. You're wanted to be at the inquest."

"But I know nothing of this affair. Who's the woman?"

The officer pulled a paper from his pocket and held it out awkwardly toward him:

"Sorry, sir, to disturb you. Miss Bradford is the victim; you are held on suspicion being the last gent, or person, seen in her company. Charge of murder!"

"Murder!" cried the horrified man.

The officer nodded as he replied:

"Ay, sir; and bad enough it is. Prussic acid was the means, sir, given in a glass of wine. Miss Elise Bradford, clerk at the Treasury Building. Body discovered by watchman early this morning."

"Great heavens!" said Sumner reeling back, "it can't be possible that the girl is dead—murdered!"

The officer's look said plainly enough,—"you know all about it." The police are quick to make victims.

"I know nothing about it. She was all right when I left her at eight yesterday after we had finished our work. I—"

"Stop, sir," said the man. "I am bound to warn you that whatever you say will be used as evidence against you."

"Let it be so," returned Sumner haughtily. "I have nothing to hide. I am absolutely guiltless of the crime as you will find."

"Maybe so, sir," replied the man civilly. "But meanwhile you must come with me."

Sumner was calm and self-possessed.

"You are free to examine my effects," he said. "I shall be ready to go with you in five minutes."

"I cannot lose sight of you, sir."

"Certainly not."

The faithful John stood by loudly protesting against the indignities put upon his master. Sumner gave him a few directions about the rooms. A herdic was called, and in five minutes the policeman and his prisoner were driven to the Police Court. The police evidence was given, and the prisoner having been remanded until after the inquest, was removed to the cells.

XXIV

Marthy Johnson knelt on the kitchen floor surrounded by heaps of fine white clothing sorting them into orderly piles. It was six o'clock on Monday morning. The gaudy little clock on the mantel, flanked by red vases elaborately gilded and filled with paper sunflowers, had just finished striking. The coffee pot was giving out jets of fragrant steam, and the pan of hot corn pone was smiling in an inviting manner from the back of the range. The square deal table between the windows held plates, mugs, knives and forks for three. The woman sang as she sorted:

> "Oh, the milk-white hosses, milk-white hosses,
> Milk-white hosses over in Jerden,
> Milk-white hosses, milk-white hosses,
> I long to see that day.
> "Oh, hitch 'em to the chariot, hitch 'em to the chariot,
> Hitch 'em to the chariot over in Jerden,
> Hitch 'em to the chariot, hitch 'em to the chariot,
> I long to see that day."

We last saw Marthy on the Enson plantation. Years have added to her weight, but other than that, hers is the same frank, fun-loving countenance, with its soft brown tint, its dazzling eyes and teeth.

Her tidy calico gown was hidden by an immense blue-and-white-checked apron, and a snowy towel tied turban-fashion hid her soft crinkly hair.

"Reckon I'd better fry that ham; it's gittin' on toward seven right smart," said Marthy with a glance at the clock. "My word, but where is mammy! I's clean worried out of my wits 'bout the child. Oliver-oh—Oliver!" she cried, opening a door which led from the kitchen to the regions above.

"What's wanting, mummy?" was wafted back in a male voice just turning into manhood.

"Your granny, Oliver; you must go hunt her child. I never knowed her to stay away all night but once befo'. You mus' git your breakfas' an' hunt her."

"Granny's all right, ma. I'm busy. Got a thesis for first recitation this morning. 'Deed I can't spare the time to go way over to the treasury from Meridian hill."

　　　　　　　　　　　　　PAULINE E. HOPKINS

"You, Oliver, you; move yourse'f now, hyar me? Your pa's never 'roun' when he's wanted, an' your sister's slavin' herse'f like a nigger to help ejekate yer. My Lord, how worthless men folks is! You've got a *teaseus*, have you?" she continued, waxing more wroth each moment. "An' your granny that's made of you like you was a baby may be daid up thar in the treasury or moulderin' in some alley an' you hollerin' down these stairs to me that you can't go an' holp her 'cause you's got a *teaseus*. I 'spec' we's all made a fool of you a-gettin' you into college. You's jes' like yer daddy; you's the born spit of him. My word, if you don't stir them long legs o' yourn out o' this lively, I'll take you down sure's I'm yer mammy; I'll take yer down if you was as big as a house." The flood of angry words ended in a flood of tears. Her face was buried in the ample folds of her gingham apron when Oliver entered the kitchen.

He was a good-looking lad, tall and slender, a shade lighter brown than his mother, but with her pleasant, kindly face, laughing eyes and fun-loving countenance. He had a gay and fearless bearing that was the pride of Marthy's heart. She often told her mother in confidence, when Oliver was out of hearing:

"Mammy, yer gran'son's a born gin'ral; I never seen any man to 'pare with the swing dat's on him outside o' ol' Gin'ral Burnsis."

And in this opinion Aunt Henny joined.

"Now, ma, don't cry," said the boy putting his arm about his mother's neck and kissing her cheek. "I'm going right off. I'm as fond of granny as can be. Don't now go and work yourself all up. I'm going this blessed moment." Marthy cried comfortably on the shoulder of her big son and allowed him to coax her into a better frame of mind. "You are a good boy, Ollie, and I didn't mean all them hard things I jes' said, honey. Don' you go an' lay 'em up agin me, son; your ol' mammy's jes' worried to death."

"Well, I ain't like dad, am I, ma?"

"No, bless yer heart, honey; yer ain't. You an' Venus is my comfits. Lawd, what a mis'able ol' 'ooman I'd be without you chilluns."

Marthy made Oliver sit down to his breakfast, waiting on him with a mother's fondness, piling his plate with the delicious fried ham and the smoking corn pone, and pouring his coffee with care.

"Do you know, ma," said Oliver between generous mouthfuls of bread and great gulps of coffee, as he ate with the hearty enjoyment of youth, "when I get through college, you shan't do a thing but wear a black silk dress every day and fold your hands and rock. I'm sick of seeing you in the washtub and Venus running to wait on the laides fit to break her neck. I'm going to take care of you both."

"When you 'spec' that time goin' ter come, silly chile? yer mammy 'spec' to wurk 'tell she draps inter the grave. Colored women wasn't made to take their comfit lak white ladies. They wasn't born fer nuthin' but ter wurk lak hosses or mules. Jes' seems lak we mus' wurk 'tell we draps into the grave."

"It won't be so always, ma. You'll see."

"Does you think money's jes' a growin' on bushes ready to shuck into your hand when you gits through college? Pears lak to me, Oliver, you'd better make up yer min' to hussle aroun' fer awhile. I don't want ter feel that a chile o' min's too biggotty to do anything hones' fer a livin'. Don' you turn up yer nose at washin', an' yer may jes' thank God ef you gits a 'ooman when you git jined that'll help you out in that business when college learnin' ain't payin'. An' don' spend yer extra money on silk dresses fer no 'ooman to lay roun' in. Caliker's done me all my life an' I ain't the worst 'ooman in the wurl' neither."

"Well, I'll wark fer you my own self, and I'll make money enough to keep you like a lady, college or no college."

"I wish it mote be so; but I jes' trimbles to have you talk that a-way, honey; jes' keep a still tongue and saw wood. Don't speak about your plans beforehan'. Never let anybody know what you reckon on doin' in the future 'cause the devil is always standin' 'roun' listenin' to you, an' that gen'man jes' nachally likes to put his cloven foot into a good basket of aigs an' smash 'em. 'Member what yer ma tells yer, honey."

"Now, ma, you don't believe all them old signs about hoodooing and such stuff. There isn't a thing in it, it's nothing but superstition."

"Don't talk to me 'bout yer suferstition; there is some things in this wurl that college edication won't 'splain, an' you can't argify an' condispute with 'em, neither. I've had my trials, Oliver, but tryin' to bring you an' yer sister to a realisin' sense of the sin in the wurl is hard on me, an' it lays on my mind. Now las' night I had a dream that a ghos' stood right up side 'o the bed lookin' at me. That's turrible bad luck; an' its bein' a female ghos' means that trouble is comin' to this family thro' a 'ooman. Now, this mornin' I gits up an fin' yer granny ain't been her all night. It's borne in on me that sumthin' is wrong. Where 'bouts did you drap her, honey, when you picked the clos' up las' evenin'?"

"The last place we went, ma, was to Senator Bowens. Granny went roun' to the kitchen to talk to Mis' Johnson while I went up to Venus.

PAULINE E. HOPKINS

Granny said she was short off for breath and Mis' Johnson gave her a cup of coffee and a cutlet. Granny's fond of chicken cutlets."

"Um," replied his mother, "Mis' Johnson's a born lady cook or no cook. Chicken cutlets," she mused. "Some new Yankee fashion cookin' chicken, I reckon, bein' Mis' Johnson's from out Bos'n way. Wha's it taste like, Oliver, didn't they ask yer to have a bite with 'em"?

"Chicken cutlets are common, ma," replied Oliver, with the indifference of familiarity. "Just slap your chicken in egg and bread crumbs, drop it into hot fat and there you are."

"Do you like 'em, son?" inquired his mother, while one could see in the watery look that lurked about the corners of her mouth a determination to try chicken cutlets at the first opportunity.

"I like 'em *fine* ma."

Marthy sighed, and then returned to the original subject. "What did granny say when you lef' her?"

"She said that she'd a right smart turn of washing up and dusting that she'd left over from Saturday afternoon because the clerks were working overtime in one of the departments. I left her at the foot of the steps on the north side."

"Well, honey, I don' kno'," and Marthy shook her head dubiously. Run along to yer pa now, an' then up to the 'partment to fin' yer granny. 'Deed, God knows I hope the ol' lady's safe, but I mistrus' mighty much, I do."

"I think you're worrying for nothing, ma; I'm not a bit anxious. Sometimes has to stop late, and she might have stayed all night because she was afraid to walk home alone."

Marthy shook her head solemnly. "Wha'd she be 'fraid of a po' black 'ooman with nuthin' to steal? 'Tain't a soul gwine tech her. She ain't young an' purty makin' a 'ticemen' fer people; men isn't chasin 'roun' street corners in Wash'nt'n after ugly ol' 'oomen's. No Oliver; fifteen year ago this blessid winter when you and your sister was twenty tots, jes' like this yer granny stayed away, an' sot all night on top o' ninety thousan' dollars wurth o' greenbacks. The night befo' it happened I dreamt I was carried up to glory 'settin' on a cloud an' playin' on a golden harp, which means suddint honors an' el'vations; nex' thing I knowed the Presidunt 'pinted mammy prominen'ly to a firmamen' persition in the 'partment at forty dollars a munf. Then I was able to sen' yer sister to school an' keep her nice in spite 'o yer daddy's racketty ways. Yer granny's holped me powful. Yer pa's money don' 'mount to a hill o' beans in my pocket, but mammy's kep' him straigh, an' ennythin'd happen the ol' lady I'd be nachally obleeged to giv' up the ghos'."

"Ef you don' fin' your granny, stop at yer pa's an' bein' as the Gin'ral's away yer pester him to try an' hunt her up. An' don' fergit to stop inter Senator Bowen's an' see yer sister. Jes' ask her ef Miss Jewel's summer wrappers is to be clar-starched or biled-starched. 'Deed, my head's clean gone runnin' after mammy this mornin'. An' ef you see the madam or Miss Jewel, make yer manners. Them white ladies is apayin' fer yer schoolin'. Git down ter bus'ness, now, hyar me, son? money talks."

As Oliver disappeared from view around the corner of the street, Marthy closed the outer door an re-entered the kitchen. Her naturally hopeful nature re-asserted itself and she took a brighter view of the situation. "I reckon I'll laugh if mammy comes in now all right. I wonder which way Ollie 'll go? Like as not he'll walk down G street an' mammy'll come on the keers. Now, I'll jes' hussle roun' an' git them clo's out o' the tub agin' they git here."

Life had been checkered for Marthy since emancipation when she had joined her lot with St.Clair Enson's Isaac, in the "holy bonds of matrimony." "Like master like man," was a true prophecy in Isaac's case, and had caused the little brown woman a world of worry.

Isaac had obtained the billet of valet to General Benson, no one knew how, for up to that time he had been a ne'er-do-well, working when the notion pleased him or when actual starvation compelled him to exert himself, at other times swearing, drinking and fighting.

It was a time of rejoicing when, upon arriving home one night, after his daily lounge about the Bay or Buzzard's Nest, looking for something to stimulate his weary system, he announced to his family that he had been "hired" by General Benson. Marthy rejoiced exceedingly although, as she told Aunt Henny,—

"What in the wurld the Gin'ral 'spects to git out o' Ike in the way o' wurk passes me."

Her mother shook her head ominously.

"De Gin'ral mus' be plum crazy. 'Twon' las'."

After three months had rolled by, the poor little brown wife began to take courage. Ike was working "stiddy" although she had not yet seen the color of his money and she was still dependent upon the washing with which a number of families supplied her, and the substantial help given by her old mother's labor at the treasury.

"Pears lak, mammy, I can see some way to raise the mor'gage."

PAULINE E. HOPKINS

"Fu' w'y, Marthy?"

"Ike's so stiddy."

Aunt Henny shook her head.

"Wha' you reckin de bill is, chile?" asked the old woman, removing her pipe from her mouth. Work was over and her chair and pipe in the warmest corner near the kitchen range, were comforting to the wornout frame. Aunt Henny was seventy, but save for rheumatism she had not changed since she left the Enson plantation. Sometimes she would bend her limbs, shake her head and sigh, "Dey neber be easy goin' 'gin, fuh sho', but I got a heap o' hope outen dem whilst dey ben limber, my soul; de bes' laigs I'll eber hab in dis wurl."

"We does owe on the mor'gage five hundred dollars," said Marthy in reply to her mother's question.

"My wurd, but de money grow slow; I got one hunder' dollars up stairs 'tween the feather bed an' de mattress. You make Ike fotch out de res'. Cayn't rightly feel de place is ourn till we's paid up. When I sees you an' de chillun under your own roof, I gwine ter gib up de ghos' in peace. An' Marthy, don't neber be a plum fool an let Ike wurrit you into raisin' money on de place, ef he gits inter scrapes let him git out as he gits in, widout any holp but de debbil. Ef you eber let dat mon take de bread outer yer mouf dat way, an I'm daid, I gwine ter riz up outer de grave an' hit yer; yas, I'll rawhide yer jes' as I user down on de plantation."

Marthy gasped but heaved a sigh of satisfaction over the thought of the hundred dollars.

"Well, I'se glad as glad 'bout the money, mammy. An' Ike's jes' got to pony up to the pint of that other fo' hundred dollars."

"Hump!" grunted Aunt Henny. "I don' trus' him. Dat niggah no leanin' pos' fer me. I'se gwine call on Gen'ral Benson myse'f, an' ef he de right kin' o' white gen'man, he gwine holp me in a 'spiracy ter make Ike raise dat money. Wha' you say to dat, Marthy?"

"I likes it *fine*," Marthy cried, overjoyed at what she considered a brilliant plan to subjugate the irresponsible Isaac.

Shortly after this conversation, Marthy applied to her husband for money.

"I ain't got no money fer ye, Marthy," he said in answer to her request.

"Ain't got no money, an' you been wurkin' stiddy fer munfs! What's gone come of it I'd like ter know." Isaac scratched his head in perplexity.

"I 'low to do better by yer, Marthy; you's ben a good gal to me, an' I 'low I ain't done the right thing by you in every way sence we was jined, but I'se turned over a new leaf; I ain't drawed a red cent o' my wages sence I went to wait on the Gin'ral. I jes' lef' it in his han's fer 'ves'men'. Major Madison an' Gin'ral's spec'latin' in mines. Dey owns de Arrow-Head, an' all my wages an' all de money, Gin'ral kin raise has ben put in dat gol' mine up in de Col'rady hills."

"The Lawd save us, Ike! Then we'll done lose this place,' she cried. "The mor'gage money done come due in June, an' Mis' Jenkins been mighty kind, but he's boun' to fo'close cause I hear he want money pow'ful bad to meet his needcessities. O, Lawd! what is we gwine do?" she moaned rocking herself to and fro while the tears streamed down her cheeks.

"Don' you take on, Marthy," her husband said soothingly. 'I'll git de money from de Gin-ral all right. I know I ain't been a 'sponsible man fer yer, but I'se got human feelin', ain't I? Ain't I proud o' my gal an' my boy what's in de college? Wha' you tink I'se turned over a new leaf fo' ef it warn't to see them chilluns holdin' up dar heads 'long wif de bes' ob de high-biggotty Wash'nt'n 'stockracy? Thar daddy's gwine ter make 'em rich an' when you an' me is moulderin' ter clay dem chillun's gwine ter be eatin' chickun an' a-settin' on thar own front do' steps jes' like de Presidun'.'"

"I don' trus' no' white man. 'Member all the money went up in the Freedman's bank, don' yer? I don' guess he'd be slow makin' a profit outen yer by keepin' yer wages. Plenty gentmen'd do it 'fore yer could bat yer eye."

"You tew ha'sh, Marthy. De Gen'ral an' de major been mighty fine ter your husban', gal. Don' you worry, dat money's safe."

"I 'spicion him jes' the same," replied his wife sullenly.

"De major do be under some repetition as a bad character, but de Gin'ral's all right. Dar's heap o' his paw in 'im," he continued in a musing voice. "Dar neber was a better man den ol' massa, an' I orter know. Law*se,*de times me an' young massa had t'gedder, bar hunts, an' gamblin' 'bouts, an' shootin' and ridin'. He goin' so fas' I skacely cud keep up tuh him. We bin like brudders. All his clo's fits me *puffick!* Our size is jes' de same as ever. En jurin' de wah I jes' picked him twice outen de inimy's han's; my sakes dem was spurious times.

"You, Isaac, wha' in the lan' you talkin' 'bout? Is you gone crazy? Them remarks o' yourn is suttingly cur'ous." Isaac started to his feet, and there was a guilty look on his face.

"What was I sayin', Marthy? 'Clar fo' it, my thoughts was miles 'way from hyar."

PAULINE E. HOPKINS

"Do hish! Ef I didn't kno' yer age, Isaac Johnson, I'd think you gone dotty. I 'clar fo' it, I hope you ain't goin' ter have sof'n o' the brain from drinkin' all Sam Smith's bad rum over to Buzzard's Nes'. I hern tell o' sech happenin's, but I pray the Lawd not to pile that trib'lation on top o' me."

After this occurrence, Aunt Henny sought General Benson's presence as the only hope of getting money out of Isaac. From this interview the old woman returned with a look of terror and consternation on her face. When questioned by Marthy as to the outcome of the interview she would say nothing of her success, only repeating the words. "I'se seed a ghos'! Lawd, my days is done."

Marthy went heavily about her work as spring approached. But for her children she would have given up the unequal struggle. Just at the darkest hour the Bowens had become interested in Venus and Oliver, and soon the little brown mother had felt a revival of hope in her breast, as she planned to make bold and go herself to Miss Jewel and ask the dear young lady to intercede with the Senator and get him to take up the hateful mortgage.

After Oliver left the house, his mother rubbed away industriously, and under her skilful fingers the delicate clothing was soon floating like snow-capped billows in tubs and boilers. When noon was signalled from the observatory upon the hill, spotless garments waved in the keen air from every line in the large drying yard at the rear of the cottage.

"'Clar fo' it, Oliver's missed his school, an' mammy ain't come yet."

Half distracted with terror and fearing the worst, Marthy sat down in the midst of her disordered kitchen and sobbed aloud.

Suddenly she heard the click of the little gate. The next moment she saw Oliver's face at the door. It needed but a glance to tell that something extraordinary had happened. He was breathless from running, his face ashen, his large eyes were distended to twice their usual size.

"O, ma, there's been a murder up to the treasury—"

"Don' tell me it's yer granny!" shrieked his mother.

"No'm; 'taint granny; it's a young lady; and Mr. Sumner that was Miss Jewel's beau is arrested, an' granny ain't been seen *nowhere* since she went into the building last night. Pa'll be home after he's been to the station to notify the police about granny, an' Venus can't leave Miss Jewel; she's taking on so."

"O, yer po' granny, Oliver! I jes' cayn't bar up under this. O, where's my mammy! Good Lawd, where's she at?"

XXV

"Terrible discovery this morning in Treasury building! Arrest, on suspicion, of Mr. Cuthbert Sumner!"

That was the startling head-line that met Jewel Bowen's eyes on that eventful Monday morning, and sent the blood back to her heart.

She had opened the paper lazily, glanced at the leaders, and with, "There's never anything interesting in the paper," turned to another sheet, and suddenly sat transfixed, her wide eyes seeing nothing but that one startling head-line that danced before her straining gaze, then stood still,—that at first appeared to be printed in great black type and then turned into blood-red letters!

In an instant the reserve and coldness of weeks was swept aside. He was again her lover. His deadly peril gripped her very heart-strings, and filled her whole being anew with all the strength and passion of woman's noblest love, that, at once, without a second's pause, throws aside all but honor itself for the being who is her world.

She had not read the account of the tragedy, but not for one instant did a thought of guilt associate itself in her mind with Cuthbert Sumner. *Guilty of a heinous crime!* She laughed aloud at the bare idea. In that moment she forgot the new duties lately assumed toward another. Promises had been forced upon her she had told herself often of late, with regret, and none could blame her if she swerved in the moment of trial from the exact path of duty. Now, she thanked God it was not yet a crime to think of the man she loved.

She calmed herself presently, and read the brief account given in the morning edition of the "Washington News." With the sheet closely clutched in her hand she sought her mother. Mrs. Bowen's maid was just serving her lady with breakfast as Jewel knocked and then entered the room. Mrs. Bowen was seated comfortably before the fire, opening her morning mail.

"Jewel, what on earth is the matter? What is wrong?" exclaimed her mother, startled at the strange look on her face.

"Cuthbert is arrested, charged with murder!"

Mrs. Bowen turned very white.

"Great heaven! Jewel! No, no, it is too horrible!"

"Read that," said the girl, laying the paper in her mother's lap.

The elder woman read the printed sheet and gazed up at her daughter with incredulous eyes.

"You do not believe him guilty?"

"*Guilty!*" the one word spoke volumes.

"What can we do to help him? It is unfortunate that your father is away."

"I have not thought yet." The determined woman spoke in the next sentence, "I shall visit him first of all."

"Jewel!" exclaimed her mother in a shocked tone. "What will the General think?"

"What he pleases," was the defiant answer.

Before Mrs. Bowen could protest, there was a hurried knock at the door, which, opening, admitted Venus. There were traces of tears on her face.

"Please, Miss, Mr. Sumner's man is in the hall asking if you will see him for a minute."

"Show him right up here, Venus."

John entered the presence of the two ladies with deep distress and alarm in his honest face. He looked years older than he did the day before. There was a strong affection between master and man. He came forward eagerly, his hands holding his cap and twitching nervously.

"Oh, Mrs. Bowen an' young Miss, I beg your pardon, but—but—I don't know what to do. I've telegraphed the ol' gent'man—

"Yes, John—when will he be here?" The ladies spoke together.

"The ol' gent'man's had shock, an' the doctor dassent to tell him, but the family lawyer will be here tomorrow to take charge; but I can't keep still, miss,—ma'am—I had to come an' see you. I've been in the Sumner family, boy an' man, for twenty years, an' they're used me white, ma-am—miss, right straight through. 'Clare, I'd do anyting on yearth for Mr. Cuthbert."

"How does your master bear it, John?"

"Like a lamb, miss—ma'am—I've been there now, jes' cam from there, been taking his orders an' things. All he says is 'John, there's a mistake; it'll be all right in a day or two.' But I don't believe it. I feel oneasy. I thought maybe you all would tell what more I can do."

"That's right, John. We will help you all we can. These are evil days that have come to us lately." But in spite of her brave words, Mrs. Bowen looked about her in a helpless, bewildered way. Then she appealed to her daughter, "Jewel, what do you advise, dear?"

"The first thing to do is to see Cuthbert; I'm going to drive down to the jail and have a long talk with him."

"Jewel!"

"Well, mamma, if we intend to benefit him, there is but one way. Venus, order me a herdic; I won't wait for the carriage," she said, turning to her maid. "Why, what are you crying about, silly child; they can't hang Mr. Sumner without a trial."

"Yes'm; I know that. But it's my granny, too, miss. We can't find her," said the girl with a burst of tears. Again John spoke, trying to explain the matter to the bewildered ladies.

"It's ol' Mis' Sargean'—"

"What did you say?" interrupted Mrs. Bowen sharply, leaning forward in her chair.

"Sergeant, ma'am, Ol' Aunt Henny Sargeant, she's Venus's gran'mother. She's a cleaner up at the department, an' she's disappeared; ain't been seen sense last night, when she went into the building to clean up. Taking that an' putting it with the murder an' other funny things that's been happening about Mr. Sumner lately, it 'pears to me that something underhand is going on," he said with a deferential bow.

"Venus, come with me. John, be good enough to order the herdic. I will look into this matter and see what can be done," and Jewel turned to leave the room.

"Please, miss, do you mind if I take a seat on the box?" asked John.

"Certainly not."

And the trio quitted the room leaving Mrs. Bowen alone.

XXVI

As the day grew older the excitement increased in the city over the murder of Elise Bradford. The circumstances surrounding the victim, as given out in the second editions of the press, the mysterious disappearance of the old scrub-woman and the high social and official position of the accused, gave rise to all sorts of sensational rumors.

"Very queer affair," said one man to another, nodding significantly. "A good deal behind it all, of course. Young men will be young men; you can't put an old head on young shoulders," he added, repeating the trite sayings as if they were original with himself.

"H'm, yes. Ugly facts, though, the wine-glasses especially. I take it the old Negress would be an important witness in the case."

"Yes. What about the wine-glasses? I haven't read the paper very carefully; just sketched it."

"Why, it seems they must have had wine together and he put prussic acid in her glass. But he denies it; says he gave her a glass of wine because she seemed faint, but he took none himself. In short, he cannot explain the presence of the *second* glass. The odd thing about it is his walking out and leaving the body there, if he did it, with no attempt at concealment."

"You don't say so! By Jove, what did he expect? And he claims to be innocent?"

"Yes; but of course, he'd do that. I suppose his lawyers will claim that it was suicide. Fact is, he must have found himself in a mess and took this method of getting clear. These young bloods are as bad as the worst when you corner them."

"It must have been that way. And then, again, what he says may be true, somehow. From what one hears of him, he is incapable of a crime like this. He is called a man of spotless honor."

"Well, perhaps, except where there's a woman in the case. We are men ourselves, and we know."

The other nodded in acquiescence.

Will Badger and Carroll West met in the corridor of the jail, one just coming from a conference with the prisoner, the other seeking an interview.

Kind-hearted Badger was feeling very much cast down over his friend's predicament.

"Think he did it, Badger?" asked West after they had exchanged greetings.

"No more than you or I," was the decisive answer. "I would not believe the blackest evidence against his bare word. I know the man."

"I'm with you, but—well—confound the jade, I say, to get Sumner in this fix. Of course, there's another man. Who is he? Have you an idea?"

Badger shook his head and sighed. "The examination is tomorrow at ten. Try and be there, West."

"I will, sure. The Madisons awfully cut up over this affair; she was almost in hysterics when I stopped in to talk it over. The Major isn't himself either."

"No wonder. Well, we shan't know anything positive until after the hearing. So long."

The friends separated.

Shortly after noon, Jewel arrived at the jail. The interview between her and Cuthbert was long and painful, but both were happier than they had been for many weeks. Sumner told Jewel the facts of his intimacy with Amelia, blaming himself greatly for all the trouble that had followed his first deception. "I should have been frank with you, Jewel, and all would have been well."

Jewel's gentle heart was at last at rest; perfect confidence was established between the re-united lovers. As she rose to go, he said:

"It may go hard with me tomorrow at the examination; indeed, I know it will. There will be difficult work ahead for my attorneys. So many things have happened to separate us, Jewel, that I dread the future."

The tears stood in her eyes. She turned her head to hide them.

"Dare I express my selfish hopes—my wishes?"

For answer she threw herself into his arms again, and as he held her thus he whispered his request with an eager look upon his face.

She blushed violently, hesitated, then drawing herself up proudly said:

"I will do as you wish."

"Tomorrow morning then, at eight, I shall be waiting."

"I will not fail you," was her low reply, as snatching her hand hastily from his detaining clasp, she turned to accompany the officer from the cell.

As she passed through the office she asked the captain for the address of the chief of the secret service.

"You mean Mr. Henson, I take it, Miss?"

"If he is the celebrated detective, he is the very one."

"Well, Miss, it's No.—Pennsylvania Avenue; but he takes no outside cases. His government duties are all that he finds time for."

"Still, I will call on him."

The man bowed, and she passed on. Months ago she remembered hearing her father speak of the great powers of this detective. Why it had lingered in her mind she knew not, but now a hidden force impelled her to seek his aid.

She shrank from nothing that might benefit her lover. Shrink! was that like it, the proud flush on the soft cheek, the warm light in her eyes? Her heart throbbed fast in the excess of happiness it was to know that he was true, that all misunderstandings were buried spectres, and that she—she alone held his heart. Let the world do its worst, she could repay by showing every trust in him. After tomorrow she would have the right to stand beside him, though all the world should frown. Her thoughts did not go beyond the present. He would be proved innocent, she was sure. Money could do anything and there would be no sparing of any moment to clear him.

The herdic seemed to creep over the space between the station and the detective's chambers. Her very heart seemed on fire under intense, suppressed excitement and the emotion that surged beneath her calm, conventional exterior.

No.—Pennsylvania Avenue was a large brick building where lawyers congregated. Jewel alighted from the herdic, leaving Venus in it. Mr. Henson's office was on the second floor. She paused before a door upon the glass panels of which appeared the letters: "J. Henson, Detective." She opened the door and entered. There were a number of clerks in the room busily writing. One elderly man near the door was in charge.

Yes, Mr. Henson was in and would no doubt see the lady if she could wait awhile, he said in reply to Jewel's inquiry. Placing a chair for her he took her card and disappeared behind a door marked "Private." Presently he returned saying that if she would come with him, Mr. Henson would receive her.

The great detective was seated at his desk writing. He did not look up as she entered, but said:

"Be seated, madam; I will give you my attention in one moment."

Jewel saw a well-preserved man of sixty odd years, middle height, and rather broad, but not fleshy. His thick iron-gray hair covered his head fully and curled in masses over a broad forehead. He was well and carefully dressed. Presently he looked up from his work and glanced in her direction; then she saw that he had expressive dark eyes and a pleasant face which might have been handsome in youth, but for a long livid scar that crossed his face diagonally. A sabre might have made that deep, dangerous cut.

The light in the room was faint, and Jewel did not perceive the pallor that spread over the man's face as he gazed at her; the words he was about to utter died away unsaid, his chest heaved an instant in a convulsive movement which he controlled by a violent effort. There was silence as the man and girl gazed at each other, mutually attracted by a hidden affinity. It was but a second that the pause endured.

"You wish to speak with me, Miss?"

Then Jewel aroused herself from the spell which had held her since she encountered the piercing gaze of the quiet elderly man before her. The sound of his voice generated a feeling of relief in her breast, of trust and confidence. She could not analyze the sensation of complete rest that came to her with the few words just spoken.

"I wish to speak with you," she replied tremulously; then, recovering herself: "When I say that I am deeply interested in the murder that has just been committed, and that Mr. Sumner is my dearest friend, you will know what I want."

"I understand, Miss Bowen," he said, glancing at the card in his hand. "I seldom take cases outside of the government; still, I will hear what you have to tell me. I think this may be an exception to my rule."

He motioned her to the chair beside him and then placed a notebook on the desk before him.

"Mr. Sumner is innocent," said the girl in a trembling voice. "He will have able counsel, I know; but I shall feel better if you will take charge. I have heard so much of your skill and wonderful powers of discernment that no one else could satisfy me."

The man looked at the beautiful girl before him with something akin to worship in his eyes. When he spoke again his voice had taken on an added softness, his words seemed to carry a caress hidden beneath their commonplace utterance.

"Thank you; I am greatly interested. Even the newspaper accounts bear evidence that this is a remarkable case, and there is generally a good deal hidden behind what they give out. Now tell me all you know of the matter."

Calmed by his gentle tones, Jewel gave a brief account of the affair as told her by Sumner. When she ceased speaking Mr. Henson, who had listened with down-cast eyes and unmoved countenance, said:

"It is a curious case, very. There seems no clue; but, if I mistake not, you have suspicions of someone." His eyes rested on her face in a peculiarly impressive manner.

"Why do you think so?"

"I trace it in the tones of your voice. Now tell me the name of the person you suspect and why."

The girl hesitated, then said in a low tone:

"General Benson!"

"Ah!" It was but a breath, but it spoke volumes. "And have you mentioned this to anyone?"

"Only to Mr. Sumner, but he will not entertain the thought. He thinks the idea absurd because the General is in New York, and can hardly know more than the bare outlines of the case as yet."

"Just so. But upon what do you base your thought?"

"Oh, Mr. Henson," and she clasped her hands and raised her wonderful, beseeching gray eyes to his face, "I can not tell. There is a feeling of conviction that he knows all about the crime if he is not the assassin. There has been an adverse fate at work since General Benson crossed my path. There has been a train of unfortunate circumstances attending our whole acquaintance. It is absurd to suspect him I know, but I cannot help it." The detective looked at her again with the immovable expression peculiar to him.

"Your woman's intuition warns you; is that it?"

She bowed her head in acquiescence.

"And I have confidence in intuitive deductions," he muttered; then, aloud, "My dear child, gentlemen like General Benson sometimes do queer things under pressure of circumstances. You may be right. I will see Mr. Sumner; he will probably be more explicit with me than he could be with you. I will do my best for you. In fact, I shall put all my powers into my work, for it is an uncommon riddle you have set me to solve."

As she rose to go she asked his terms. He named a fair price. "But if you succeed in clearing him, and I know that you will, Mr. Henson, you shall receive a princely reward." Jewel laid her check for a goodly retainer, upon the desk before him. Henson looked and tapped the desk with his pencil, but did not notice the check. Then he rose, touched a bell, and accompanied his fair client to the door.

BEFORE NINE O'CLOCK ON TUESDAY morning, attended by her maid, with the jail officials for witnesses, Jewel Bowen became the wife of the suspected murderer, Cuthbert Sumner.

XXVII

The evening of the eventful day that made Jewel, Cuthbert Sumner's wife, closed in heavy and sombre. The hearing had the expected ending, and Sumner was held for trial in the following September, before the grand jury for wilful murder. The evidence was circumstantial, but damaging in the extreme. It showed exclusive opportunity for reasons unknown, but it was whispered about town that the girl had been an unwedded mother. Added to this was the knowledge of the broken engagement between the prisoner and Miss Bowen, and the fact that Miss Madison had at one time been affianced to him, and it was expected that she would be called by the prosecution to show the fickle nature of his relations with women.

At seven o'clock in the evening of that same day, robed in black velvet, Jewel paced restlessly up and down the floor of the library, sometimes pausing to listen to sounds from without, sometimes approaching the window and trying to pierce the gloom. The dinner bell rang; for no matter what our griefs, or how dark the tragedies which are enacted about us, meals are still served and eaten, just as if the hearts assembled about the board were never wrenched nor broken.

The points brought out in the evidence were soon making their way about the city, and excitement and interest grew momentarily. Sumner smiled in bitterness of heart. He hardly knew himself in the picture drawn. Jewel sat in an obscure corner of the audience room of the court, heavily veiled, and listened to the testimony with a heart bursting with indignation. Each moment the load at her heart grew heavier. They both realized at last that this was no child's play but a struggle to the death. Sumner clenched his hands and registered a vow to spend his fortune, if necessary, to clear his name, for the sake of the dear incentive, the thought of whom warmed his heart and made him bold to meet impending disaster.

The two ladies took their accustomed places at table, each secretly regretting the absence of the Senator. With him at home, dinner was wont to be a festive meal, where laughter and wit cheered the household or chance visitor. A dismal air hung over the room now; the servants moved to and fro with unaccustomed solemnity. The mother and daughter addressed each other seldom: each was buried in her own thoughts. Presently both rose from the table and passed into the library, where coffee was served.

After the servants had retired and they were safe from intrusion Mrs. Bowen broke the silence that brooded over them. She had watched Jewel closely all through the meal, studying her looks, thinking over her words and striving to arrive at satisfactory conclusions. At length she said quietly:

"Now, my dear, you have told me next to nothing, nor have I asked seeing how pale and tired you are, but I must talk with you about this marriage. I fear you have been very rash. My dear, I positively dread your father's return; dearly as he loves you, he will be very angry." After a pause she continued, clasping and unclasping her fingers nervously. "Oh, the talk there will be when this affair is known! Why didn't you consult me, child? I could have devised some way of helping the poor fellow without requiring you to sacrifice yourself. I am disappointed in Cuthbert Sumner."

"Do not use the word 'sacrifice,' mamma; I am glad to have the right to stand by Cuthbert in this dark hour. And why say anything to you of our intention? No one can blame you now. Beside, we have agreed to say nothing at present, about the marriage."

"But your whole life will be spoilt if he is found guilty."

"Mother," said the girl, sinking on her knees by Mrs. Bowen's side, "don't despair; it will all come right in a little while, I am sure it will. And you have always called yourself his friend, even when I was against him. You *cannot* believe him guilty; you are too just in your judgment, mamma."

Jewel was kneeling in the full light of the glowing fire, the ruddy glare fell on her white face, and the plaits of bright hair wound closely around her small head. Mrs. Bowen sighed as she gazed in admiration at her daughter. The great gray eyes glowed like diamonds, but there was a world of passionate anguish in their depths. The flower-like mouth was compressed with the intensity of the pain which filled her breast.

Again Mrs. Bowen sighed and moved uneasily in her seat.

"Yes; but this is so different—a man accused of murder."

"How so, mamma? Is friendship in sunshine so different from friendship in shade?" There was sarcasm on the delicately chisseled features.

"What a champion you are, Jewel; once, perhaps, I should have acted and felt as you do."

"But now, mamma—?"

"Now, my child, I am of the world—worldly."

"Do you think papa will be very angry?" asked the girl with trembling lips after a short silence.

"We can expect nothing less. He is too fond of you to hold his anger long, however. I shall stand with you, Jewel, if it is any comfort for you to know it. I am glad, glad, glad, that you cannot marry General Benson." Jewel marvelled much at the strange look on her mother's face as she uttered these words.

"My dear mamma!" and the two women embraced each other. Then followed another silence broken by the elder woman.

"What impression did you receive from the evidence—I mean apart from the conclusions drawn by the jury?" A quiver went through the girl as she replied:

"I was confirmed in my belief in his innocence, although everything seemed to point the other way. Aurelia Madison's evidence was against him. She gave the impression that he came and went at her beck and call."

"She is false to the core—a dangerous woman."

"I agree with you, mamma. But her beauty blinds men. I dread her influence on the jury."

"There is no soul there—nothing but sensuality."

"Soul! there is no need for soul in a woman's beauty for it to dazzle most men," was the bitter answer.

"I marvel much over the matter. It seems to me there is something incomplete in the case—something to be explained. That poor girl! I can see no reason for murdering her. She may have been killed by mistake."

"That is scarcely likely."

"Cases of mistaken identity are common enough. It's a mysterious affair; I hope it may be cleared up without any delay."

"I hope so," added Jewel. "Murder will out; there lies my hope for our success in tracing the murderer."

"What does Mr. Henson say?"

"Not much; we have had no time to talk. He has hardly got to work yet; but he told me to keep my courage up, and that he thought he should be able to throw some light on the dark points of the story. He has talked with Cuthbert."

Before Mrs. Bowen had time to reply the lace and satin portière was pushed aside and Venus advanced toward them with a solemn and awe-stricken face.

PAULINE E. HOPKINS

"What is it, Venus?" asked Mrs. Bowen, regarding her with surprise.

"Please, Mrs. Bowen," she said hesitatingly, "Senator Bowen—"

"Oh, papa is come," cried Jewel in delight.

"No. Miss—"

At this point General Benson's well-known figure appeared in the entrance.

"Mrs. Bowen—Jewel—" he exclaimed as he hurried toward them. "I am the bearer of evil tidings. Senator Bowen was taken ill in New York, and we have hastened to bring him home as soon as it was possible to move him. Have a room prepared instantly, the ambulance will arrive almost immediately."

Before another hour had elapsed, the great hush—which is the shadow of the grim visitant, whom no earthly power may shut out—had fallen on the Bowen mansion. The servants walked with noiseless tread and spoke in whispers.

Senator Bowen was ill until death. He had been suddenly striken down by a shock. The Washington delegation had been tendered a banquet at a famous New York club, and a hilarious time had been enjoyed. The New Yorkers had outdone themselves in catering for the amusement of their guests.

Senator Bowen had enjoyed himself hugely. Along in the early morning hours a servant passing the door of his room had caught the sound of some one struggling for breath within. Entering, he beheld the Senator lying on the bed, one hand pressed to his heart, the other hanging inert. His eyes were wild, his pale countenance lined with purple marks.

The man went for help and soon medical aid had rendered all the relief possible. As soon as he could make himself understood the stricken man urged them to take him home.

After the first burst of grief, Mrs. Bowen and Jewel took up their places in the sick room along with the trained nurses. Each looked at the other in awe and consternation over the awful suddenness of this event. Surprising events had followed one another rapidly the past few days. They dared not think of the next cruel blow that Fate might deal them.

The doctors and nurses came and went softly. The hours drew out their long, anxious length. At the close of the third day the sick man fell into a heavy stupor, from which the doctors said he might rally— probably would—and he might linger two or three days longer; but the end was inevitable. Should he rally he must be kept quiet, and on no account excited; his heart was weak.

Mrs. Bowen undertook to see these instructions carried out. Jewel, pale and distressed, shared her mother's watch. She was in agony; her love for her father was strong, deep and tender. She was his idol, and he was hers, and until she met Cuthbert Sumner she had always felt that if he died she should not care to live another hour. She could never remember his having been cross to her in his whole life. In her eyes his very faults were virtues.

At midnight Mrs. Bowen persuaded her daughter to go and lie down.

"Keep your strength, my child, there is much to go through. If your father wakes I will surely call you."

When alone she drew her chair to the fire and sat there in shadow, watching the face of the silent figure on the bed that looked so ghastly in the light of the shaded light. It was very still; the tired nurses in the next room, dozed. Events long passed, returned in full force and pictured themselves vividly before her inner senses. How kind this man had been to her; how much she owed to his love and care. And now the hour had come for her to lose a protector who had never failed her. Wealth she might have, but it would not supply the tender deference and loving solicitude of wedded life that had been hers.

She shuddered at her thoughts. Why did the past haunt her so persistently? Presently she found herself weeping softly.

There are brave natures—women's perhaps, more often than men's—which bear up in a sea of adversity, and present a bold front to the buffeting winds of life's uncertainties. And sometimes these brave natures fine a safe haven for their frail barks. Mrs. Bowen was one of these. She had never known trouble, save by name, since she met Zenas Bowen some twenty years before; and now behold, she is confronted by a very tempest of sorrow. In the midst of her reveries she was startled to hear her own name pronounced:

"Estelle."

It was Senator Bowen who spoke. In an instant his wife was at his side.

"Dear Zenas, you are better?" she said cheerfully.

"Yes, my brain is clear. I have been watching you, Estelle. Where is Jewel?"

"In her room; I made her lie down. Do you want her?"

"Poor child; let her sleep."

His eyes roved restlessly about the familiar room.

"It is good to be at home—so good."

"Yes—but you must not talk. Drink this and sleep." She held a soothing draught to his lips, lifting the powerless head in her arms with all a mother's tenderness. He drank it obediently and then lay back on his pillow and a satisfied look of peaceful rest overspread his pale features. He held his wife's hand in a nerveless grasp.

"We have been happy, Estelle. You have been a perfect wife. I have left you well provided for. Them rascals got some of it, but not the whole of it by a durned sight; Zenas ain't such a fool as he seems," a gleam of his old fun-loving spirit was on the pain-worn face.

"If Jewel marries the General—"

"No, Zenas," she interrupted; then she stopped remembering the doctor's caution. But the sick man did not grasp the significance of her words. His mind wandered.

"No you don't, General; my little girl shan't be forced. I, her father, say it. When, where and who she likes; that's my idea. I tell you, no!"

Then he looked at his wife with fast-glazing eyes, and said:

"The little hair trunk—tell her—no difference—just the same."

Feebly he raised his arm. His wife knew his desire. She placed it about her neck. Then he drew her head nearer. A soft light radiated his features.

"My faithful wife!" he whispered. The cold lips touched her cheek.

"Zenas, Zenas!" exclaimed Estelle with a burst of emotion as she kissed the chill brow.

There was one long-drawn breath. The distracted wife sprang to the bell and rang a peal that brought the nurses hurrying in.

"Senator Bowen is worse!" she cried, wringing her hands helplessly.

The head nurse bent over the bed, then rising, said:

"Senator Bowen is dead, madam."

Again Washington society was stirred by an unexpected calamity among its leading people. Interest was heightened because of the close association which existed between the Bowens and the chief actor in the Bradford tragedy. The ill-starred trip of the delegation that had started so gaily on its Canadian mission was the talk of the capital.

XXVIII

The funeral was over. Senator Bowen was at rest in the handsomest cemetery of the capital after many honors had been paid to the sterling worth of the rugged Westerner. Condolences flooded the widow and orphan. The contents of the will were not yet known, but it was supposed that both ladies were left fabulously rich.

One event had crowded so closely upon another that General Benson was given no opportunity for confidential conversation with the woman he desired to make his wife.

The loss of her father was a terrible shock to Jewel, and she kept to her rooms, weeping passionate tears and refusing to be comforted. A sense of horrible loneliness, of grief, apprehension, and the weight of some unknown calamity weighed her young heart down. Young, beautiful, well-born, and wealthy, surrounded by every luxury money could purchase or a cultivated taste long for, Jewel was supremely wretched. Her father dead, her husband a prisoner, accused of the deadliest of crimes, the girl was a prey to a thousand vague fears and haunting suspicions. She dreaded, too, the coming of the day set apart for reading the will, for General Benson could no longer be avoided. She had written him a letter asking a release from promises made, but as yet had received no reply.

Senator Bowen had been buried two weeks when, at an early hour, the family lawyer appeared at the house and was ushered into the breakfast room where, attired in deep mourning, Mrs. Bowen sat in solitary state making a pretense of eating.

Mr. Cameron was a pale, small, dark-haired man, with sharp eyes and thin lips; a hard, but honest face, and a short temper.

Somewhat alarmed by the troubled look on the solicitor's face, Mrs. Bowen asked anxiously—

"Is anything wrong, Mr. Cameron?"

"Well, madam, I hope not; but I thought I would ask you for a cup of coffee, lay the case before you and talk it over. I heard some surprising news last night," he continued, as he seated himself and swallowed the steaming beverage that Mrs. Bowen poured for him, the discreet servant having left the room at a glance from his mistress. "Did you know that your husband made a will while in New York?" he questioned abruptly, watching her with keen, bright eyes.

PAULINE E. HOPKINS

"A will in New York? No—surely not!"

"There is such a will in existence; it is held by General Benson, who came to me last night with the astonishing information. He will be here by eleven to have the instrument read. Of course, this later document leaves the one in my possession null and void."

Mrs. Bowen had grown very white as she listened to the lawyer, and a fixed look of intense thought was in her eyes.

"What are the terms of this new will? do you remember?"

"Not all of them; but Major Madison is left sole trustee, and General Benson executor and guardian of Miss Bowen until she is of age. Think of it!" cried the excitable man, "all the immense business of the estate, ready money, etc., *absolutely* in the control of these men!"

A wonderful change came over Mrs. Bowen at these words. She was stung to the quick. She sprung from her chair as if moved by a spring; her lips quivered, her eyes dilated with what seemed like terror.

"General Benson and Major Madison!" she exclaimed in a hoarse voice, "surely you jest."

"Would it were a jest, my dear madam. Think of it! This magnificent estate and fortune to be left in the hands of two such villains as General Benson and his pal, Major Madison. Yes, villains, madam; and I will undertake to prove my position should they bring action against me for slander. What could my old friend, Bowen, have been thinking about! He must have lost his head completely," continued Mr. Cameron, looking with accusing eyes at the black-robed figure across his second cup of coffee. "Madison had done him out of a million in his bogus company already. A child could see that it was a cheat and a sham."

For one instant, at these words, Mrs. Bowen's face wore the look of a lioness bereft of her young; but her alarm seemed to subside as quickly as it arose. The lawyer was too excited himself to notice the expressions of consternation and alarm that flitted across the pale face of the silent woman before him. After a silence, she asked: "Have you examined this will, Mr. Cameron? Are you sure it is genuine?"

The old attorney put his cup down with emphasis and said with a bow: "Madam, it is a pleasure to talk with you. You have expressed my own thoughts in your question. The Bowen millions would be a great temptation to a set of sharpers. I have not examined the document, but I will; and you may trust me to find any flaw that exists."

"Let us be calm. If it is as we suspect, we shall gain nothing by allowing these men to see that we suspect them. Do not oppose them, but use every legal means to retain control of the estate until we prove our suspicions groundless."

The expression of her face was intense, even fierce; her mouth was tightly closed, her eyes strained as though striving to pierce the veil which hides from us the unseen.

Mr. Cameron looked his admiration of the fearless woman before him, and after a few more words they settled themselves to calmly wait developments.

At this same hour General Benson and his honored associate, Major Madison, sat in the former's room talking earnestly of the business in hand.

"Now, Madison, we have started on the last part of our enterprise and it is full of peril: one flaw will destroy the whole structure which we have labored so hard to raise. We must preserve all our trumps. Aurelia has failed in her part: we must not fail."

"Pshaw!" said the Major, "we shall succeed. What is there to fear? the man is dead."

"There will be many questions asked, and, doubtless, that old fox of a lawyer is even now hunting for evidences of fraud. Don't underrate the danger, Madison. Our projects are dangerous, and the slightest mistake will prove fatal. But while there are one hundred chances against us, there are the same number in our favor. We know this, too, Madison,— necessity knows no law; we must go ahead!"

"There's the old woman: she'll kick on the will, and kick hard. What'll you do with her?"

There was a peculiar smile on the General's face as he said:

"She'll struggle a little: the scene today will be a stormy one, so be prepared; but I hold a trump ahead of her."

"The deuce you do!"

"She can't escape from us any more than the girl can."

The Major whistled softly as he murmured "Amen," and then said: "I have faith in your judgment, Benson."

Benson took several turns up and down the long room and finally assumed his favorite attitude before the mantel.

"You do well to feel so, Major. I anticipate no difficulty in assuming full control of the Bowen millions, and how sorely we need them, you and I know, Major."

"But the girl—how will you manage her?"

Benson's face darkened, but he only waved his hand significantly. "Be calm. I wish the whole business was as easily disposed of as the girl."

PAULINE E. HOPKINS

"She's the only link in the chain that appears weak to my thinking, and she is the key of the old man's cash-box. Who would ever have thought of her kicking over the traces so completely and marrying Sumner?" and the Major relighted his cigar, which had gone out while he was talking.

"Keep quiet about that, Madison; let them think us surprised by their news today. Pray observe my caution; I will explain later.

"I am glad it is all right. That old attorney worries me, too. Women are deceitful hussies; a man never knows what they are at." General Benson laughed softly at the Major's suggestion.

"What!" he said, "shall the foolishness of a mere girl stop us now, when we are so near the goal? By no means. If she attempts to thwart me, so much the worse for her. Wait for me, Major," and General Benson left the room to speak with Isaac.

Left alone, Major Madison went to the window and stood looking out at the passing throng.

"It is impossible not to admire Benson's nerve and his infernal penetration," he thought half-aloud. "He reasons out a position and plans from the most trivial circumstances. He always falls on his feet. How many close calls we have had since we joined forces: yet, thanks to his luck, we have come out first best every time. Yes, he has wonderful ability and his extraordinary audacity and nerve may be trusted to carry us safely through a difficult undertaking like the present one. What a profession we have adopted and practised for twenty years. Justice never sleeps, the old fogies tell us, but I'll be dog-goned if the old woman ain't in a dead swoon when Benson's on the rampage."

Shortly after this the two friends stepped from their carriage before the Bowen mansion. The Major, in his black clothes, white cravat and spectacles might readily have passed for an eminent divine about to administer consolation to the bereaved widow and orphan.

Jewel stood in the great library waiting for General Benson, who had requested an interview. The reading of the will had shown her how dependent she would be upon this man. The thought of him as a guardian made her sick at heart. What could her father have been thinking about? She was bewildered by the difficulties which had suddenly beset her path. She who had been petted and shielded all her life saw an existence of strife and danger opening dimly in the future.

"How will it all end," she asked herself drearily, "if Cuthbert should be condemned? He shall not be; he must not be," she told herself, shutting her teeth hard and drawing a long breath.

Presently General Benson entered the room closely followed by Mrs. Bowen, who crossed the room to Jewel's side and took her hand tenderly in hers. Together they faced General Benson, and this silent defiance filled the man with rage. He came to a halt immediately in front of the pale girl, who had risen to her feet on his entrance.

"I want to tell you, Jewel, in answer to your letter, that I shall not give you up," he began abruptly. "Nothing is changed since you gave me your promise and I shall hold you to it. Your father expected it, too, when he made me your guardian."

"Sir," said Jewel, in a voice almost unintelligible from agitation, "I know that my conduct is extraordinary, but so are the circumstances surrounding my acts; I do not propose to justify myself. It is a great favor that I ask at your hands, but I entreat you to relinquish a project so fraught with unhappiness for both of us. Your generosity will spare me many sad and sorrowful hours, and surely you could not desire an unwilling bride."

"All is fair in love, Jewel," replied the General, who had listened apparently cold and unmoved, but inwardly a passion of rage and jealousy was gnawing at his heart. Then he continued with a malicious smile, "Why not yield gracefully to the inevitable?"

At these words the girl's every instinct arose in arms. She contrasted this scene with her father's fond indulgence and in hot anger longed to show this usurper how she despised his brief authority. There was a look of utter disgust on her face.

"I would have spared you, General Benson, but you need no leniency from me. There is no hope that I shall ever become your wife. I am already married to—Cuthbert Sumner!"

In a moment the man's manner changed.

"Ah!" he said, and the exclamation burst from his lips in a hiss; the elegant society man disappeared—hideous passion gave glimpses of depths of infamy—one beheld the countenance of a devil. "I have heard something of this before; but it does not concern me; it does not alter my plans. I should be foolish to allow a dead man to mar my future; and a dead man Sumner will be, for the law will remove him from my path. Nothing can save him." Jewel measured the man before her

PAULINE E. HOPKINS

with flaming eyes; she turned from him toward the door with a gesture expressive of loathing; she halted on the threshold.

"Hear me, General Benson, I will never become your wife; never, I swear it. Now do your worst."

As the door closed behind the angry girl the man turned to Mrs. Bowen, who stood watching the scene. "And you, madam, are you in league with the misguided girl who undertakes to defy my authority and rights?" The cool sarcasm of his tones was a combination of insolence and impudence.

"You are speaking to Senator Zenas Bowen's widow. You will kindly alter your words and tone when we are conversing, General Benson." Mrs. Bowen spoke in her usual calm, dignified tone. The General's face became purple, then pale; his white teeth gleamed savagely. His elaborate bow was full of mockery as he replied:

"I await your answer, madam, to my question."

"You shall have it," Mrs. Bowen exclaimed in exasperation. "I shall support Jewel in her desires. I am convinced her father would never force her to act against her inclinations."

There ensued a moment of intense silence when she had finished speaking. General Benson was utterly transfigured. There was not the slightest vestige remaining of the elegant chief of a high official bureau; the sweet voice was changed—it was hard and rasping and had a ring in it that reminded one of the slums. He advanced toward Mrs. Bowen and seized her roughly by the arm.

"So you will assist that headstrong girl to defy me, will you? Well, do it at your peril! Do it, and I will tell your story to the world. I know you; I knew you instantly the first night I saw you in this house. This girl is not your child; why should you care. I have no desire to harm you. Just let things take their course and I will never disturb you in any way."

Uncontrollable terror had spread over Mrs. Bowen's features at these words. Her lips moved but gave forth no sound.

"You do not answer, madam!" exclaimed her tormentor. Then with a diabolical smile of evil triumph he added, "I am correct then in my surmise; you do not deny it?"

The white lips moved: this time her words were distinguishable,— "No! I do not understand what you mean." "I mean—," and he bent toward her and whispered in her ear. That whisper seemed to arouse her benumbered faculties. She moved toward him with disheveled hair, foaming lips and one arm outstretched in menace. He sprang back from her with a smothered oath: "It is true: you cannot deny it."

"I admit nothing; I deny nothing. Prove it if you can," she muttered in a strained tone.

"Then it is war, is it? Very well, I give you until May to think it over. If you do not come to your senses by that time, I shall proceed to act. Think of it, madam; think well," and the General turned and abruptly left the room.

Mrs. Bowen stood there panting, crushed; her eyes alone gave signs of animation; they glared horribly. As the door closed behind her enemy she sighed; she sunk on the carpet. She had fainted.

XXIX

Time passed on, bringing in the early summer. It was the close of a beautiful June day and the sunset was still glowing and burning as it reluctantly bade the world good-night. Venus stood by an open window gazing anxiously into the twilight. Jewel had gone to the jail early in the day, leaving her maid at home. Mrs. Bowen had been in the room a number of times asking for her daughter. She was always uneasy now when Jewel was away from her, and her face wore a strained look of expectancy pitiful to see.

General Benson's anger seemed to have spent itself in the dire threats he had made on the day the will was read; he had left the women in peace, being scrupulously polite when they met to transact business.

Mrs. Bowen was anxious to leave the hot city, and it was agreed between her and Jewel to go to Arlington Heights, where the latter could still be in close proximity to the prisoner and continue her visits with ease. She had gone that day to tell him not to be depressed if the time between her calls was longer than usual.

The glow of sunset faded from the sky, and the summer twilight deepened into night, still Jewel did not appear. It was a warm night; the upper windows were all open; the diamond-studded sky was like a sea of glass. Another hour went by. Mrs. Bowen was pacing the floor restlessly. Venus came up from the servants' quarters with soup and wine for her mistress.

"Now do be persuaded to eat something, madam," said the maid. "You're just as white as death, and you've sat here waiting for Miss Jewel, without your dinner and you must be quite faint. Here it's nine o'clock, and you always dine at half-past seven. I reckon my young lady's all right. She'll turn up presently as bright as a dollar, sure's you're born."

So Mrs. Bowen smiled and allowed herself to be cheered by the devoted girl, and took some soup and a little of the wine; but she could not rest, and listened to every sound that came faintly to the great mansion from the outside.

Hour succeeded hour and it was eleven o'clock; nobody thought of going to bed. As she sat listening there came a sharp quick ring at the outer bell. Venus herself, anxious for tidings from her loved mistress, rushed to the door ahead of the butler. It was a note which was handed her by a man well muffled up, who instantly disappeared in the thick shrubbery about the lawn. Venus hastened to Mrs. Bowen. With a smile she opened the envelope. The next moment she uttered a cry and gasped for breath.

"Whatever is the matter?" cried the frightened maid.

"This letter—this letter! Help me—help me! Your lady has been abducted!" Mrs. Bowen fell back unconscious in her chair.

The terror-stricken maid opened the letter with shaking hands and read the following lines:

"I always keep my word. If you value your reputation and your step-daughter's *welfare*, you will not seek to find her. In due time she will reappear."

MEANWHILE WHAT HAD BECOME OF Jewel? She had elected to walk to the jail and back because of the beauty of the day. At the jail she found Mr. Henson, and they had stayed talking over the difficulties of the case until twilight was falling. But that did not disturb her for Mr. Henson would walk back with her, and the Washington streets, famous for their loneliness and seclusion, stretching like immense parks in all directions, would be robbed of their usual terrors for lone female pedestrians.

Mr. Henson accompanied her to the great entrance gates; there he left her, and she started up the carriage path at a rapid gait. Along the edges of the drive the underwood was so thick, and the foliage of the trees arching overhead so full and dense that towards the centre of the drive it was in semi-twilight, and thick shades of darkness enveloped all things. In the half-light Jewel thought she discerned a vehicle—a close carriage, she fancied—standing at one side of the drive.

Surprised, but not startled, because of the close proximity of the house, the girl advanced. The next moment she was startled enough; a chill of fear went through her woman's heart and it stood still for one instant with a thrill of sickening terror, for suddenly out from the gloomy shade of the trees, into the drive, stepped two men, rough-looking ruffians wearing black half-masks.

The one who was evidently the leader said in a hoarse voice, probably disguised:

"Now, Jim."

Instantly both moved toward her.

Jewel was a Western girl. She did not scream. She had been brought up on a ranch; one of her early habits remained fixed, and even in

Washington she was never unarmed when without male escort. The jewelled toy she carried was a present from her father, and he had taught her to use it with deadly effect. Many a day they had hunted together, the young girl bringing down her game in true sportsmanlike style.

Instantly now her hand sought her pocket, in the very instinct of self-defense and desperation; she drew her revolver with intent to fire, but quick as flash the leader flung himself upon her and wrenched the weapon from her hand. He then threw his arm about her slender form, drawing her towards the carriage.

The passion of terror and desperation lent the girl unnatural strength in her frantic struggle for freedom. The man was forced to place his other hand to stifle her screams.

"You come along quietly, missee, an' you'll be all right; but ef yer screams it won't be pleasant."

"You coward!" she gasped, as he bore her to the carriage. "You coward! Name your price, and let me go."

"Thar you are, now, slick as grease." She was in the carriage then. "Yer money won't help you with me, missee. You're a brave gal, but what's your strength to a man's? Drive on like h—, Jim."

The cold drops of agony stood on the girl's brow as the horror of her position grew upon her each moment.

"Where are you taking me?"

"I'm goin' ter take yer jes' a little journey outside o' Washington fer a few days. Don't you be feared; thar's nuthin' goin' hurt ye."

Who was this man holding her, refusing bribe, yet vowing to protect her from harm. She looked into the masked face in an agony of appeal and doubt and fear in the great grey eyes. The man was touched.

"Don't now, *don't,* missee, look that skeered. Nothin' ain't goin' hurt you, I tell you. Ise got a little gal o' my own."

The girl did not answer. Like a light it flashed across her who was the author of this outrage.

"I know your employer!" she said fiercely. "But he shall learn that I fear him not. I defy him still."

XXX

When Jewel came to herself she was lying on an old-fashioned canopied bed with a coverlet thrown over her. The room was evidently, originally designed for a studio, and was lighted by a skylight; even now a flood of sunlight streamed from above, making more dingy and faded by comparison the appearance of the dusty canvases and once luxurious furniture scattered about the apartment. Evidences of decay were everywhere; a broken easel leant against the wall, and on a table odds and ends of tubes, brushes and other artistic paraphernalia were heaped in a disorderly mass. There were also a couch and easy chairs in faded brocade.

The girl looked about with lanquid interest scarcely realizing what had happened to disturb the serenity of her daily life. Presently, however, the power of thought returned and with it a flood of memories concerning the outrage of the night before. She was a prisoner, but where?

What a terrible sensation it was to wake to the conciousness of being a prisoner! A prisoner! she, Jewel Bowen, who until recently had never known a care in her short existence of twenty years. Now all the waves and billows of life were passing over her threatening to engulf her. Could it be that all her bright hopes for the future were to end here in this lonely chamber?

With the thought she arose hastily from the bed and began walking despairingly about, examining the room. After a tour of the apartment she gave it up. Her prison was well-chosen. The doors were bolted, and no window gave a possibility of escape. There was no chance of attracting attention, by her cries, from passers-by, even if scores of persons traversed the streets about this house; no one would know that within its walls a desolate girl suffered the keenest of mental torture.

She paced the room frantically, and shook the doors of her prison violently until she was obliged to sink exhausted upon the couch. "They will hardly let me die of hunger," she told herself, resolving to save her strength for questioning whoever should bring her food.

Crouching upon the couch, she listened. Not a sound broke upon her ear. It seemed to her that desolation engulfed her. Presently, as she sat there, the sound of a football came to her strained ears, then a key grated in the lock, the door swung open, and a tall, pleasant-featured black man entered the room, bearing a tray. He carefully locked the door behind him, removing the key from the lock. He wheeled forward a small table and deftly arranged the contents of the tray upon it.

Jewel launched an avalanche of questions at him, but he returned no answer. He went and returned a number of times, bringing her clothing, books and luxuries of the toilet, all indicating that a long captivity was in prospect. At lunch time an aged Negress brought her food, but all efforts to engage her in conversation were unavailing; a more morose and repulsive specimen of the race Jewel had never met.

After this there was a monotonous interval of time passed in the agony of silence. Her meals were furnished regularly and all other needs lavishly supplied. One day was the record of another.

Four weeks must have passed since she was brought to this place, still she had no knowledge of her captors, nor where her prison was located. One change, however, was made—they gave her the freedom of an adjoining room as the summer heat increased, but the windows were barred and looked out upon extensive gardens filled with the ruins of what must once have been buildings and offices of a large plantation. The once well-kept walks were overgrown with weeds, and a heavy growth of trees obstructed the view in all directions.

One night she sat by the window gazing at the stars and eating her heart out in agony and tears. She could not sleep; insomnia had added its horrors to her other troubles. Suddenly the sky became overcast and the stars disappeared. A storm threatened. Low mutterings of thunder and gusts of rising wind foretold a summer shower. At intervals a lightning flash lit up the inky blackness of the scene. Finally the flashes became so vivid that the girl moved her seat from the window to a less exposed position with a scornful laugh at her own fear of death. "Truly," she thought bitterly, "self-preservation has been called the first law of nature. How we strive to preserve that which is of so little value."

Up and down the sides of the room her eyes wandered aimlessly; sometimes she felt that she was losing her mind. Presently a painting fixed into the wall arrested her attention. It was the portrait of an impossible wood nymph, but so faded that its beauty—if it had once possessed any—was entirely gone.

As she gazed at it indifferently the centre bulged outward, and a small strip of canvas swung to and fro as if from a draught of air.

Jewel sprang to her feet and ran to the picture. She trembled with sudden hope. Where did the draught come from? Carefully she raised the torn strip of canvas and inserted her hand beneath it, feeling along the wall back of the picture. There was a narrow recess behind it. Greatly excited by this discovery, she flew to the table where her dinner-service still remained, seized a knife and cut the canvas close to the frame for a good distance up. Then she trembling raised the cloth.

Oh! Joy! it revealed a passage usually closed by a door which had become unfastened and now swung idly in the breeze made by the raising wind.

Thank heaven, it was an hour when she was free from interruption. No one would disturb her until morning. She took the lamp in her hand. Escape seemed very near. Scarcely waiting to widen the aperture, she crept through, and soon stood, covered with dust, trembling shaken with emotion, in the dark passage which the canvas had hidden.

She paused and strained her ears to listen for sounds in the silent house. None came. Then she crept on very, very cautiously.

The passage was dark. It had evidently lead to the servants' quarters at the back of the house when mirth and gaiety held high revel in the glorious old mansion. She went swiftly on, till she came to a black baize door. She pushed it open with difficulty. Here she paused irresolute, for this door gave admission to the front of the house; there was a passage at right angles with the one just quitted, with stairs leading above and below. She glided toward the latter, seized hold of the banisters, descended into another passage with many doors opening into it. The doors were all closed.

What a rambling old place it was. In the excitement of the instant she had felt no terror, but now an icy chill seized her and her heart throbbed heavily.

She noticed now that one of the doors in the passage was ajar! Dare she pass it? To advance was appalling, but the case was a desperate one. With her heart throbbing wildly she stood motionless one instant, then she ventured past the unclosed door.

She shaded her lamp with one hand and with fascinated gaze took in, in one brief instant, the contents of the room. Her eyes wandered from the bare floor and walls to the table, the two chairs, and then to a bed in one corner. There her gaze lingered, for on the bed lay a woman of dark brown complexion and wrinkled visage; about her head was wound a many-hued bandanna handkerchief. The woman's eyes were open and fixed in terror and amazement upon the girl who had just entered the room. They gazed at each other for one moment, these two

PAULINE E. HOPKINS

so strangely met, then the old woman threw her arms above her head, exclaiming:

"Bless Gawd! I'se ready! Praise the Lor'! He done sen' his Angel Gabriel to tote me home to glory."

The sound of her voice broke the spell that bound Jewel.

"Who are you, Auntie, and what makes you think me an angel?"

"Lor', honey, is you human sho' nuff? Why when I seen yo' face er'shinin' on me dar, an' hearn yer sof' step comin' en de lonely night, I made sho' it was de Lor' come to carry dis' po' sinner to er home in glory. I 'spec' I been shut up her so long I'se gittin' doaty. I'se a po' ol'black 'ooman, been dragged 'way from my home an' chillun an' locked up here by a limb o' de debbil 'cause he's 'fraid I tell his wicked actions. But 'deed chile, whar'd you come from? Does you live in dis place?"

Jewel shook her head sadly.

"I'm a prisoner, too, Auntie. I've been shut up here for four weeks now. I happened to find a way out of my room tonight, and I thought I might possibly escape. Can you tell me where I am?"

"Yes, honey, I can. You's down on de ol' Enson plantation in Ma'lan. I was born on de nex' joinin' place myself. But who brung you here? What's your name, chile?"

"I haven't seen my captor yet, but I believe it to be General Benson. My name is Jewel Bowen."

"Mercy, King! My lovely Lor'd, but ain't dis curus?" exclaimed the old woman, greatly excited. "My gran'darter is yo' waiter, Venus Johnson!"

It was not Jewel's turn to become excited.

"Then you are—?"

"Aunt Hennie Sargent; dat's me."

XXXI

Meanwhile there was mourning at the Bowen Mansion, for the joy of the house had fled with Jewel. Mrs. Bowen sent for the family lawyer and then went to bed; trouble was wearing her out, and there was danger of her becoming a confirmed invalid.

Mr. Cameron put the machinery of the law in motion to find the missing girl, but there progress seemed to end.

Now the sorely tried mistress discovered what a treasure she had in the maid Venus. The girl was everywhere attending to the business of the house and waiting on the invalid mistress. She visited the jail with news for the restless unhappy man confined there, never seeming to weary in well-doing. Venus preserved a discreet silence concerning the letter received on the night of the abduction, but the brain of the little brown maid was busy. She had her own ideas about certain things, and was planning for the deliverance of her loved young mistress.

When Jewel had been absent about two weeks, Venus asked leave to pay her mother a visit one evening. Marthy had heard nothing from the police in relation to Aunt Hennie, and she was overjoyed to see her daughter; it gave her an opportunity to pour her sorrows and griefs into sympathetic ears.

She bustled about the neat kitchen setting out the best that her home afforded for supper, and Oliver dropped his books in honor of his sister's visit, making it a festival.

When the meal was on the table, smoking hot,—corn pone, gumbo soup, chicken and rice and coffee of an amber hue,—the children ate with gusto. The mother's eyes shone with happiness as she watched their enjoyment, pressing upon them, at intervals, extra helps.

"Have some mo' this gumbo soup, my baby. I reckon you don' git nothin' like it up yonder with all the fixin's you has there."

"Well, my Lord, ma, I won't be able to walk to the cars if I keep on stuffing myself," replied Venus as her mother filled her plate again with the delicious soup.

"Say, Venus," broke in Oliver, with a grin on his mischievous face, "who's the good-looking buck that came to the end of the street with you the last time you were home?"

"What's that?" cried Marthy, sharply.

Oliver laughed and clapped his hands, "Ma's like a hen with chickens; she's afraid of the fellows, Vennie."

Venus laughed, too, a little shame-facedly. "Oh, now, Ollie, ain't you got no cover to your mouth? That was Mr. Sumner's man, John. I had to see him about a message from Mrs. Bowen to Mr. Sumner, and so he was polite enough to come with me to our street, it being pretty dark."

"That's all right," said Marthy in a relieved tone. "Mr. Williams is a perfec' gent'man. You're only a leetle gal, Venus, if you is out to work, an' there's time 'nuff for you to git into trubble. You don' wan' to fill yo' head up with 'viggotty notions 'about fellars yet. I got married young when I'd doughter been playin' with baby rags; I don' want my gal to take on eny mo' trubble en her haid than she can kick off at her heels. You, Venus, mark my wurds, an' 'member what I tell's you ef I'm moulderin' in the clay to dus' an' ashes tomorrer,—gittin' jined to a man's a turrible 'spons'bility, 'specially the man. You want to think well an' cal'ate the consequences of the prevus ac'. Mymy, mymy!"she continued musingly, "how that carries me back to the las' time ol' Mis' Sargeant whopped me. She says to me, 'Marthy, did you take the money off my dresser table? tell me the troof,' and I dussan' lie, an' so I said: 'Ys'm; Ike Johnson tol' me to do it an' he'd buy me a red ribbin fer my hair.' Ol' miss says 'Marthy, you's 'mitted the *prevus' ac'*, an' I'm gwine whop you,' an' the ol' lady laid it onto me right smart with her slipper. Ike Johnson's been gittin' me inter tubble ever sense that time.

Oliver, when you was born an' I foun' you was a man chile I said to myself, "Lord, how come you let me bring one of them mule critters into the wurl to make trubble for some po' 'ooman? An' ef ever you git jined, an' treat yo' wife as yo' pa's treated me, I hope you'll git yo' match, an' she'll wallop the yearth with you, 'deed I does."

"Daddy been home lately?" asked Venus carelessly after the meal was cleared away.

"No, chile, he ain't,"replied her mother. "He was home—le' me see—jes' befo' the fus' of the munf. He brought me the mor'gage money."

"How much was it?"

"Four hundred dollars Venus, chile, you could have knocked me down with a feather, I was so outdone from 'stonishmen' when he throwed it into my lap and said 'dar's you' mo'gage.'"

"Now, ma, where'd he get *all* that money I'd like to know? He never got it honest, that's my belief."

"Yes, I reckon he did, honey, this time. Gin'ral Benson give it to him. Yo' granny asked the Gin'ral about it 'way in the winter."

"Hump!" exclaimed Venus.

"He ain't been home sense. Gin'ral's bo't a plantation out o' Baltimo' a bit, an' yo' pa's holpin' to fix it up. I reckon he'll be thare 'bout all summer. He took a few clo's an' things with him when he was home." Venus looked at her mother intently, but remained silent.

"Dear, dear, Venus," Marthy continued beginning to cry, "ef I only knew where was yo' granny or what had come to her, I'd be a happy 'ooman this night. An' to think of Miss Jewel, too, that dear beautiful girl with a face like an angel out of glory. The ways of the Lord is pas' follerin', an' that's a fac'."

"What's dad say about granny?" asked Venus suddenly.

"*He* ain't worried none, bless yo' soul. He ain't studyin' 'bout the dear ol' so'l. He ain't got no mo' blood in him than a lizard. He's the onerist man! Says to me, 'quit frettin'; the ol' 'ooman 'll turn up safe quicker'n scat', he says. 'She's tuf; nothin' ain't gwine kill the ol' hornet.' Them's yo' pa's words to me."

"What do you expect from dad, ma? You know him. You ought to if anybody does. Granny makes him toe the mark, that's why he dislikes her."

"That's so, sho' 'nuff, baby; an' what we know 'bout Ike Johnson's mean capers would fill a book. It's twenty years come nix Chris'mus sense we jumped the broomstick together. We was the very las' couple jined befo' the s'render, an' ef it hadn't been for yo' granny, we'd all been in the po' house long ago an' fergit."

When it was time to start for home Oliver escorted his sister to the car. On the way she questioned him closely and learned many things concerning her father that her mother had failed to mention.

"It's as sure as preaching," she told herself late that night as she was preparing for bed, "it's as sure as preaching that somebody who knows something must take hold of Miss Jewel's case or that son of Sodom will carry his point. The police are slower 'n death. Dad's up to his capers. He can fool ma, but he can't pull the wool over my eyes; I'm his daughter. Hump! well, we'll see about it. It's a burning shame for dad to go on this way after all Miss Jewel's kindness to us. But I'll balk him. I'll see him out on this case or my name ain't Venus Johnson."

"I'll see if this one little black girl can't get the best of as mean a set of villains as ever was born," was her last thought as her eyes closed in slumber.

PAULINE E. HOPKINS

Mr. Henson sat in his office the next morning thinking deeply. He had just returned from New York, where he had carefully examined the ground, trying to find a flaw in the Bowen will, drawn and signed in that city, but not a particle of encouragement had rewarded his efforts. He was much depressed over his failure to obtain a clue to what he was convinced was clever forgery committed by two dangerous men. His vast experience did not aid him; he was forced to declare that the criminals had covered their tracks well.

Mr. Cameron had just left him after acknowledging *his* inability to fix a point that would legally stay the enforcement of the will.

All was dark; but the man felt that if he could obtain the slightest clue, he could unravel the whole plot without difficulty. But how to gain a clue was the question. He had determined to start the next day for Kentucky in the hope of finding Elise Bradford's aunt and the child of the dead woman, hoping that this might furnish the key to the mystery.

The morning sunshine streamed into the room. The intense heat was enervating. He drew his chair before the large open window on the side where the sun had not reached and directly in the wake of an electric fan. He leaned his head upon his hand and thought over the situation.

All his efforts had been to ascertain if there were any real grounds for the suspicions, which had been aroused in Miss Bowen's mind, and which his interviews with Sumner had confirmed. The news of her abduction had come as a distinct shock to him when it was given him upon his return from New York. The beautiful girl had aroused all the man's innate chivalry; springs of tenderness long dead to any influence had welled up in his soul, and he felt a mad desire, uncontrollable and irresistible, to rescue her, and take dire vengeance on her captors.

Her haunting influence was wrapped about him; he could see her, feel her presence and almost catch the tones of her low voice in the silent room. Ever and anon he glanced about him as if seeking the actual form of the fair spirit that had so suddenly absorbed his heart and soul.

He was satisfied in his own mind that General Benson was the criminal, but to this man who had become a legal machine, tangible evidence was the only convincing argument that he knew.

Presently a clerk entered the room and announced that a woman wished to speak to him.

"Show her in," he replied to the man's query.

A few seconds passed, and then the opening door admitted a young colored girl who had an extremely intelligent, wide-awake expression.

Venus was not at all embarrassed by the novelty of her surroundings, but advanced toward the chief with a businesslike air, after making sure that the retiring clerk had actually vanished.

"I'm Miss Jewel Bowen's maid," she declared abruptly. The detective whirled around in his chair at her words, and in an instant was all attention. His keen eyes ran over the neat little brown figure standing demurely before him, with a rapid mental calculation of her qualities.

"What is your name?"

"Venus Camilla Johnson."

"How long have you been in Miss Bowen's employ?"

"All the winter."

"Who sent you here?"

"Nobody. I keep my business to myself. Things are too curious around Wash'nton these days to be talking too much."

The shadow of a smile lurked about the corners of Mr. Henson's mouth.

"Well, what do you want? Time is precious with me."

"Yes, sir; I won't keep you long, but you see Miss Jewel's been my good angel and I jus' had to come here and unburden my mind to you or burst. You see, sir, it's this way,—the Bowen family is *white* right through; mos' *too* good for this world. They've got piles of money, but mymy, mymy! Since the Senator's gone, and Mr. Cuthbert's done got into trouble from being in tow with Miss Madison, they be the mos' miserablest two lone women you ever saw."

Venus forgot her education in her eartnestness, and fell into the Negro vernacular, talking and crying at the same time.

Mr. Henson waited patiently. He knew that she would grow calmer if he did not notice her agitation.

"It's hard for me to go back on my own daddy," continued the girl, "but it's got to be done. I suspicion him more and more every minute I'm alive, I do. Miss Jewel's stolen away, and the old lady's taken down to her bed, an' my daddy is waltzing through the country looking after General Benson's business down on a plantation in Maryland. I'm no fool, Mr. Henson; he's my daddy, but Isaac Johnson's a bad pill. He's jus' like a bad white man, sir,—he'll do anything for money when he gets hard up."

Mr. Henson sat with pale face regarding the woman before him. His eyes gleamed and were fixed searchingly upon her.

Finally he asked:

"Who are your parents? I take it they were once slaves. Where were they born?"

"Ma's Aunt Henny Sargeant's daughter Marthy, and daddy's Isaac Johnson. They lived on adjoining plantations in Maryland. Dad belonged to Mr. Enson, and Ma to Mrs. Sargeant. Ma says it was a terrible misfortune that she did live next door to the Ensons, leastwise Oliver and me'd never had Ike Johnson for our daddy."

"Any relation to the Aunt Henny who was employed by the government and who has disappeared?" the detective asked.

"Yes, sir; that's her," replied the girl, nodding her head.

"Poor granny; I reckon she's dead all right. Ma takes it terrible hard. Does nothing but cry after granny all day while she's working. I tell her I *cain't* cry till I find Miss Jewel. Ma says I'm unfeeling; but, Lord, you cain't help being just as you're built. Say, Mr. Henson, I've made bold to bring you something. I took it away from the madam the night Miss Jewel was stolen."

Mr. Henson took the envelope that the girl extended to him, and read the note contained therein.

"Who do you think sent this, Venus?"

"No one but old Benson."

Again the chief smiled at the quaint answer. But he looked at her still more searchingly, as he asked:

"Did anything of a particularly suspicious nature occur to make you hold that opinion?"

"Well, yes, sir; there did. Something I overheard General Benson say to the old lady."

"Oh, then, you were listening."

"I reckon I was, and a good job too, or I wouldn't have this to tell you. It was the day the will was read. Mr. Cameron was gone, and the three of 'em—Mrs. Bowen, Miss Jewel and General Benson were in the library. Miss Jewel went out and left the other two together.

He hollered at the madam like he was crazy, and I was standing there outside the door with the old Senator's boot-jack in my hand, expecting that I'd have to go in and hit the General over the head with it to protect the madam. He says to her, 'So, you will assist that headstrong girl to defy me, will you? Well, do it at your peril!' then he went close up to her—so close that their noses almost touched, and I thought it was about time for the boot-jack, sure,—but all he did was to whisper to her, and the old madam gave a screech and keeled over on the floor like she was dead.

"I 'clare to you, Mr. Henson, I was skeered enough to drop, but I didn't say a word, no sir; I just went in as soon as the General went out, and I picked the old lady up and got her to her room, and when she came to her self there was nobody to ask her what was the matter because they didn't know what I could have told them. But Madam hasn't been herself since. I believe my soul that he skeered the life out of her. When Miss Jewel didn't come home, and that note came instead, I just made up my mind it was Venus for General Benson, and that I'd got to cook his goose or he'd cook mine."

"You do not like General Benson, I see."

"Like him! who could, the sly old villain. He's mighty shrewd, and—" She paused.

"Well, what?"

"Foxy," she finished. "He tries to be mighty sweet to me, but I like a gentleman to stay where he belongs and not be loving servant girls on the sly. I owe Miss Jewel what money cain't pay, and I'm not ungrateful."

"*I* believe the old rapscallion has got her shut up somewhere down in Maryland, and dad's helping him. Oh, I didn't tell you, did I, that dad's his private waiter?"

"Ah!" exclaimed the chief, for the first time exhibiting a sign of excitement.

"Now we're getting down to business, my girl. I understand your drift now. You have done well to come to me.

Venus smiled in proud satisfaction at his words of praise. The man sat buried in deep thought for a time before he spoke again. Finally he said:

"I need help, Venus; are you brave enough to risk something for the sake of your mistress?"

"Try me and see," was her proud reply.

"It comes to just this: someone must go down to this plantation in Maryland, and hang around to find out if there is truth in our suspicions. Can you wear boys' clothing?" he asked abruptly.

Venus showed her dazzling teeth in a giggle. She ducked her head and writhed her shoulders in suppressed merriment as she replied:

"*Cain't* I? well, I reckon."

"Then you'll do. There's no time to be lost. Disguise yourself as a boy. Be as secret about it as possible. Tell no one what you are about to do, or where you are going, and meet me at the station tonight in time for the ten o'clock train for Baltimore. My agent will be waiting for you on the Avenue, just by the entrance, disguised as your grandfather Uncle Henry, a crippled old Negro, fond of drink. You are to be Billy, and both of you are going home to Baltimore. We will fix the rest of the business after you reach the village.

God grant that this plan may hasten the discovery I have been seeking."

XXXII

Enson Hall reminded one of an ancient ruin. The main body of the stately dwelling was standing, but scarcely a vestige of the once beautiful outbuildings remained; the cabins in the slave quarters stood like skeletons beneath the nodding leaves and beckoning arms of the grand old beeches. War and desolation had done their best to reduce the stately pile to a wreck. It bore, too, an uncanny reputation. The Negroes declared that the beautiful woods and the lonely avenues were haunted after nightfall. It had grown into a tradition that the ghost of Ellis Enson "walked," accompanied by a lady who bore an infant in her arms.

The Hall was in charge of an old Negress, known all over the country as "Auntie Griffin." She was regarded with awe by both whites and blacks, being a reputed "witch woman" used to dealing and trafficking with evil spirits.

Tall and raw-boned, she was a nightmare of horror. Her body was bent and twisted by disease from its original height. Her protruding chin was sharp like a razor, and the sunken jaws told of toothless gums within.

Her ebony skin was seamed by wrinkles; her eyes, yellow with age, like Hamlet's description of old men's eyes, purged "thick amber and plum-tree gum." The deformed hands were horny and toilworn. Her dress was a garment which had the virtue of being clean, although its original texture had long since disappeared beneath a multitude of many-hued patches.

Auntie Griffin only visited the village for supplies; she was uncongenial and taciturn. She made no visits and received none. Lately, however, it was noticed that the old woman had a male companion at the Hall, an elderly, dudish colored man whom she announced, on her weekly visit to the store, as her brother Ike, come to spend a short time with her.

It was well along in August when an old Negro calling himself Uncle William Henry Jackson, accompanied by his grandson Billy, a spritely lad, scarcely more than a boy, wandered into the village and took possession of one of the dilapitated antebellum huts, formerly the homes of slaves, many of which still adorned the outskirts of the little hamlet.

Uncle William Henry claimed to be a former inhabitant who had belonged to a good old Southern family of wealth, made extinct by the civil strife. The oldest resident—a Negress of advanced age who was an authority on the genealogy of the settlement—claimed to remember him distinctly, whereupon he was adopted into their warm hearts as a son of the soil and received the most hospitable treatment, in two weeks he had settled down as a fixture of the place. The old man claimed to be a veteran of the late Civil War, and that he was in receipt of a small pension which provided food for himself and grandchild. Uncle William spent most of his time sitting on a half-barrel at the door of the general store, chewing tobacco, making fishing rods from branches which Billy brought him from the woods and telling stories, of which he had a wonderful stock. The rods he turned out were really pieces of artistic work when they left his hands, and the owner of the store agreed to find a market for the goods.

Thus the old man was happily established, to quote his own words, "fer de res' ob my days," sitting in the sun with a few old cronies of his own cut—white and black harmoniously blended—spinning yarns of life in camp, and, for the truth must be told, drinking bad moonshine rum.

He never tired of describing the battle scenes through which he had passed.

"Do I know anythin' 'bout Wagner? I should say so, bein' I was in it," was his favorite prelude to a description of the famous charge.

"No, honey, I didn' lef' dat missin' leg dar. I lef' dat leg ober to For' Piller. But fer all dat, Wagner was a corker, yes, sah, a corker. From eleven o'clock Friday 'tel four o'clock Saturday we was gittin' on the transpo'ts, we war rained on, had no tents an' nothin' to eat. Thar was no time fo' we war to lead de charge. We came up at quick time an' when we got wifin 'bout one hunde'd yards, de rebs open a rakin' fire. Why, mon, they jes' vomited the shot inter us from de fo't, an' we a-walkin' up thar in dress parade order; they mowed us down lak sheep. De fus' shot camed down rip-zip, an' ploughed a hole inter us big 'nuff to let in a squadron, an' all we did was ter close up, servin' our fire; but I tell you, gent'men, we looked at each other an' felt kin' o' lonesome fer a sight o' home an' fren's.

Colonel Shaw walked ahead as cool as ef he war up to Boston Common, singing out, 'steady, boys, steady!' Bymeby de order come in a clar ringin' voice, 'charge! Foreard, my brave boys!' We started on a double-quick, an' wif a cheer an' a shout we went pell-mell; wif a rush into an' over de ditch them devils had made an' fenced wif wire. But we kep' right on an' up de hill 'tel we war han' to han' wif de inimy. Colonel Shaw was fus' to scale de walls. He stood up thar straight an' tall lak de angel Gabrul, urgin' de boys to press on. I tell you, sah, 'twas a hot time.

Fus' thing I 'member clearly after I got het up, was I seed a officer standin' wavin' his sword, an' I heard him holler, 'Now, give 'em h—, boys, give 'em h—!' an then thar come a shot; it hit him—zee-rip—an' off went his head; but, gent'men, ef you'll b'lieve me, dat head rolled by me, down de hill sayin' as it went, 'Give 'em h—, boys, give 'em h—!' until it landed in de ditch; an' all de time de mon's arms was a wavin' of his sword."

"Come off, Uncle," exclaimed one of the circle of listeners. "Who ever heard of a man's talkin' after his head was cut off?"

"Gent'men," replied Uncle William solemnly, "dat ar am a fac'; I see it wif my own two eyes, an' hyard it wif my own two ears. *It am a fac'*."

"I've heard lies on lies," drawled another on-looker, "from all kinds of liars—white liars and niggers—but that is the mos' *infernal* one I ever listened to."

"I'll leave it to Colonel Morris thar ef sech things ain't possibul. Ain't you seen cur'us capers cut when you was in battle, sah?"

"Don't bring me into it, Uncle William Henry, I'm listening to you," laughed the Colonel, who had just driven up and was about entering the store to make a purchase.

"It am a fac'; I 'clar it am a fac'," insisted the old man. "Thar was the officer talkin', and' then the shot hit him so suddint dat he hadn't time to stop talkin'. Why de water in de ditch mus' have got in his mouf fer *I seen him when he spit it out!*" At this there was a roar of laughter from the crowd, and the first speaker slapped Uncle William Henry on the back with a resounding blow.

"That's a tough one for a professor, Uncle. I know you're dry. Come, have a drink."

When they had all returned to their places, the old man resumed his narrative.

"When I looked agin, Colon Shaw was gone. The Johnnies had pulled him over the parapet down onter de stockades, an' dat was de las' seen of as gallan' a gent'man as ever lived. I tell you, mon, when I seen dat, I fel' lak a she wil' cat, an' I jes' outfit a blin' mule. I tore an' I bit lak a dog. I got clinched wif a reb, an' dog my cats, fus' thing I know'd I was chawin' him in de throat an' I never lef' go 'tel he give a groan an I

PAULINE E. HOPKINS

seed he was gone. Jes' then I seen three or fo' Johnnies running 'long de parapet toward me shoutin', 'S'render, you d—nigger.' I looked an' seen dat all 'bout me they was clubbin', stabbin' an' shootin' our boys to death, an' our men was fightin' lak devils themselves.

"Well, sah, when I seen them Mr. Whitemen makin' fer me, I jes' rolled down de hill to de ditch, an' plantin' my gun ba'net down in de water, I lepped acrost to de other side. I was flyin' fer sho, you may b'lieve, an' fus' thing I heard was, 'Halt! who goes thar?' It was de provy guard, a black North Carolina regiment stationed thar to return stragglers to their posts. I sung out, clar an' loud, thinkin' I was suttinly all right then: 'Fifty-fourth Massachusetts!' But I felt de col' chills creep down my back when I heard de order: 'Git-a-back-a-dar, Fifty-fourth!' an' every mon's gun said 'click, clack.' You may b'lieve, gent'men, dat I got back.

"I wandered aroun' fer a spell lak a los' kitten; finally, I stumbled into de lines, an' I crep' unner a gun-carriage an' slep' thar 'tel mornin'."

Now it happened that Isaac Johnson was lonely in his enforced solitude, and being of social disposition, soon made it a habit to wend his way to the corner store and listen to Uncle William Henry's stories. Having plenty of money, he treated freely and was soon counted a "good fellow" by all the frequenters of the place.

At first Isaac drank moderately, mindful of his responsibilities, but soon his old habits re-asserted themselves. Moreover, Uncle William liked the social glass also; and finally the two became so intimate that they would wend their way to the hut in the woods, where the latter had taken up his residence, and there enjoy to the full the contents of a gallon-jug which was concealed under a loose board in the floor. In short, Isaac got drunk, and losing all sense of caution, remained away from the Hall two days and nights, hidden in the hut from prying eyes. The first time this happened, old William Henry recovered control of himself as soon as Isaac was locked in drunken slumber upon Billy's bed, behind the curtains, which divided the one room into sleeping apartments.

He went to the door then and waved a handkerchief three times, nailed it to the side of the hut and retired.

Ten minutes after this act, the lad Billy entered the woods which led to Enson Hall.

The path, though often ill-defined, was never quite obliterated, and he came at last to where the trees grew thinner, and the Hall was visible.

Then he emerged upon the broad stretch of meadow and crossing it was soon on the grounds. There he paused and looked cautiously about. Twilight was falling. The scene was wild and romantic. There was no sight nor sound of human beings.

He passed the rusty gates and sped swiftly across the law to the shelter of bushes near the wide piazzas. He sank down in their shadow and waited.

Nothing occurred to break the heavy silence. Not a human creature crossed the unkept grounds. The soft summer wind lazily stirred the grass growing in rank luxuriance. The scene was desolate and depressing enough. So it continued for over an hour. Darkness finally succeeded the soft twilight. Then the lad re-appeared and skirted the sides and front of the building carefully.

Presently he espied a wild honeysuckle that had climbed to the third story of the house and blended its tendrils gracefully with the branches of a giant sycamore that stretched its arms so near to the house that they tapped gently against the irons that barred a window high above its head.

With the agility of a cat, the boy was quickly finding his way up, up to the window of the room where Jewel was allowed to exercise and breathe the sweet summer air from the woods and fields. A subdued light gleamed in the window behind the iron bars.

Hush! what noise was that? It was the sound of voices in conversation. The lad ceased his climbing and rested, listening intently for a repetition of the sound. Again it came—first a sweet young voice that had a weary, despondent note; then, in answer the tones of an aged Negro voice in the endeavor to comfort and encourage.

The listener waited no longer, but rapidly mounted to the window just above his head, reached the lower end of the rusty iron bar which divided the broken casement into two, and drew himself up to the ledge, and peered in.

Mr. Henson was aroused from slumber at midnight that night to receive an important telegram, which read: "All O.K. Just as we thought. Come on and bag the game."

XXXIII

By the middle of September Washington awoke from the stagnation incident to the summer vacation, and was ready to begin the business of another working year. The departments were re-opened and hundreds of stragglers returned to work in the great government hives, all eager for the excitement of the great murder trial.

Sunday, the day before the opening of the trial, Cuthbert Sumner sat in his cell looking pale and careworn but still preserving his outward composure though racked by inward torture. Jewel's abduction had been a worse blow to him than his own arrest, and uncertainty as to her fate had nearly driven him wild; but today Hope had smiled her April smile from amid the clouds that threatened and he was at peace. His lawyer had just left him, bidding him to be of good cheer for all things pointed to a happy ending of his troubles.

Absorbed in thought he sat dreaming of the future and planning for a period of felicity that should atone for the suffering of the present time. Suddenly the key grated in the lock and the door swung open to admit a visitor. He recoiled as from a blow when he met the gaze of Aurelia Madison who stood staring at him with a glance in which curiosity, fear and love were mingled. She stood in the center of the gloomy, cell like a statue, her dazzling beauty as marvelous as ever, the red-gold hair still shining in sunny radiance, the velvet eyes resting upon the man before her with a hidden caress in their liquid depths. Sumner shuddered as he gazed and remembered the dead girl's story. When alone with this woman, she had always possessed an irresistible attraction for him, and in spite of the past the old sensation returned in full force at this unexpected encounter, mingled with fear and repulsion. She broke the spell which held them silent.

"Bert! my Bert!" She stretched out her hand to him, but he made no move to take it. The blood flushed her cheek.

"Why will you not take my hand?" She moved a step nearer to him; but he rose to his feet and drew back.

With a passionate cry she fell on her knees before him, seized his hand and covered it with kisses.

"Do not repulse me. See me at your feet. Bert! let me save you. Do not spurn me, I beseech you."

"Save me? Miss Madison, you jest," replied Sumner in a voice made quiet by a strong effort.

"I do not jest. I can and *will* save you." Her eyes were fixed upon his face in eager intensity. With a shock of surprise Sumner was convinced that she spoke the truth; but he stood there looking down upon her with all the coolness and sternness of a judge.

"You tell me news," he said at length.

"Great God! do not doubt me now. I can save you. All I ask in return is that you take me to your heart again as your affianced wife, and I shall be content."

"Ah! I thought so. There is a price attached to your generosity."

"Do not be so merciless. If you only knew—"

"I *do* know!" broke from Sumner's lips as he flung her off. She reeled back, gasping for breath. Still upon her knees, she gazed up into his immovable countenance. For a full minute there was dead silence. Then Sumner spoke.

"Do not let us have any more mistakes. If my acquittal depends upon the plan you have mentioned, Miss Madison, I shall never be free."

"Why do you speak thus?" she asked as she rose to her feet.

"For many reasons," he replied, significantly.

The woman looked utterly despondent. There was a pause—an exciting pause.

"Surely," she said at length, "you can have no hope that Jewel will return to you. Even if you were free, General Benson will hold her to her promise."

"Do not speak her name," cried Sumner, fiercely. "It is sacrilege for your perjured lips to name her whom you have so tricked, deceived and abused. A bad promise is better broken than kept, and *my wife*, formerly Miss Jewel Bowen, felt the truth of the old adage when she consented to *marry me in this very cell.*" He could not repress the note of triumph in his voice as he uttered the words, but he was not prepared for what followed.

"No!" she cried out, with a passion terrible to see. "You have not dared—you could not dare—"

"Stop!" said Sumner sternly. "I warn you; do not try me too far. You will act wisely if you drop this whole matter and leave Washington and the society where you have queened it so long under false pretenses, for solitude and seclusion where you may escape the scorn of the world."

"What do you mean?" she demanded, her features pale to the very lips. She stood at bay, but in her face it could be seen that she measured his strength struggling with a new and horrible dread.

"God forbid that I should make you a social outcast!" he replied. "Need I speak plainer?"

Aurelia listened to him with the watchfulness of a tiger, who sees the hunter approaching, her strong, active brain was on the alert, but now her savage nature broke forth; she laughed aloud ferociously and then began a tirade of abuse that would have honored the slums.

Weary of the whole proceeding, disgusted with himself and the infatuation that had once enthralled him, he said at last, in desperation:

"Let us end this scene and all relations that have ever existed,—if you were as pure as snow, and I loved you as my other self, *I would never wed with one of colored blood, an octaroon!*"

Wordless, with corpse-like face and gleaming eyes she faced him unflinchingly.

"If I had a knife in my hand, and could stab you to the heart, I would do it!"

"I know you would!"

"But such weapons as I possess I will use. I will not fly—I will brave you to the last! If the world is to condemn me as the descendant of a race that I abhor, it shall never condemn me as a coward!"

Terrible though her sins might be—terrible her nature, she was but another type of the products of the accursed system of slavery—a victim of "man's inhumanity to man" that has made "countless millions mourn." There was something, too, that compelled admiration in this resolute standing to her guns with the determination to face the worst that fate might have in store for her. Something of all this Sumner felt, but beyond a certain point his New England philanthropy could not reach.

He bowed his head at her words and said,—"As you will, I have warned you!"

She stood at the full of her splendid stature, her eyes gleaming, her ashen lips firmly set, then she turned from him and gave the signal that brought the warden to let her out. Silently, without a backward look, she passed from the cell, and the prisoner was once more left in solitude.

At nine o'clock that same night, Chief Henson stood near a gas-lamp on the platform of the Baltimore & Ohio railroad station, glancing through a few lines from his colored agent, placed in his hands by plucky little Venus Johnson that very morning. The latter had gone on to the Bowen mansion to prepare the mistress for an unexpected arrival.

Chief Henson was particularly pleased with the ability shown by his colored detectives. Smith, the male agent, was a civil war veteran who had left a leg at Honey Hill, and on that account a grateful government had detailed him for duty on Chief Henson's staff of the secret service, and he had helped his chief out of many a difficult position, for which Mr. Henson was not slow nor meagre in his acknowledgments.

Five minutes after the train was in, Chief Henson saw Smith advancing toward him, accompanied by two females, closely veiled.

From out the swarming crowd the great detective stepped and motioned the man to follow with one of the females while he himself led the way with the other to the Bowen carriage outside the depot on the Avenue. Having placed the women in the carriage, and given the coachman his directions he and Smith entered a herdic and were driven rapidly to his office where they remained talking until the first hours of the morning.

Meanwhile Venus had resumed her duties as suddenly as she dropped them. The servants wondered among themselves, but not a comment was made. The news that the faithful girl brought seemed to restore Mrs. Bowen's lost vitality; she insisted on rising and being dressed, and received Jewel in her arms at the great entrance doors.

Supper was served in Mrs. Bowen's private parlor. Anyone who had entered the room would have been surprised at the kind solicitude and graciousness shown old Aunt Henny who was an honored guest. Mrs. Bowen's attention was evenly divided between her step-daughter and the old Negress. Venus waited on the company and for the time all thoughts of caste were forgotten while the representatives of two races met on the ground of mutual interest and regard.

Again and again Venus was called upon to repeat the story of her adventures.

"Yes, Mis' Bowen," she said for the twentieth time, "when I peeked in through that window and saw Miss Jewel an' gran sitting there talkin', I was plum crazy for a minute. Then I climb down as fas' as any squirrel an' I made tracks fer Mr. Smith, an' I told him what I'd seen. He says to me, says he, 'now, Venus, how in time 'm I goin' to get you into that house? We can't break the windows an' git in because they're ironed. 'Clar, says he, 'I don't know where I'm at.' Well, you know Mis' Bowen, I ain't a bit slow, no'm, if I do say it, an' I jus' thought hard for a minute, an' then *it*

PAULINE E. HOPKINS

struck me! Says I to him, 'git a move on dad there. You and me together mus' tote him to the house. When we git there you knock up the ol' woman an' make her let you put dad in; keep up all the fuss you can,' says I, 'an' in the kick-up why I'll sneak in and hide. You be waitin' by the front door, an' I'll have 'm out in a jiffy.' 'Good!' says he, 'two heads is better'n one if t'other is a sheep's head.' 'Much 'bliged for callin' me a fool,' says I. 'Welcome,' says he, 'but I take off my hat to you, young lady, I does, an' I'm goin' to give the chief a pointer to get you on the staff,' says he. 'Here's something to help the cause along,' an' he gave me a big bunch of keys an' a dark lantern. 'Try the keys on the big front door,' he says.

"Well, everything worked preticularly fine, Mis' Bowen. Dad was so drunk he couldn't stand, an' he didn't know whether he was afoot or ridin'. I slipped in all right, got my lady an' gran, an' got away as slick as grease.

"Dad ain't shown his head since; Mr. Henson's lookin' fer him, but I know he'll keep shy. I reckon he don't want to see ol' Ginral Benson fer one right smart spell. He's skeered all right—skeered to pieces."

Aunt Henny said nothing but once in a while she would nod her turbaned head in seeming perplexity, as she furtively watched every movement made by Mrs. Bowen. For her part, Mrs. Bowen seemed uneasy under the old woman's persistent regard.

XXXIV

A t last the eagerly looked for day of the Bradford murder trial came. Society had been on the qui vive ever since Sumner's arrest, and in twenty-four hours preceding the opening of the trial, public interest had gone up to almost unparralled intensity of excitement, which the facts already known of the case increased as the time for the crisis approached. Among these facts was the one of the disappearance of the principal witness for the defense. Extraordinary disclosures were anticipated, and the wildest rumors were afloat, some of which contained a few grains of truth.

The police told off for duty at the court had their work cut out for them, for crowds began to gather long before the opening hour, some to get in—some to see the notables in society, and the government swells arrive in quick succession. Before ten the room was crowded in every available place, and further admission was refused except to those engaged in the case.

Will Badger and Carroll West made their way slowly to their places among a nest of their set, including Mrs. Brewer and Mrs. Vanderpool and other friends of Sumner. Badger and West expected to be called by the defense.

The entrance of General Benson and Major Madison caused a flutter as they took their places in the space reserved for witnesses by the prosecution. Aurelia's tall, graceful form in a handsome dark gown followed the men. She received the various salutes which came to her from all parts of the crowded room with her usual polished elegance, but the fashionable world was puzzled; there was that in her appearance which suggested tragedy.

"Good heaven!" thought Carroll West, "I wonder if there can be any truth in the rumor I have just heard! How exquisite she looks, and pale—yes, and anxious too. I wonder if she cares for Sumner. I wonder what it all means anyhow. Heaven help her safely through this ordeal."

And she had need of all the sympathy that his kind heart could bestow, for the close of the trial would see her homeless, friendless, moneyless, under the ban of a terrible caste prejudice, doubly galling to one who, like herself, had no moral training with which to stem the current of adverse circumstances that had effectually wrecked her young life.

But all society missed its queen, Jewel Bowen, about whom the wildest reports were circulated, but no one knew the truth concerning her trip out of town. Jewel had an interview with her husband early in the morning, and it was decided that Mrs. Bowen and she would not enter the court room until the day when Aunt Henny was to give her testimony. Sure now of Cuthbert's acquittal the ladies were content to wait patiently the law's course.

General Benson was ignorant, as yet, of his prisoner's escape. Isaac had disappeared and Ma'am Griffin did not dare send him word. So in ignorance of the true state of affairs, he was his own imperious self.

Presently counsel were in their places. The Attorney General and a distinguished advocate for the government; and for the defence, ex-Governor Lowe, of Massachusetts, brilliant in criminal cases, had associated with him the Bowen family lawyer, Mr. Cameron, and—mightiest of all in interest of the accused, was the guidance and keen incisive intelligence of the sleuth hound E. Henson, Chief of the Secret Service Division.

Just after ten the buzz of talk suddenly ceased, hushed by the indescribable settling of a crowd long in expectancy, as the officials took their seats. The hush became breathless as the spectators waited the appearance of the one man for whom they had all gathered here that day—the prisoner. A buzz of admiration passed through the crowd as the accused passed to his seat. Erect, easy, dignified, Sumner took his place with the same grace that had marked his entrance into the crowded halls of pleasure. He met the steady stare of those thousand eyes cooly, steadily.

"How splendidly he bears himself!" whispered one to another. He had made a distinctly good impression.

Now came the necessary formalities. The jury to be called a mysterious algebraic proceeding to the uninitiated, where the value of the x is evolved to the amazement of the onlooker. The twelve men good and true were selected in this instance with very little trouble for a case so widely known and discussed. They were unchallenged and so, presently, were duly sworn; then the official question was put:

"How say you, prisoner at the bar—guilty or not guilty?"

The answer came in clear tones, low and steadily:

"Not guilty!"

The Attorney-General arose and began the trial with a recapitulation of the circumstances attending the murder of Elise Bradford, and the evidence adduced at the inquest. "And," said the learned counsel, "there can be little doubt that the secret of the crime lies in the victim's past. Clever detectives are of that opinion, and they argue logically enough that the fear of exposure of a guilty secret has been once more the motive of a terrible tragedy. The prisoner admits that he had been particularly attracted by the murdered girl at one time. It is known that they were alone together all that fatal Sunday afternoon in the deserted Treasury Building. He alone had exclusive opportunity to commit the crime. He admits that he gave her a glass of wine from the store kept for the chief's private use, but tells us that he left the victim in her usual health at eight that night, she refusing his escort home on a plea of wanting to pack up her belongings as she did not intend to return to work the next week having resigned her position. All this story will be proved a tissue of falsehoods unless the prisoner has the power to prove who *did* administer poison to the dead woman—if he did not do it himself—after he left the office on that fatal night.

The learned counsel weighed strongly all these stubborn facts, in an eloquent speech, which told with the audience. The case looked black for the accused. But the brilliant ex-governor smiled serenely as he glanced over the sea of faces. The trial dragged itself along with varying interest through two days. On the third day Aurelia Madison was called to prove the prisoner's gallantry and fickleness.

She did not glance at the prisoner as she passed to the witness box, impassive and lovely, but gave her evidence in a clear, concise manner that carried conviction with it. When she had finished, the tide of public opinion was strengthened against the prisoner. Like a whited sepulchre, full of hatred, she attempted to swear away the life of an innocent man to gratify her wish for revenge. By her testimony society learned for the first time the secret of the broken engagement between the accused and Jewel Bowen. Her story caused a sensation.

"Heavens! It looks strange!" whispered Mrs. Vanderpool to her neighbor Mrs. Brewer. But the end was not yet. As the witness turned to leave the stand, Governor Lowe said blandly:

"One moment, Miss Madison; I wish to ask you a few questions."

The girl paused; a white shade passed over the classic features.

"You are Major Madison's daughter?"

"Yes."

"He is your father?"

"Yes; so I am told," this last haughtily.

"Describe your mother as you remember her."

PAULINE E. HOPKINS

"I do not remember my mother—I never saw her. I know nothing of her."

"Where were you born?"

"In Jackson, Mississippi, I am told."

"How much money were you to receive the day Mr. Sumner married you and General Benson married Miss Jewel Bowen?"

"I don't understand your meaning."

"Weren't you to have a million given you the day you married Mr. Sumner? Yes or no."

"My dowry was a million dollars, if that is what you mean."

"Call it what you like, young lady; that was your share of the boodle with the man thrown in. That is all."

A buzz of excitement went over the crowded room. The prosecution looked at each other in blank amazement. Major Madison moved about uneasily in his seat. He was the next one called.

He knew very little of the prisoner. He was abroad at the time the engagement was made between the accused and Miss Madison, and could add little to the testimony already given. Knew Mr. Sumner as a visitor at houses where they were mutually acquainted, and had invited him to card parties in his own home.

Again the brilliant advocate asked but few questions.

"Miss Aurelia Madison is your daughter?"

"Yes."

"Born in Mississippi?" The Major nodded.

"Who was her mother?"

"My wife."

"The servant—slave or what might you call her—that stood to you in that relation? Is it not so?" blandly insinuated the questioner.

"We object," interposed the Attorney-General hurriedly to the evident relief of the enraged witness.

"Your objection is sustained," returned the judge.

Not at all disconcerted, Governor Lowe bowed pleasantly to judge, jury, lawyers and witnesses, in token of submission.

"Well, Major, did you ever know a man by the name of Walker? Or, weren't you known by that name once yourself?"

"Yes, I took that name when I was in money difficulties and hiding from my creditors."

"The man I mean was a slave-trader, notorious all over the South, who was one of the band of conspirators that murdered President Lincoln. Did you ever meet him?"

"I never have," replied the witness visibly disturbed.

"Business good, Major? How are the Arrow-Head gold mine securities turning out?"

"As well as I can expect."

"But not so well as you could wish; meantime you run a faro bank with your daughter as the snare and incidentally black mail and bunco a rich family to repair your shattered fortunes. That is all, major."

The excitement increased momentarily among the spectators. It was easy to perceive that Governor Lowe was but reserving his forces. The last witness called by the prosecution was General Benson, and nothing was elicited from him but the fact that the murdered woman had worked in his department for five years, was competent and faithful. He had no knowledge of her family nor connections outside the office. He had noticed that Mr. Sumner was somewhat partial to the good-looking stenographer, but he attached no importance to that fact, he had been young once himself. The audience was captivated by his winning manners and genial smiles. Governor Lowe took all his rights in the cross-examination.

"You gave your name as Charles Benson, General? Ever known to the public by any other name?"

For a moment the General was nonplussed.

"Sir!" with freezing haughtiness, "I do not understand you."

"My question was a plain one; but I will put it in another form—Weren't you originally known as St. Clair Enson? Isn't that the only name you have a right to wear?"

Sensation in the court room.

"We object," from the Attorney-General.

"Your objection is sustained," from the judge.

Governor Lowe was in no wise disconcerted. Again he bowed to the judge, then faced the witness still bland and smiling.

"How old was Miss Bradford when she entered your employ?"

"Eighteen, I believe."

"Awhile back you said you thought nothing of Mr. Sumner's attentions to the good-looking stenographer because you were young once yourself. I hear you are still very partial to the ladies, age has not deadened your sensibilities to their infinite charms. Did you not also offer attention to your good-looking stenographer? Did not your attentions become so warm that for various *pressing* reasons you promised Miss Bradford marriage?"

"Your questions are an outrage sir!"

"Plain yes or no, that is all I want."

"Most emphatically *No!*" thundered the witness, livid with rage. Again Governor Lowe bowed.

"Just one question more. Where were you on the night of the murder, in New York or Washington?"

"I was in New York."

The silence in the room was intense. One sensational question had followed another so rapidly that the vast throng of people found no expression for their wonderment save in silence. What was this man showing?

"Thank you, General, that is all."

That closed the prosecution.

"By Jove! more lies under this than we can see," whispered West to Badger.

Still the testimony of the state was clear on all essential points strengthened by numberless details pointing toward the guilt of the prisoner. So the third day ended, and the public felt repaid for their interest; it bade fair to go down in history as an extraordinary criminal incident.

XXXV

Thursday there was a settling down for a fresh start, an intense expectancy throughout the court. All felt that they were nearing a crisis. There were many new faces seen amid the throng and among them were the well-known features of Mrs. Bowen and Jewel, both closely shrouded in their sombre mourning robes.

Speculation was rife as to the line of the defense. What were they to hear now? What was, what could be the defense that could overpower the weight of evidence already given which seemed to make a fatal verdict a foregone conclusion? And yet, somehow, from the highest to the lowest of that hushed, excited throng, there was a curious, subtle feeling that some such resistless power lay in that reserved defence now about to be launched.

Perhaps the wish was "father to the thought." The calm confidence and lack of anxiety on the part of the defense hinted of powerful resources.

One lawyer remarked to another, "It looks as if he had a reserve force that will absolutely reverse the battle."

The prisoner sat with folded arms, cool, motionless as a statue, outwardly, but within, the man's blood was on fire.

Now Governor Lowe, with courtly manner and in sonorous tones, took up his part in the drama, beginning with the prisoner's alleged reckless youth as brought out in Miss Madison's testimony, mainly. He admitted that his client had been wild but not to the point of profligacy. He spoke tenderly of the absent, aged father—a helpless invalid—and his indulgence of an only child—motherless, too, from birth—proud, passionate, high-spirited, indulged, uncontrolled personally and in the expenditure of money, and that at this most dangerous period of a lad's life, the young man had met Miss Madison and succumbed to her fascinations, whom he intended to show was but a beautiful adventuress.

"The court," he said, "has been prejudiced against my client more by this woman's evidence than by any other testimony introduced for the government, added to that the sympathy of the whole audience has been aroused by the spectacle of a helpless woman's trust betrayed. Bah! Let me briefly unfold to you, gentlemen of the jury, the truth of the garbled tale so skilfully woven by a designing woman."

PAULINE E. HOPKINS

Governor Lowe then related the story of the past winter and the broken engagement, as known to our readers, with added facts to show that his client had in no way wronged the woman, who knew perfectly well what she was about, having previously become a party in a conspiracy designed to force Cuthbert Sumner into marriage, and at the same time, give control of the wealth of a well-known family into the hands of 'the gang' through the daughter of the house, the bethrothed of the accused.

Counsel then told of Aurelia's proposition of the day before the opening of the trial, and that the warden was a listener to the conversation between the prisoner and the witness; of her offer to give testimony at the trial which should free him, as she *knew the guilty party;* of the prisoner's scornful rejection of the offer, and his final retort when he told her that if she were as pure as snow, he would *never wed with one of colored blood!"*

Here the astute counsel paused for his telling point to take effect. Nor was he disappointed in his calculations, for its action was as an electric shock upon the aristocratic gathering. "And now, your honor, and gentlemen of the jury," he resumed with solemn impressiveness, "I am going to prove that my client's version of his connection with this affair is absolutely true; that he was not the perpetrator of the deed, but by the irony of Fate he has been placed in a position where it was next to impossible for him to prove his innocence. After Mr. Sumner left Miss Bradford in the office on that fatal Sunday night, a person who shall be nameless still, for a time, a man high in official life, a leader in society, did enter said office and talk with the murdered woman whom he had promised to marry in a short time. While there they took wine together, he himself pouring it out and placing in her portion the arsenic, grains of which were found in the empty glass, and in the woman's stomach after death, as testified to before you by the coroner, et al."

Again he paused, for he could feel the horror that thrilled the crowd.

"This man, gentlemen of the jury, was aware of the relation formerly existing between Miss Madison and the accused, and scoundrel that he is, used the woman as a tool for the base purpose of blackmail which fortunately a higher power has frustrated; and for other reasons as well, planned to leave Mr. Sumner so surrounded and connected with Miss Bradford as to render it impossible for him to extricate himself from the charge of murder."

The counsel's manner was most effective as he made his charges; the whole scene so dramatic that only a sensational melo-drama could have rivalled its power. A subdued "whew-w!" went from mouth to mouth as a faint glimmer of the truth began to show something of the possibilities of the line taken by the defence.

"Finally, thanks to the astuteness, experience and daring of the very clever detective, who has really had active charge of the whole case, and to whom the highest praise is due, a *witness of the crime will be produced!*"

The audience was astounded; they had hoped for a sensation; their desire was more than realized.

Governor Lowe wound up his brilliant effort with a slight peroration—knowing well its good effect upon a jury—and amidst murmurs of applause, was ready to call his witness.

The first was John Williams, Sumner's valet, who testified to the regularity of his master's habits and his abstemious living. During the cross-examination, John got angry and told the Attorney-General that the Sumners were top-crust, sure; and never one of them had been known to show up as underdone dough no half-and-half's, if it wasn't so he'd eat his own head; he didn't object to meeting any man who disputed the "pint," in a slugging match, the hardest to "fend" off. The judge called him to order and the witness took his seat in a towering rage over the "imperdunce" of Southern white folks, anyhow.

Then West and Badger took the stand to refute the charge of inveterate gambling that had been made against the prisoner by Miss Madison. West was questioned only about Sumner and not of his own connection with the Madisons for which he was devoutly thankful. The fact was brought out that the Madison house was a gambling palace where men were fleeced of money for the sake of the smiles of the beautiful Aurelia, by the young fellow's tale of Sumner's warning to him against allowing himself to be ensnared by the Madison clique.

The watchmen and one or two cleaners were also placed upon the stand to prove that Mr. Sumner *did* leave the Treasury Building at the hour sworn to by him.

After that the motherless and worse than fatherless child—a beautiful fair-haired boy, was led forward and stood upon a chair in the witness-box to give emphasis to the point made by counsel that the dead woman had a pressing claim upon some man who wished to rid himself of her as encumbrance. Some of the women spectators wept, and many men felt uncomfortable about the eyes. Then Gov. Lowe said: "I call Aunt Henny Sargeant." Two officers led the tottering old Negress from the ante-room to the witness chair. Aunt Henny had aged preceptibly since her imprisonment, but her faculties were as keen as ever. As she entered the crowded court-room, there was a cry, quickly suppressed, from the back seats of the room:

"Oliver, that's yer granny! My God, she's livin' yet!"

"Aunt Henny, I believe you have been in the employ of the government at the Treasury Building?"

"Yes, honey, I has."

"Tell the court how you came to be employed."

"Well, honey, I foun' a big pile o' greenbacks—mus' a bin 'bout a million dollars, I reckon,—one night when I was sweepin', an' I jes' froze to 'em all night. I neber turned 'em loose 'til de officers come in de mornin'; money's a mighty onsartin' article, chillun. People won' steal if they don' get a chance, dat's my b'lief. Then de Presidun' an' lots of other gemman made a big furze over me, an' dey done gib me my job fer life."

"Now, Aunt Henny, do you remember where you were on Sunday evening, March 20, between six and ten o'clock?"

"Yas, honey, I does, fer I warn't in bed, nuther was I to home. I was at the Building doin' some dustin' in Gin'ral Benson's 'partmen', that I'd lef over from the afternoon befo'."

"Yes; well tell us what happened that evening at the Building."

"Well, honey, I wen' in pas' the watchman, who arst me wha' I was after, an' I tol' him. Den I wen' up to Gin'ral Benson's 'partmen', which was whar I'd lef' off. I has a skilton key dat let's me git in whar I wants to go. After I'd been in 'bout an hour, I hearn people talkin' in one ob de rooms—the private office—an' I goes 'cross de entry an' peeks roun' de corner ob de po'ter—"

"The what?" interrupted the judge.

"Po'ter, massa jedge; don' yer kno' what a po'ter am?"

"She means, portière, your honor," explained Gov. Lowe, with a smile. "Go on, aunty."

"I peeked 'roun' de corner ob de po'ter, an' I seed Miss Bradford an' de Gin'ral settin' talkin' as budge as two buzzards. He jes was makin' time sparkin' her like eny young fellar, an' fer a mon as ol' as I kno' *he* is, I tell you, gemmen, he was jes' makin' dat po' gal b'lieve de moon was made o' green cheese an' he'd got the fus' slice."

A suppressed laugh rippled through the room.

"What happened then?"

"Honey, my cur'osity was bilin' hot to see what was gwine on, an' I keep peekin' an' peekin'; byme-by I hearn de glasses clickin', an' I took another look, 'cause, tho' I'm a temprunce 'ooman, an' I b'long to de High Co't o' Gethsemne, an' de Daughters ob de Bridal Veil, I neber b'lieve dat good wine is gwine ter harm on' ol' rheumatiz 'ooman like me; no, sah; dar ain't none o' yer stiff-necked temprunce 'bout yer Aunt Henny; I ain't no better than quality. I know'd dat was good stuff dat de chief had in thar 'cause I'd done taste some ob it befo', and' I'd promis' myself to taste it agin dat very night as soon as dat couple was gone. While I was thinkin' bout it, de Gin'ral turned his back to Miss Bradford as he poured de wine from de 'canter, an' dat brung him full facin' me what I was a peekin' at him, an' bless my soul, gemman, I seed dat villyun drap somethin' white inter de glass an' then turn 'roun' an' han' it to Miss Bradford. I was dat skeered I thought I'd drap, an' while I was a makin' up my min' what do so, suddintly she throwed up both arms an' screeched out *"My God, Charles, you've pizened!"*

Great sensation in the court, and the crier restored order.

"What happened then, Aunty?"

"Bless my soul, honey, I don't know what did happen, somethin' dat neber come across me in all my life befo'. I tell you, gemmen, it takes somethin' to make a colored woman faint, but dat's jes' wha' I did, massa jedge; when I seed dat po gal fro up her arms an' hern her screech I los' all purchase ob myself, and I ain't got over it yet."

The old negress rocked herself to and fro in her chair. She made a weird picture, her large eyes peering out from behind the silver-bowed glasses, her turbaned head and large, gold-hoop earrings, and a spotless white handkerchief crossed on her breast over the neat gingham dress.

"And then, Aunty?" gently prompted Gov. Lowe.

"When I come to myself agin, I was in prison, an' my own son-in-law was a keepin' me locked up."

"Was that the reason you did not inform the authorities of what you had seen?" asked the judge.

"Yas, sah; yas, massa jedge."

"Now, Aunt Henny, I want you to tell the court when and where you knew General Benson before you saw him in the employ of the government," said Gov. Lowe.

"We object, your honor," promptly interrupted the Attorney-General.

"The objection is not well taken, Mr. Attorney-General. I think Gov. Lowe has a right to put the answer in evidence. We are not here to defeat the ends of justice. Proceed, Aunt Henny."

"He ain't Gin'ral Benson no more'n I'm a white 'ooman. His name's St. Clair Enson; he was born nex' do' to de Sargeant place on the Enson plantation. Ise one ob de fus' ones what held him when he was born. Ise got a scar on me, jedge, where dat imp ob de debbil hit me wid a block ob wood when he warn't but seven years ol'. Fus' time I seed him in dat 'partmen' I know'd him time I sot my eye on him, an' den I know'd thar'd be rucktions kicked up, fer ef eber der was a born lim' o' de debbil it's dat same St. Clair Enson."

"That will do, aunty. Perhaps my legal brother may wish to cross-examine."

The Attorney-General then took the witness in hand and conducted a skilful cross-examination without shaking the old woman's testimony. Finally he said:

"One last question and I am through; you spoke of your son-in-law—what has he to do with General Benson?"

"He!" snorted Aunt Henny indignantly, "thar ain't no kind ob devilmen' St. Clair Enson was ever mixed up in dat Ike Johnson warn't dar to help him. Ike's my gal's husban'; he's Gin'ral Benson's valley; he was gave to St. Clair Enson when dat debbil was a baby in de cradle."

During the testimony of this last witness, Gen. Benson and Maj. Madison were busily talking to each other, with an occasional word to the Attorney-General.

As Aunt Henny retired to her seat in the ante-room. Gov. Lowe arose, and in an impassioned speech moved the prisoner's release, and the taking into custody of the man really guilty—General Benson.

Scarcely waiting for him to finish, the Attorney-General sprang to his feet and attacked the defense fiercely. Then ensued a scene unparalleled in the history of courts of justice.

"On what would you base such an unheard of precedent? on the evidence of a Negress? Would you impugn the honor of a brilliant soldier, a brave gentleman—courteous, genial, standing flawless before the eyes of the entire country? Such a man as General Benson cannot be condemned and suspicioned by the idiotic ramblings of an ignorant *nigger* brought here by the defense to divert attention from the real criminal, who attempts to shield himself under the influence of the Bowen millions. In the same spirit that has actuated my legal brother, while deprecating violence of any kind as beneath the dignity of our calling, I would feel myself justified in sounding the slogan of the South—lynch-law! if I thought this honorable body could be influenced to so unjust a course as is suggested by Gov. Lowe."

Instantly a chorus of voices took up the refrain—"That's the talk! No nigger's word against a white man! This is a white man's country yet!"

For a brief space, judge, jury and advocates were non-plussed; women shrieked and men flinched, not knowing what the end might be. But above the uproar, which was answered by the crowd outside, rang the voice of the police-sargeant as he formed his men in line at the door ready to charge the would-be violators of the peace. Before the determined front of the police, the crowd quieted down and order was restored.

Then Gov. Lowe arose once more:

"May it please your honor, and gentlemen of the jury, I have still another witness to present, and the last one, I call the chief of the Secret Service Division."

Once again there was silence in the room. Curiosity was on tiptoe. Many men in high places knew the chief well by reputation but had never met him. He had successfully coped with many important cases and had saved the government millions of dollars. He entered the witness-box calmly as if oblivious of the curiosity of the crowd.

"Mr. Henson, I believe that for any years you have been in the secret service."

"Yes, for fifteen years I have served the government in the capacity of a detective. Previous to that time I was a soldier and served three years, on the Federal side, at the front."

"Now, Mr. Henson, we will ask you to tell the court what you know of this case, in your own way."

At the first sound of his voice, Mrs. Bowen, who up till this time had been sitting with lowered veil, suddenly swept it one side and stared at the man in the witness-box with a strained, startled gaze. His eyes, wandering over the audience, rested on her white face. For one instant he wavered and seemed to hesitate, then by an effort he regained his composure and began his story.

"I was first called into this case by Miss Jewel Bowen. I took hold of it because of the interest she aroused in my mind, and out of pity for her distress. After I met and conversed with Mr. Sumner, I was satisfied in my own mind of his innocence, and that he was the victim of a conspiracy."

In a brief, incisive way, which carried weight to many doubting minds, he detailed the substance of the information he had obtained.

"Being brought into the issues growing out of the intimacy between General Benson and the Bowen family because of his engagement to Miss Bowen, I, very naturally, was placed in charge of the business of accumulating the facts in regard to Senator Bowen's death in New York. I have found out that he made no will while there, and that the one offered here for probate by Gen. Benson *is a forgery.*

"After Senator Bowen's death his daughter was abducted, and in the search which I caused to be made for her, we found, concealed in the same house, the Negress, Aunt Henny. So, step by step, we have been able to fix the murder of Miss Bradford, the forged will of Senator Bowen, the abduction of Miss Bowen and of Aunt Henny—the most important witness in this case—upon a band of conspirators numbering three people, all well known in society and having the entrée to the best houses."

"Do we quite understand you, Mr. Henson," asked the judge, "that in your opinion the prisoner at the bar has been the victim?"

"Yes, your honor, but only because he stood in the way of their obtaining the Bowen millions. That was the intention in the start— to obtain that immense fortune. Other than the strong attachment existing between Miss Bowen and Mr. Sumner, he would never have been molested.

"It now becomes my duty to make a statement in regard to the testimony of the last witness."

His face was set and stern. It was evident that he struggled to maintain his composure.

"What she has said concerning Gen. Benson is absolutely true. It is a long story, gentlemen, but I will be as brief as possible."

Then in graphic words that held the vast crowd spellbound, he told the story of Ellis and St. Clair Enson, as our readers already know it up to the discovery of Hagar's African descent. The judge forgot his dignity, a shock waved over the court-room. People seemed not to breathe, the interest was so intense, as they listened to the burning words of the speaker.

"When Ellis Enson returned home after completing his arrangements for taking his wife abroad, he was set upon in Enson woods by his brother and the unprincipled slave driver, Walker, and beaten into unconsciousness. When he came to himself he was in South Carolina enrolled as a member of the Confederate army. Here he remained until a good opportunity offered, when he deserted and returned home to find that his wife, child and slaves (of whom Aunt Henny was a valued house servant), had been driven to the Washington market, where his wife in desperation had thrown herself and infant into the Potomac river.

"Stripped of his fortune, home and family, cursing God and man, he entered the army on the Federal side, seeking death, but determined to carry destruction first to those who had so cruelly wronged him. But death comes not for the asking, and the ways of God are inscrutable."

He paused and passed his hand over his beaded forehead. Gen. Benson sat like a marble statue, and his nails reddened where he gripped the arms of his chair. The sound of voices came in from the street through the open window. Inside there was silence like the grave.

"Ellis Enson always supposed that his brother St. Clair stayed abroad where he had hidden after he was found guilty as one of the conspirators against the life of President Lincoln, but when I was called into this case, I found that he was in this country, serving the government he had basely betrayed, and still steeped in crime, along with his pal, Walker. Gentlemen, General Benson is St. Clair Enson, and his friend, Major Madison, is the notorious trader, Walker.

"As for me, I no longer need to conceal my identity. Gentlemen—" he gasped and faltered, and put his hand to his throat as though the words choked him.

"General Benson is my brother—I am Ellis Enson!"

As he finished speaking Mrs. Bowen sprang to her feet with a scream; she made a step towards him—then stopped—while these words thrilled the hearts of the listeners:

"Ellis! Ellis! I am Hagar!"

PAULINE E. HOPKINS

XXXVI

At Mrs. Bowen's impassioned cry, Chief Henson turned an appealing look upon the judge, who bowed his head as if understanding the mute question; he reached the fainting woman's side with one stride, and lifted her tenderly in his strong arms, then he bore her from the crowded room, followed by the maid and weeping step-daughter. The spectators fell back respectfully before the stern man over whose white face great tears, that did not shame his manhood, coursed unheeded.

When the excitement incident to Chief Henson's story (or Ellis Enson, as we must now call him) had somewhat subsided, the trial was resumed.

Governor Lowe called no other witnesses, but at once rose to address the jury for the prisoner, and never, perhaps, had the great politician and leader been more eloquently brilliant than on that occasion. He ranged up the whole mass of evidence with a bold and masterly grasp that could not be outrivalled.

In burning words he laid bare the details of the plot for millions, explaining that when General Benson found himself defeated in all directions, and threatened with exposure by the woman he had ruined, if he persisted in marrying Miss Bowen, he had conceived the idea of a diabolical deed—to murder Miss Bradford and allow the guilt to rest upon Cuthbert Sumner, thus ridding himself of two obstacles at one stroke.

He painted vividly the stealthy return of General Benson from New York to Washington, his arrival at the Treasury Building, his concealment in the great wardrobes, with which his department was supplied, his long wait for the departure of Mr. Sumner, during which he heard the dead woman's confession to the secretary; his meeting with Miss Bradford, down to the last awful move in the tragedy witnessed by the old Negress, Aunt Henny, who fainted with horror at the tragedy of the night. "He returned to New York as secretly as he left the city," continued the Governor, "because his flight had occurred on the Sabbath, when all the members of the committee were bent on individual pleasure, and as he was in his place on Monday morning no one noticed his absence. Then, in his devotion to his employer's interests, the faithful servant and ex-slave, Isaac Johnson, knowing no law save the will of his former owner, faithful to the traditions of slavery still, concealed the only witness of the crime, failing only in one point—that he did not murder the old woman (his mother-in-law) as commanded by General Benson, but kept her in confinement. In attempting to force Miss Bowen to marry him by abducting her and concealing her in an old country house, detectives searching for her found the missing witness, whom we have heard here today.

"The romance of the situation is enhanced by the fact that in just retribution the brother so inhumanly betrayed and abandoned, even as was Joseph of old, by his brethren, was the Nemesis placed upon the criminal's track to put him in the power of outraged justice."

With a splendid peroration, and a tender reference to the unexpected meeting of the cruelly-separated husband and wife, the Governor sat down and the Attorney-General followed him in a speech of great ability; but he knew the verdict was a foregone one, that his own remarks were but a form, that the weight of evidence in "this most extraordinary case" left him but one course. He felt, too, a savage bitterness towards Benson or Enson, that made him pant for the trial which he knew must come. In fact, officers were already stationed near the precious trio ready to take them in charge the moment all preliminary proceedings were over.

The Attorney-General concluded his speech with the words, "Justice is all that we are seeking, gentlemen of the jury, and in your hands I leave the prisoner's interests, knowing that you will return a verdict in accordance with the evidence given, that will give us all the right to welcome Mr. Sumner among us again fully reinstated in the confidence and esteem of the whole country."

The judge's charge followed, with a finely-balanced summing up which displayed all the power and glory of English jurisprudence; even the prisoner followed him with admiring forgetfulness of self. Finally the case was given to the jury; they consulted together a few minutes for the sake of appearances, without leaving their seats, then the foreman rose and announced: "We find the prisoner not guilty."

"Is this your verdict, Mr. Foreman?" asked the clerk.

"It is," he answered.

"So say you all, gentlemen of the jury?"

"We do," in chorus from the box.

If there had been much doubt which way public opinion and sympathy had set during the trial, there was absolutely none when the verdict "not guilty" was given, for the long-repressed excitement found vent in an outburst of applause that for a time defied official control. Like wildfire the news spread to the people outside, and cheer after cheer rent the air, the crowd swaying and pushing in a vain attempt to get a glimpse of the late prisoner; but as soon as he could, Sumner left in a carriage with Badger and West, faithful John Williams on the box, for his apartments, and later the Bowen mansion.

Sumner could never have told very precisely what passed after the verdict had been given, save that as in a dizzy dream he heard applause within and cheers without; then he saw the fetters on the wrists of General Benson and saw him hurried from the room between two officers, followed by Major Madison and Aurelia. The two villains had sat nonplussed and dumbfounded during the stirring events just chronicled, making no effort to escape. Governor Lowe rushed the business of their arrest, and this was ably seconded by the judge and the Attorney-General.

Presently Sumner found himself in a mass of humanity in a room with Governor Lowe and Mr. Cameron, receiving congratulations and invitations. He thanked all in his pleasant way and declined; he could not bear society just yet.

That verdict gave back life to Jewel and to him, but he was unhappy and anxious over her situation with her stepmother; the wonderful revelation of Mrs. Bowen's identity with the slave Hagar was a shock to him. It was a delicate situation, but, of course, he told himself, Mrs. Bowen could see that with all sympathy for her and her sad story, it was impossible for Jewel to be longer associated with her in so close a relationship as that of mother and daughter. He comforted himself with the thought that the unfortunate woman was the second wife of Senator Bowen, and that was a fortunate fact. He would do all that he could for Mrs. Bowen, but the social position of Mrs. Sumner demanded a prompt separation.

Cuthbert Sumner was born with a noble nature; his faults were those caused by environment and tradition. Chivalrous, generous-hearted—a manly man in the fullest meaning of the term—yet born and bred in an atmosphere which approved of freedom and qualified equality for the Negro, he had never considered for one moment the remote contingency of actual social contact with this unfortunate people.

He had heard the Negro question discussed in all its phases during his student life at "Fair Harvard," and had even contributed a paper to a local weekly in which he had warmly championed their cause; but so had he championed the cause of the dumb and helpless creatures in the animal world about him. He gave large sums to Negro colleges and on the same princpal gave liberally to the Society for the Prevention of Cruelty to Animals, and endowed a refuge for homeless cats. Horses, dogs, cats, and Negroes were classed together in his mind as of the brute creation whose sufferings it was his duty to help alleviate.

And Jewel? She, too, felt that straining of the heart's chords as she waited in her private sitting room for her lover-husband. She was alone. Ellis Enson was with her stepmother. After Mrs. Bowen returned to consciousness, Jewel had stolen away unnoticed by the strangely reunited pair, leaving them in sacred seclusion.

She held the evening paper in her hand. It contained a column headed, "Sensational Ending of the Famous Bradford Tragedy."

After detailing the day's events, the editor gave the story of the white slave Hagar (Mrs. Bowen), and her extraordinary recognition of her former husband and master in the person of Chief Henson of the Secret Service Division. The editor went on to say:

"No trace of woman or child was found after her leap over the bridge into the river. She was supposed to have been drowned. The woman, however, was picked up by a Negro oyster-digger and concealed in his hut for days. At the breaking out of the war she drifted to California and in a few years married the wealthy miner, Zenas Bowen. This story, showing, as it does, the ease with which beautiful half-breeds may enter our best society without detection, is a source of anxiety to the white citizens of our country. At this rate the effects of slavery can never be eradicated, and our most distinguished families are not immune from contact with this mongrel race. Mrs. Bowen has our sympathy, but we cannot, even for such a leader as she has been, unlock the gates of caste and bid her enter. Posterity forbids it. We wait the action of Mr. Ellis Enson (Chief Henson) with impatience, praying that sentiment may not overcome the dictates of duty."

Jewel's tender heart was full of pity and love for her stepmother. Now she knew for the first time whence came the fountain of love so freely lavished upon her by this heartbroken mother.

"How she must have suffered," murmured the girl to herself. Then, as she mentally counted up the years that had passed since the events chronicled by the paper, she said aloud in some surprise, "Why, I must be about the age of the poor baby girl. How wonderful!" She was glad to be alone after all these weeks of tempest and today's climax, with its reaction. Mingled with her own joy at Cuthbert's release was a silent, wordless awe of Chief Henson's declaration in the court room and her stepmother's avowal. But, strange to say, the girl felt none of the repugnance that the announcement of Mrs. Bowen's origin had brought to Sumner. Her own happiness was so great that all worldly selfishness was swept away.

Hush! She suddenly rose from the couch where she was sitting, with wide eves and quivering form, hearing the soft musical voice outside, so yearned for all these dreadful weeks, now fast disappearing like a horrible nightmare before the rosy glow of Hope's enchanting rays. She saw the door open and shut—saw Cuthbert's tall form enter—she sank upon the couch, putting out her hands to him in a trustful, childlike way.

Without a word he flung himself beside her and folded her in his arms with a passion and strength that were resistless.

"Mine at last! My darling! My one love—my wife!" For a second there was a blank—life itself seemed to stand still, and time and space were obliterated. "Husband!" she said at length with smothered passion. He stopped and kissed her in a strange, awed way—silently, solemnly, as a man might who had been so near the grave—heart to heart, soul to soul, conscious only in that supreme moment paradise was touched! So for some minutes they sat in soul communion. Sumner broke the silence after a time. "Heaven only can reward Chief Henson and Venus Johnson for their rescue of you, my treasure. May heaven forget me if I ever forget their devotion to my dear wife. I tell you, Jewel, I was maddened when the news was brought to me of your abduction. I would have been a murderer in truth could I have been free for one moment to meet Benson!"

The wife's lips touched his softly, lovingly—true woman to the core—as a "ministering angel."

"But, dearest, God protected me."

There was another eloquent pause. Then Sumner said abruptly:

"Tomorrow our marriage must be properly advertised. It is Thursday now; on Monday you must come with me to my father. After you have seen him, you shall plan our future."

Jewel laid her head against him. "Your wishes are mine, Cuthbert."

Then they talked a while of the strange revelations made at the trial, of the discovery of Negro blood in Aurelia Madison and Mrs. Bowen.

"With the knowledge that we now possess of her origin, we can no longer wonder at her wicked duplicity," said Sumner.

"That is true in her case," replied Jewel, "but a truer, sweeter, more perfect woman than mamma does not live on the earth; how do you account for it?"

"Depend upon it, those characteristics are but an accident of environment, not the true nature of her parent stock. I have always heard that the Negro race excelled in low cunning."

"True," repeated Jewel, dreamily, "but then there are Venus and Aunt Henny."

"Yes, and my faithful John. I suppose these exceptions prove the rule. Still I am thankful that Mrs. Bowen is only your step-mother."

Then they drifted back into their lovers' talk once more.

> *"Look thro' mine eyes with thine, true wife,*
> *Round my true heart thine arms entwine;*
> *My other dearer life in life,*
> *Look thro' my very soul with thine!"*

It was midnight when the wedded lovers separated. In the hall they met Ellis Enson, as we shall hereafter call him.

The man's face wore a look of solemn joy. He shook Jewel's hand silently. He urged Sumner to go to his room with him and spend the night, for he had much to say to him in regard to the late trial. Sumner felt obliged to accept the invitation, and the two men went away together.

The early morning hours found them still talking over the trial, but their greatest interest was in the story of the elder man—the strange trials in two lives.

"How do you intend to fix it?" questioned Sumner.

"Of course Mrs. Bowen is very much shaken, but we shall be quietly remarried on Sunday, and then I shall take my wife away. When we return I hope to have possession of Enson Hall, where we shall take up our permanent abode. I hand in my resignation today, to take immediate effect."

"I honor you for your resolution, Enson, but indeed I have not your strength of character. I could never solve the social problem in that high-handed manner. Have you no fear of public opinion?"

"My dear boy, I know just where you are. I went all through the old arguments from your point of view twenty years ago. I wavered and wavered, but nature was stronger than prejudice. I have suffered the torments of hell since I lost my wife and child."

He rose from his seat and strode once down the room, then back again, pausing before the young man.

"Sumner," he said, with impressive solemnity, "race prejudice is all right in theory, but when a man tries to practice it against the laws which govern human life and action, there's a weary journey ahead of him, and he's not got to die to realize the tortures of the damned. This idea of race separation is carried to an extreme point and will, in time, kill itself. Amalgamation has taken place; it will continue, and no finite power can stop it."

"But, my dear Enson, you do not countenance such a such a—well—terrible action as a wholesale union between whites and blacks? Think of it, my dear man! Think of our refinement and intelligence linked to such black bestiality as we find in the slums of this or any other great city where Negroes predominate!"

Enson smiled at the other's vehemence.

"Certainly not, Sumner; but, on the other hand, take the case of Aurelia Madison. Did you ever behold a more gorgeously beautiful woman, or one more fastidiously refined? Had her moral development been equal to her other attainments, and you had loved her, how could you endure to have a narrow, beastly prejudice alone separate you from the woman pre-destined for your life-companion? It is in such cases that the law of caste is most cruel in its results."

"I think that the knowledge of her origin would kill all desire in me," replied Sumner. "The mere thought of the grinning, toothless black hag that was her foreparent would forever rise between us. I am willing to allow the Negroes education, to see them acquire business, money, and social status within a certain environment. I am not averse even to their attaining political power. Farther than this, I am not prepared to go."

"And this is the sum total of what Puritan New England philanthropy will allow—every privilege but the vital one of deciding a question of the commonest personal liberty which is the fundamental principle of the holy family tie."

"When one considers the ignorance, poverty and recent degradation of this people, I feel that my position is well taken," persisted Sumner. "Ought we not, as Anglo-Saxons, keep the fountain head of of our racial stream as unpolluted as possible?"

Enson smiled sadly; a holy light for one instant illumined the scarred face of the veteran:

"'A boy's will is the wind's will, And the thoughts of youth are long, long thoughts,'" he quoted softly. "You will learn one day that there is a higher law than that enacted by any earthly tribunal, and I believe that you will then find your nature nobler than you know."

"You make me feel uncanny, Enson, with your visionary ideas. Thank God, I have my wife; there I am safety anchored."

"Amen!" supplemented Enson softly, as they clasped hands in a warm goodnight.

XXXVII

O n Friday the court room was again crowded to the doors by spectators eager to view the closing scenes in the celebrated case.

The soi-disant General Benson was arraigned on a charge of wilfully murdering Elise Bradford, and was committed for trial in October. Major Madison, or Walker, the ex-slave driver, and his daughter Aurelia were also in court, Madison for forgery in connection with Senator Bowen's will.

Nothing criminal was charged against Aurelia; in fact, no one desired to inflict more punishment on the unfortunate woman, and when she left the court room that day she vanished forever from public view.

Deadly pale, but proudly self-possessed, Ellis Enson gave his testimony at the hearing, fixing a steadfast, unflinching gaze on the livid, haggard face that glared back with sullen hate and fear in every line. So for a moment of dead silence, of untold pain to one, those two men, sons of one father, but with a bridgeless gulf between them, stood face to face after many years.

The story had to be told again, however deeply it racked one soul to be forced to give deadly testimony against the murderer, who, outcast by his own evil deeds, was still his father's son. The ghastly facts stood out too clearly for hesitation, and St. Clair Enson, alias Gen. Charles Benson, was remanded for trial.

Owing to the unsavory character of the prisoner extra precautions were taken by the warden to prevent a rescue or an escape.

At one o'clock Saturday morning the guard upon the outer wall that surrounded the jail saw a shadow that seemed to move. At first he thought it a stray cat or dog, then as he watched he saw that it stole along the wall suspiciously; obedient to orders, he fired; the shadow fell to earth.

The men who came running at the sound of the shots bore the wounded man back into the jail, where they found that their burden was the body of St. Clair Enson, and that he was dead. The guard's bullet had taken a fatal effect.

In the prisoner's bed crouched Isaac Johnson in a vain endeavor to cover up his former owner's flight. A gaping hole at one side of the cell told where an entrance had been effected. How Isaac had managed to cut his way through the solid masonry always remained a mystery to the authorities.

Thus ended St. Clair Enson's career of vice and crime. Walker, alias Major Madison, died in the state prison.

XXXVIII

Late Saturday afternoon, Hagar, so long known to us as Mrs. Bowen, reclined in semi-invalid fashion on the couch in her boudoir. She had exchanged her deep mourning for a house dress of white cashmere, profusely touched with costly lace. Her dark hair, showing scarcely a touch of silver, was closely coiled at the back of her shapely head. In spite of a shade of sadness her countenance was serene.

She was happy—happier than she had ever hoped to be in this life. True, no callers begged admittance into the grand mansion, no cards overflowed the receivers in the spacious entrance hall, since the sensational items disclosing her identity had appeared in the columns of the daily press; that fact did not disconcert her in the least. One thing alone troubled her,—Sumner's determination to separate her from Jewel.

The tender-hearted woman who had been his champion and friend throughout dark days of suspicion and despair, could not understand his antipathy to her. The two ladies did not worry themselves unduly, however, trusting that time and their united persuasions would win him to a better frame of mind.

The ceremony of the morrow would see her united to the husband of her youth. She thought only of that.

Ellis wished to settle the whole of Senator Bowen's immense fortune upon Jewel, but the latter would not hear of so unjust a proceeding. So the mansion was to be left in the care of Marthy Johnson, Aunt Henny and Oliver, while Mr. and Mrs. Enson were abroad. Venus was to go to Massachusetts with her young mistress, and the plan was that she and John Williams should be married about Christmas. The travellers were to start on their journeys early Monday morning. Suddenly Senator Bowen's last words, "The little hair trunk!" flashed across the lady's mind. It had been his in his first wife's time. He had clung to it through poverty and prosperity. It was in the late Senator's dressing-room which opened into the room where she was lying. Secretly blaming herself for neglecting the shabby object of his love and care, Hagar rose hastily and passed into the adjoining room.

Everything was as he had left it. How lonely it seemed without the jovial, genial presence of the man who had saved her from despair. Tears came to her eyes as she stood gazing upon familiar objects, each bearing the personality of the man who had gathered them about him.

Over in a corner stood the little hair trunk. She moved slowly toward it, and presently was on her knees before it with the lid thrown back.

She sat there, prone upon the floor, for a time, gazing in mute sadness upon the contents—shabby, peculiarly made garments of the fashion in vogue before the war, mementoes of that other wife of his young manhood, and, strange mixture, a number of clay pipes, burned black by use, and fishing tackle, all mingled in a motley heap.

She took up the first wife's picture, opened the case and gazed into the eyes of the blowzy girlish face in its hideous cape bonnet, the long spiral curls falling outside the ruche that faced the head covering. Not a pretty face; no, but honesty and kindliness of heart were written there, silently claiming their tribute, turning the contemptuous smile to gentle reverence.

Hagar closed the case softly and placed it beside her on the floor with the other articles which her sense of neatness and order had caused her to fold carefully in regular piles, ready to replace in the shabby receptacle.

She had often wondered who Jewel resembled and where she had obtained the dainty, high-bred elegance of face and figure; surely not from father nor mother. Today her curiosity was again aroused; the desire to know pursued her so persistently that she was amazed.

The small velvet case containing Senator Bowen's daguerrotype, taken in early youth, had a peculiar fascination for her. His face smiled up at her, round, jolly, rubicund, a dimple in his chin and a laugh in his eyes, which the straight hair, combed flatly to the sides of his head, could not render sedate. Hagar felt a film gather to her eyes. What a god he had been to her! How devoted! How gentle! And he was a man of strong intellect and staunch integrity. She had no cause to be ashamed of him. He had saved her from despair. Next to her God she placed this man, whom she knew instinctively would never have forsaken her, never for one instant would he have wavered from his constancy to her, no matter what the cause, were she but true to him.

Ellis had come back to her; yes, but although love forgave, love worshipped at his shrine, love could not blot out the bitter memory of the time when he had failed her.

She closed the case with a nervous click, and went on with her sorting and folding. The very last thing that she found was a brown paper parcel, tied with coarse string. She undid the knot with the feeling of pride which attends the operation of succeeding in untying a

PAULINE E. HOPKINS

string without cutting it. She smoothed out the kinks and curls and laid it carefully at her side ready for use again; then she removed the paper, expecting to see a man's wearing apparel; to her surprise a roll of white cashmere, yellow with age, met her eyes; it was wrapped about other articles. The kneeling woman felt the room spinning round her as she held the packet in her hand. There was something vaguely familiar in that ordinary piece of yellow cashmere; one side being visible showed a deep embroidered design tracing the edge of the deep hem. She could not move. Every muscle was paralyzed, and a flood of memories rushed in turmoil through her brain.

Trembling, breathless with excitement, she began to unroll the bundle. The last fold, as it fell apart, revealed the outer covering to be an infant's cloak of richest material and beautifully embroidered. With quivering fingers the agitated woman continued to shake out the garments that the cloak enfolded—a tiny dress, dainty skirts, a face cap—in short, all the articles necessary to make up the attire of a child of love and wealth.

"Oh, merciful heaven! How came these here?" she whispered with white lips, as she pressed each tiny garment to her lips, and rained tremulous kisses on the exquisite lace cap. "My baby, my baby!"

She threw herself upon the floor and lay there weeping scalding tears. Before her lay the garments that her own hands had fashioned twenty years before, for the little daughter who had come to bless the union of Ellis Enson and herself. Half in terror she gazed upon them as upon the ghost of one long since departed. She made a movement and a metallic sound drew her attention to an object that slipped from among the clothing to the floor. It was a gold chain, from which depended a locket.

"My mother's locket!" she gasped. "Ah! Until this hour I had forgotten it; it was about my darling's neck when last I dressed her. My God! How comes it here? Why do I find it in Zenas Bowen's trunk?"

She touched a spring and the outer lid sprang back, showing a piece of paper pressed in the space usually devoted to pictures. The paper fell upon the floor unheeded. The writing was in Senator Bowen's hand, but she did not notice it; she was pressing her fingers along the margin of filagree work which decorated the edge of the locket; presently the back fell apart; then she pressed again and a third compartment opened and from it the face of Ellis Enson in his first youth smiled up into her own.

How well she remembered all the minute details of the history of the locket in the shadowy past, brought so vividly to her memory by the dramatic events of the last few days. Her mother had given her the locket at the time of her father's death, and had told her that it was a valued heirloom, and had explained to her the intricate working of the triple case. Probably no one had ever discovered the secret spring, and the case was supposed to be empty. After Mrs. Sargeant's death, she had in turn explained to Ellis, and placed his pictured face there, and when, tortured and tormented by persecution, she was driven from her home to the slave market, she had placed the locket about the baby's neck; why, she knew not.

Gazing at it now with sick and whirling brain, there came a step outside in her sitting room. She dragged her leaden limbs to the door and beheld Ellis. The bright smile on his face at sight of her seemed to chase away the years and renew his lost youth.

"My darling," he began, "you see I have managed to return earlier than I expected. I could not support the purgatory of absence from you longer. But what is the matter?"

Hagar could not answer him. Leaning against the doorframe, she looked him in the eyes, then extended her hand, the open locket lying on her palm.

"Ellis," she said, in a husky whisper, "I have just found this—here—in this room—in Senator Bowen's old trunk of relics. What can it mean? For God's sake, try and explain it to me. I cannot grasp the meaning of it at all."

Ellis's face was as white as her own, but he spoke soothingly to the distracted woman. Then his trained eye travelled beyond her to where the folded paper lay forgotten.

Taking her in his arms, he placed her upon the couch in the sitting-room, and then picked up the paper, first tenderly straightening each tiny garment and placing them all together in a pile upon a chair. Closing the door carefully behind him, he drew a chair to the side of the couch where Hagar lay weeping.

"Now, Hagar, my dear," he said, coaxingly, "you will try and be good and command yourself. God grant by these tokens that we may trace our darling's last resting place—a message from heaven!"

"Oh, how selfish I am, Ellis! You need comfort as much as I do," she cried, her love on fire at sight of the tears in his eyes, which he tried in vain to suppress. And then for a little while the childless parents held each other's hands and wept. Presently Ellis opened the paper from the locket. It seemed but a leaf from a memorandum book, but what a change it wrought in the lives of four people!

> March, 1862
>
> Went up the Potomac on the "Zenas Bowen" for oysters. Brought off 100 guns, 300 pounds of ammunition, Charleston, S. C. Picked up log floating outside the bay with a girl baby less than one year old attached to it by clothing. Must have floated many hours, but the sleeping child was unhurt. Clothing rich; no clue to parents or relatives.

> November, 1862
>
> Have adopted child and shall call her "Jewel." I have placed this mem. inside locket found on child for future reference.
>
> Zenas Bowen
>
> Mary Jane Bowen

There was a sound of weeping in the quiet room. "The Divine Father hears all prayers, sees all suffering. In His own good time the All-Merciful has had mercy." The solemn words broke from Ellis.

"And I have said in my anguish, there is no God. He does not heed my woes. Blasphemer that I am!" cried Hagar.

"And she is here in this very house! My God, I thank Thee! Ellis, do not fear, I am strong; go, I beseech you, lose not a moment, bring her to me—bring my Jewel, my daughter, to my arms. Ah, did not my heart yearn over her from the first, when, as a tender baby girl, I held her to my aching heart, and soothed my deep despair? Go, go—at once—Ellis! This suspense is more trying than all that has gone before. You do not know a mother's feelings. Shall I live till your return?"

Ellis, alarmed at her state, choked down his own feelings, and left the room in search of Jewel.

WHO CAN PAINT THE MOST sacred of human emotions? Clasped in her mother's arms, and shown the proofs preserved by her adopted father of her rescue from the death designed by her distracted mother, Jewel doubted not that she was Hagar's daughter.

XXXIX

All night the new-found daughter and husband watched beside Hagar's couch. They feared for her reason. But joy never kills, and at length she slept, and Jewel stole away to take her needed rest.

When alone again in her room, after the startling revelation that had come to her, she sat a long time, trying to realize the complete change in her future which this discovery would bring. She did not deceive herself; the cup of happiness was about to be snatched from her lips. Cuthbert, who was the one object of her passionate hero worship, would turn from her with loathing. There were dark circles about her eyes and her cheeks were ghastly. She loved her mother, she was proud of her father but feelings engendered for twenty years were not to be overcome instantly. It was horrible—a living nightmare, that she, the petted darling of society, should be banned because of her origin. She shrank as from a blow as she pictured herself the astonishment, disgust and contempt of her former associates when they learned her story. The present was terrible, the future more awful still. Overcome by her thoughts, moans burst from her overcharged heart; she stretched out her arms in an abandonment of grief and dropped senseless in the middle of her room, and so Venus found her in the early morning hours. Heaven help her, for it must also be written for her as for her ill-fated mother:

> *"Better the heart strings had never known*
> *The chord that sounded its doom."*

Venus knew the whole story. Mr. Enson had called Marthy, Aunt Henny and Venus into the room and told them very solemnly the facts in the case. There was much weeping and rejoicing.

"My soul," cried Venus to her mother when they were alone, "what about Mr. Sumner? If he goes back on Miss Jewel it'll kill her; it will break her heart."

"It's my 'pinion dat it's already broke, honey; a gal brung up like her has been's gwine break her heart to fin' herself nuthin' but common nigger trash. I jes' hope de debbil's give St. Clair Enson a good hot place down thar to pay him for his devilmen' here on yearth, 'deed I does," said Aunt Henny.

Jewel sent for her father and they talked the matter over. Mr. Enson could give her little hope. He was forced to acknowledge that Sumner was strongly prejudiced. He promised to see him, however, and tell him the story and hear his reply to Jewel, who sent also a pathetic note bidding him farewell:

"I know your prejudice against amalgamation: I have believed with you. My sin, for it is a sin to hold one set of God's creatures so much inferior to the rest of creation simply because of the color of the skin, has found me out. Like Miriam of old, I have scorned the Ethiopian and the curse has fallen upon me, and I must dwell outside the tents of happiness forever. I know you pity my poor mother; she has been so unhappy. I am proud of my father; he is a noble man. I will write again tomorrow and perhaps see you; but, oh, pray not today!"

Twenty-four hours passed and left Sumner as they found him, in mental torture. Then his good angel triumphed. He swore he would not give her up, and then he learned the power of prayer. He was ready to overlook and forgive all if only Jewel were left him. As his entreaties went up to a compassionate God the words rose ever before him.

"Many waters cannot quench love, neither can the floods drown it. All Thy waves and Thy billows have gone over me, but the heart is not easily closed. Love is strong as death."

Evening found him hastening toward the Bowen mansion. The house looked desolate. He rang the bell at the great entrance doors. Marthy Johnson answered the imperative summons.

"Lor', Mr. Sumner, Lor', sir!"

"Where are they all, Marthy?" he asked abruptly.

"Gone to de continen', Mr. Sumner. Massa Ellis say, you young folks'll git better lef' by your lonesomes; dat's what he tol' me tell you, Sir."

Sumner left her in deep despair. He went home to his father for a brief time and then started for the Continent himself.

At the end of a year, mindful of poor John's devotion, for he vowed not to marry Venus till his master settled down, Sumner returned to America and again sought the Bowen mansion. Again Marthy answered his summons, and told him that the family were at Enson Hall. He did not notice the pity on the woman's face.

He never paused until he reached the pretty little rustic town in Maryland that held his heart, his dove of peace. And then a great fear fell upon him, undefined and foreboding. He sent John on with his luggage to the Hall, and wandered up the country road with beating heart and feverish pulses. In a few minutes he would see her, she would be beside him, loving, forgiving. The tears came into his eyes, and he whispered a prayer. He drew his hat over his face and wandered off across a daisied field until he had overcome his emotion. A little graveyard nestled close beside the road. He was on the broad Enson acres, and in that enclosure dead and gone Ensons had slumbered for centuries. It was cool and shady and restful, and unconsciously he stepped into it.

Suddenly with a great cry he stood still before a fair, slender shaft of polished cream-white marble,

Jewel, aged 21.
"Not my will, but Thine be done!"

He fell down with his face upon her grave. She had died abroad of Roman fever.

CUTHBERT SUMNER QUESTIONED WHEREIN HE had sinned and why he was so severely punished.

Then it was borne in upon him: the sin is the nation's. It must be washed out. The plans of the Father are not changed in the nineteenth century; they are shown us in different forms. The idolatry of the Moloch of Slavery must be purged from the land and his actual sinlessness was but a meet offering to appease the wrath of a righteous God.

Across the lawn of Enson Hall a child—a boy—ran screaming and laughing, chasing a gorgeous butterfly. It was the child of St. Clair Enson and Elise Bradford, the last representative of the Enson family.

Cuthbert watched him with knitted brows. In him was embodied, a different form, a lesson of the degradation of slavery. Cursed be the practices which pollute the soul, and deaden all our moral senses to the reception of the true doctrines of Divinity.

The holy institution of marriage ignored the life of the slave, breed indifference in the masters to the enormity of illicit connections, with the result that the sacred family relation is weakened and finally ignored in many cases. In the light of his recent experiences Cuthbert Sumner views life and eternity with different eyes and thoughts from what he

PAULINE E. HOPKINS

did before he knew that he had wedded Hagar's daughter. Truly had Ellis Enson spoken when he judged him nobler than he knew.

"A boy's will is the wind's will,
And the thoughts of youth are long, long thoughts."

THE END

A Note About the Author

Pauline E.h Hopkins (1859–1930) was an African American novelist, playwright, and historian. Born in Portland, Maine, Hopkins was raised in Boston by her mother and adopted father. Supported in her academic pursuits from a young age, Hopkins excelled at Girls High School, where she won a local competition for her essay on the raising of children. In 1877, she began her career as a dramatist with a production in Saratoga, which encouraged her to write a musical entitled *Slaves' Escape; or, The Underground Railroad* (1880). In 1900, she published "Talma Gordon," now considered the first mystery story written by an African American author. Having established herself as a professional writer, she published three serial novels in the periodical *The Colored American Magazine*, including *Hagar's Daughter: A Story of Southern Caste Prejudice* (1901–1902) and *Winona: A Tale of Negro Life in the South and Southwest* (1902–1903). Often compared to her contemporaries Charles Chestnutt and Paul Laurence Dunbar, Hopkins made a name for herself as a successful and ambitious author who advocated for the rights of African Americans at a time of intense violence and widespread oppression.

A Note from the Publisher

Spanning many genres, from non-fiction essays to literature classics to children's books and lyric poetry, Mint Edition books showcase the master works of our time in a modern new package. The text is freshly typeset, is clean and easy to read, and features a new note about the author in each volume. Many books also include exclusive new introductory material. Every book boasts a striking new cover, which makes it as appropriate for collecting as it is for gift giving. Mint Edition books are only printed when a reader orders them, so natural resources are not wasted. We're proud that our books are never manufactured in excess and exist only in the exact quantity they need to be read and enjoyed.

Discover more of your favorite classics with Bookfinity™.

- Track your reading with custom book lists.
- Get great book recommendations for your personalized Reader Type.
- Add reviews for your favorite books.
- AND MUCH MORE!

Visit **bookfinity.com** and take the fun Reader Type quiz to get started.

Enjoy our classic and modern companion pairings!

Classic & Modern

Printed in the USA
CPSIA information can be obtained
at www.ICGtesting.com
JSHW022329140824
68134JS00019B/1383

9 781513 280134